A Promise Of Forever

MaryEllen is originally from Rockaway Beach, NY. She resides in Middletown, NY with her husband Kevin of 36 years. They have three grown children and two grandchildren, so far. MaryEllen has always dreamed of becoming a published writer and she loves the idea of sharing her stories of love and romance with other people. She's grateful to have a supportive family and terrific friends who have always encouraged her to continue writing. Her dream was kept was kept alive and continues to flourish, thanks to them.

A Promise Of
Forever

Aunt Mary

Enjoy! Thank you
for all your support !!
Love
M.E. Brady
AKA
Mary Ellen

M.E. Brady

Happy Birthday !   *2014*

Edited by Dennis DeRose dderose@hvc.rr.com
Cover design by Donna Casey http://DigitalDonna.com
Formatted by Maureen Cutajar www.gopublished.com

ISBN 13: 978-1500603175
ISBN 10: 1500603171

Chapter One

Katelyn sighed; this was the third time today that Adam brought the same discussion to her. "We've been over this before, Katelyn; you need to decide where we are going with this relationship. I hadn't intended on being your friend forever," he said in an irritated but polite voice. "How do you feel about me?" he questioned yet again.

He had that look on his face, the same look he had when he first tried to convince her that it was time for them to take the next step. The look that said he knew better than she what was good for both her and her daughter. He maintained his conviction that it was time that her daughter had a man in her life, a father figure.

"You and I are good together. Besides, you said yourself, Jenny could use a father figure in her life, now that Kevin lives in Montana."

Katelyn hated feeling cornered like this but she did understand the way Adam felt. *There is no doubt in my mind that he deserves better from our friendship; Jenny deserves a father in her life too, but at what expense to me?*

"You continually evade the subject whenever I bring it up. This time we both need to make a choice." Adam stared out at the traffic that sped by the restaurant window, glancing away from the eyes of the woman he loved so deeply; he had never felt this way about anyone before. *How insignificant each car is in the big scheme of things;* that was exactly how he felt at this moment. Katelyn loved another man and he knew that. He wished that she could feel that way about him and believed in time it

1

would happen. He knew, by looking into those emerald eyes, that she was second-guessing their entire relationship. He turned back, held her hand in his and focused his attention on her. He studied her eyes and all the secrets that she kept hidden behind them. As beautiful as her eyes were, he sometimes resented the lies they couldn't hide.

Adam let out an exasperated sigh; he let her hand drop to the table. "I don't know how to convince you that it's time to move on? I'm not sure what else I can do or say to you. Whoever he was, Katelyn, he's a part of your past and that's where he should stay. He didn't care enough to stick around. If he did, he never would have left you to raise a child on your own. I promise, I'll take care of both of you," he assured her.

Her heart beat a little faster as she contemplated what to say in return. Katelyn knew, in her heart of hearts, that she couldn't possibly give him the answer he was searching for. She wasn't ready to commit and didn't know if she would be ready any time soon.

"I have no doubt in my mind that your intentions are noble. I know that I've kept you waiting, inadvertently leading you to believe that I would be able to take this friendship to the next level. Truthfully, I'm afraid it's always been just me and Jenny. I know I haven't told you anything about Jenny's father. Honestly, I've never told anyone about him. I promised myself a long time ago that I would never let Jenny get hurt by him or any other man in my life. And, for that reason, dating has been out of the question for me since him." For the first time since this conversation started, she caught a glimpse of a smile on his face. Katelyn knew Adam cared about her deeply but she also knew that his family would never accept Jenny as one of their own. So, to her their friendship was always safe and non-threatening. Katelyn felt sorry for Adam as he gently stroked her hand. He was a good man and had been a good friend to her for a few years now.

"I hadn't expected this subject to come up with you. I thought you understood," she said feeling a little cornered.

His father, Jack Taylor, would always see Jenny as a liability, not measuring up to his idea of the perfect family. He would never accept another man's child into his family. To him, Jenny would always be another man's bastard child. She had come to know Jack Taylor, perhaps better than his own son knew him. She had had numerous run-ins with him at work. It took years to prove herself to him. Jack Taylor was old school and he believed that women should know their place; though he never acted so, openly.

She gently stroked the side of Adam's face and hoped that he would acknowledge that they were inevitably going to be friends and nothing more.

"I'm flattered that you want more but..." she wanted to begin to explain but, once again, he interrupted her train of thought. It was obvious to her he didn't want to hear what she had to say.

"No buts," he said.

Katelyn smiled, bit her lip nervously and then continued. "I'm not ready to make the commitment you're looking for and it wouldn't be fair to keep you waiting, hoping that I'll change my mind." she added.

Adam looked intently into the green eyes that had captivated him since the first time he saw them and smiled. "I won't take no for an answer. As a matter of fact, don't answer me today. Think about it, give it a week. You said yourself that you missed your brother and that you wanted to go out to Montana to visit him. Call Kevin tonight; make arrangements and go. While you're both there, take time to think about us. Write down all the reasons you can think of, pro and con, about our relationship. If, at the end of the week, you feel that there are more reasons for us to go our separate ways, rather than stay together, I promise to accept your decision."

Katelyn knew that Adam was hoping that Kevin would side with him. It had been a long time since she and Jenny had seen Kevin and Sylvia, her brother and sister in law. Kevin had been the focus of her life for a long time, before Jenny was born. He was all she had left when their parents were killed in a car accident while on their first vacation away from them. She was still in high school at the time and she didn't think she would have survived without her brother. Adam was right; she should go visit Kevin, but for different reasons.

"I just finished the Matlin story. I only hope that your father appreciates all the work that went into getting it done on time, without my getting killed."

Adam rested his hand on the table thoughtfully. He knew the amount of time she put into that story and the danger she put herself into by getting it. Katelyn had a way of making people talk, even the ones who never shared their lives with anyone. It was one of the reasons he was drawn to her.

"I will arrange everything with my father. If I have to, I'll threaten to do his next story myself if he throws a wrench into your vacation. I promise that will scare him enough not to interfere." They both laughed, lightening the mood of their conversation. Adam was not a journalist, nor did he ever want to be. His father pushed him into the family business and Adam's only job was to pretty much stay in the background. He was a huge disappointment to his father. These days he handled the finances in the accounting department. He oversaw all the investments made on behalf of the magazine. It was the one place his father thought he couldn't get into trouble. He had a great team behind him who did all of the work and Adam's only job was to report back to his father with the spreadsheets. Jack Taylor was sure his son couldn't screw up in that department. He was a figure head and everyone knew it. Adam kissed her hand, almost afraid that by kissing her she would deny him the future he craved.

Adam is so different from Gianfranco Broccolini. Funny, but up until this moment, I never compared the two. She tried not to think about Gianfranco these days. Thinking about him and what they had once shared only caused her pain. It was as though she could feel him in this room, warning her against making any hasty decisions about a future with Adam. *Nothing is ever easy.* It was sort of amusing that she found herself in this position.

Years ago, I would have given anything not to have had to raise Jenny alone. She spent most of her young adult life fantasizing about the return of the infamous Gianfranco Broccolini. He never came and she had long ago given up her childish dream of their becoming a family. Her only consolation was the child he had unknowingly fathered.

Katelyn and Adam stood for a moment before leaving the restaurant and then walked out the door. They walked back to the office instead of using the car that had been waiting for them. The two of them walked

4

the entire way without exchanging a word and entered the building in the same fashion. The silence between them was deafening. They knew that their relationship was at a crossroad and each had very different ideas about where it was taking them. As they came to her desk, she shuffled papers that were in a manila folder, trying to act as if it were intended. Before she had time to look up and speak to Adam, her intercom sounded and the receptionist broke in. "Miss Donavan, Jack Taylor is on line three for you. He would like to set up a meeting with you for this afternoon if that is convenient for you." Margie, the receptionist, said into the intercom.

"That would be fine, Margie. Could you set it up for me? Anytime would be great." She glanced over at Adam, who had already started to walk away; she told him she would talk to him later in the day. "I have a meeting with your father this afternoon. I'm sure it's about the Matlin story and I'm hoping it meets with his satisfaction. If everything goes well, I could be packing and on my way to Montana by this evening," she added.

Adam smiled and left Katelyn to finish the work that was quickly accumulating on her desk. When Margie called her back later on that morning with the details of her meeting, Katelyn found it odd that Jack chose to meet at a restaurant, rather than his office, but she didn't have time to think about it. *I'll never get to my meeting if I don't start to clean up this mess.*

All morning, she made one error after the other, simple mistakes that only a greenhorn would make. She wasn't superstitious or anything but it seemed like fate was trying to tell her something or, better yet, warn her of some impending futurity. She shook her head and quickly dismissed that notion as ridiculous. *What's wrong with me? Why can't I shake this crazy feeling?*

She was feeling completely dumbfounded and frazzled. Something had her on edge and this was not the way she wanted to feel going into a meeting with Jack Taylor. She needed to be on her game but her sixth sense was working overtime. Even as a child she had the gift of premonition. She reached for the phone and had the receptionist confirm that her meeting was still on and that its location was the same. She was glad to hear it was confirmed because anything to get her away from her ominous thoughts was a good thing.

Glancing at the clock, Katelyn knew she should leave. She had just enough time to go to the ladies' room and freshen up before her meeting. She sparred with herself in the ladies' room as she looked into the mirror. *I have to forget about all this doom and gloom.* She dabbed her face with cool water and reapplied what little makeup she did wear. Her thoughts returned to Kevin; calmness followed close behind. Thinking of him could always make her feel settled and secure. She couldn't wait to see him. She needed to see him. Perhaps she was getting worked up over nothing or maybe it was Adam's suggestion that they take their friendship to the next level that had her on edge. She didn't know. Katelyn had always hoped that when the time came to make the decision to marry someone that that someone would be Gianfranco Broccolini.

Adam was tall, blonde, rich and safe, or so she thought. He was everything many women desired but she wanted his friendship and nothing more. She was sure of that.

The elevator doors opened and the Taylor limousine was waiting at the curb as she came through the revolving door. The driver opened the door for her and greeted her warmly.

"Mr. Taylor went on ahead I'm afraid; he asked that I deliver you safely to the restaurant of his choice. If there is anything I can get you, just let me know," the chauffeur added politely. Katelyn just smiled and shook her head. There was nothing she needed but… *I wonder if he can get rid of this feeling of uneasiness, I'm experiencing.*

She tried to get some work done on her laptop but quickly dismissed the idea; the words refused to flow. She never had a problem with words before; words were her livelihood. It had always been easy for her to put thoughts to paper. When everything else in her life failed to make sense, she had always had the gift of pen and paper to see her through. As she gazed out at the Manhattan skyline, she couldn't quite believe the difference the missing towers made in everyone's life. *What a travesty and waste of life.* New York City and its people would never be the same. It took years before she could bring herself to recall what she had witnessed herself so vividly.

Trying very hard to push the foreboding thoughts from her mind, Katelyn glanced across the street and caught her breath at what she saw. *No, it can't be. Yet, there he is.* She stared, mesmerized by the vision before her.

Her palms began to sweat as she watched him walk with two other men, almost in slow motion. The three of them were dressed in suits; yet no man was quite like him. He stood out in a crowd; it didn't matter who he was with, he always stood out. He had a presence that few men had but many aspired to be like him. It came naturally to him. His hair was jet black, except for the feathering of grey along his ears. She wanted to feel differently toward him; she couldn't hide what her heart was feeling, not from herself. It was definitely Gianfranco Broccolini standing right there in front of her. He was back in the United States; he'd vowed he'd never return. Yet there he was, in the flesh. It was then that he turned toward the car and looked in her direction. Her stomach did flip-flops. This was silly; he couldn't see her through the smoke-colored glass. He couldn't possibly sense that she sat in the stalled limousine.

"Is something wrong, madam?" the driver asked with a note of concern. She realized then that she must have blurted some kind of outward response, seeing Gianfranco.

"No, I'm fine; it's just the traffic." *Who am I kidding? I'm not fine. He is no longer a phantom in my life. He is here in the States and he is just as handsome as I remembered.* Katelyn felt a horrible stab of pain pierce her heart as the car came to a halt directly across from where he stood. He looked even more distinguished and sexy than the last time they'd seen each other, if that were at all possible. No matter how many times she tried to blink away his image, it was impossible. It became more uncomfortable seeing him; she felt as though he was the one watching her and she was suffocating.

"Excuse me, Miss Donavan, would you like me to call ahead and let Mr. Taylor know that we've run into a bit of traffic?" the driver queried. Then, as if Gianfranco himself willed it to be so, the traffic suddenly opened and granted them access to continue.

"I guess there won't be any need of that now," she said. "By the way, I never asked you your name?" she murmured, thinking that she had been so preoccupied with her own thoughts that she hadn't talked to the driver at all. It wasn't like her to be so dismissive.

"Martin Burke," he said, pleased that she had bothered to care to inquire at all. Mr. Taylor barely spoke three words to him on any given day. "You seem upset; is it your meeting that's bringing about those frown lines?" he asked seeming genuinely concerned.

"I'm afraid my problems are a little more complex than this meeting. I'll be fine Martin but thank you for asking," she added with a smile.

Martin continued to speak to Katelyn and before she knew it she had found out that Martin was married for thirty-five years and had two children. He had a boy, James, who was away at Boston College, and a daughter, Emily, who would graduate this year from high school. He told Katelyn that as much as he sometimes hated his employment, he couldn't afford to give up this job. He wanted his children to succeed and he would put up with whatever was necessary to assure that he made that happen for them.

Katelyn hadn't given her meeting with Jack Taylor too much thought until now and suddenly found herself wondering what it was he wanted to see her about. She was confused over the secrecy of the meeting. She still hadn't been able to shake or dismiss the nervousness she was feeling but, being the professional she was, she put her fear aside and concentrated on what lay ahead. She had to deal with this meeting but when it was over she would call and make travel arrangements to Montana, anything to take her mind off this latest development.

The car was beginning to slow and Katelyn realized that they were approaching the restaurant. She thanked Martin for being so kind and caring toward her. She could tell that he was shocked by the conversation. Knowing Jack Taylor, she doubted that Martin had ever been treated decently before.

"It was wonderful meeting you, Martin. I enjoyed our conversation and I wish your children the very best. After meeting their father though, I don't doubt they will succeed at whatever they choose to pursue."

Chapter Two

Katelyn arrived at the restaurant with barely seconds to spare. If there was one thing Jack Taylor expected from his employees, it was punctuality. Jack was already seated and waiting. She had read somewhere about people like him; they purposely sat themselves so they could watch their prey and study them as they approached. She was sure this was true of Jack Taylor. He was definitely paranoid and egotistical, if it were possible to be both. He seemed to enjoy those quiet moments of observation while his victims were unaware he was watching them. He believed it told him a lot about the person because they would let their guard down during those rare moments of isolation. Who was she to doubt his philosophy? It seemed to work for him; he was rich and powerful because of the way he was.

He stood and welcomed her as she approached his table. "Miss Donavan, I'm glad you could join me. Before I tell you the reason I invited you here, let me congratulate you on the Matlin story. It was your best work yet. I don't think I need to tell you; I've always been impressed with your work." He held her chair for her as she sat and Katelyn became skeptical. *What does he want to talk to me about, if not about the Matlin story?* He ordered a drink for himself and asked if she would like to join him; she declined and asked the waiter for a de-caffeinated tea instead. The conversation suddenly changed course to a subject that she found infuriating.

"I wanted to talk to you about Adam. It was necessary to use the Matlin story as a cover so that my son wouldn't ask me why I wanted to see you." He reached for his drink and raised a brow, as if she understood he was warning her that they keep this meeting confidential.

"I fail to see the reason for the secrecy but whatever it is we need to discuss privately shouldn't cause either of us any unnecessary embarrassment." Katelyn gave him a look of uncertainty as she waited for his reply.

"I agree with you and, by all means, correct me if I'm wrong, Miss Donavan. You strike me as the type of woman who likes all the cards on the table, figuratively speaking, of course. I'm sure you're aware that Adam is my only child. I mean no disrespect to you by what I'm about to say but the idea of my son marrying a woman with a child is simply ludicrous. Adam is the only heir to the Taylor fortune and, as such his children. He has informed me that, should you marry him, he wants to adopt your child. I know things are different these days but I'm old-fashion. I'm not thrilled about the prospect of a match between the two of you and neither are my attorneys. I cannot stand idly by and allow this union to happen, whatever it is that is developing between the two of you. This relationship has to end. I have no intention of allowing this child, your bastard child to inherit one dime that belongs to me and mine," he stated deprecatingly.

She watched him; disgusted by the way he had just described her child. No one had ever called Jenny a bastard before. Though the definition by all sums was correct, it was degrading and demeaning to them both. He tried to diffuse the situation immediately when he saw how irate she had become but his poor choice of words did little to alleviate her mood.

"I'm not here to insult you. As a matter-of-fact, under different circumstances, my feelings toward you would be quite different. I find you to be a very attractive woman with the good fortune to have the brains to go with your looks. I'm not at all surprised, after working with you through the years, that you're as successful as you are. However, I find it hard to understand how you got yourself into this predicament in the first place," he added so nonchalantly.

Unlike his usual followers, Katelyn didn't sit idly by while he insulted her and her child. She stood up as if gesturing to leave, which was what she wanted to do desperately. Escaping seemed the best solution for all.

He immediately caused her to stop in her tracks when he added, in a commanding voice, "The Roe vs. Wade decision came into effect long before your child was conceived. You could have gotten rid of **it** then and we would be having a very different conversation. I would have gladly welcomed you into my family had we not found ourselves discussing this child from your past."

This is incredible. She wanted to take the glass of water sitting on the table and pour it over his head. *What an arrogant ass. Could this conversation get any worse? And why, pray tell, am I still standing here listening to him?*

Katelyn knew the answer to that question. It was simple. She had a daughter to support and the only way she could do that was to keep her job. Jack Taylor was her source of income, the source of her paycheck. He grabbed at her wrist as she turned to leave and Katelyn couldn't help but feel skeeved by his touch. "Please sit down, Miss Donavan. I may have come up with a solution to both our problems. A last resort if you will," he added without any sense of wrongdoing.

"I don't need to tell you that when Adam announced his intentions towards you, I had your background thoroughly checked. I understand you have a brother, Kevin, I believe his name is?" he queried. He opened a folder; a dossier of sorts and continued to read from it. "I'm aware that your brother and his wife have been unable to bare children. I also see that he's an attorney and, from what I see here, quite successful. He's wealthy enough so that any family of his would be well taken care of. I understand he already loves your daughter as if she were his own child," Jack added, as if that would somehow make what he was stating less vulgar to hear. He couldn't even bring himself to recognize Jenny as her child and instead addressed her as *this child from your past.*

Katelyn couldn't believe it; she could feel the bile rising from deep within her throat. *What is he suggesting? Is he proposing that I give my daughter away*? Jenny was her life, her blood, her reason for getting up in the morning. Not to say that she didn't believe that Kevin and Sylvia would not be great parents, they absolutely would. She had spent many a night praying that they would conceive a child of their own. "I don't believe we need to be having this conversation, Mr. Taylor." She felt open hostility for the man sitting across from her.

"I'm willing to supply an allowance for your daughter's care. All you have to do is legally sign adoption papers. Your brother and his wife would make excellent parents. It's a win-win proposal; they would have the child they yearn for and you would have the opportunity to see her anytime. It's the only way that I'll allow any relationship between you and my son. The problem, as I see it, would go away and all would be forgiven. This is my final offer," he stated without feeling.

Too stunned to talk, Katelyn sat back down to relieve the jelly legs she had just acquired and rehashed what he had just openly suggested. She couldn't believe that Jack Taylor was capable of such cold, loathing thoughts. Suddenly, she felt pity for Adam, the man who had professed his love for her earlier in the day. *Was this the kind of home he was raised in?* He didn't deserve a father like this. How had he escaped unscathed from that relationship? Her voice quivered with anger as she gathered her thoughts to react. "Let me make something very clear to you; my child is not for sale. What you're suggesting is something I would never consider."

He seemed taken aback by her words. It was almost as if he believed his son, who had never gone against his father before, would choose her and her daughter over money; she could see that realization frightened him. "I want you to know that I will cut him out of my will if it becomes necessary. I wonder, if it comes to that, will he seem as intriguing to you?" Jack Taylor lifted his head and, for a moment, Katelyn thought he looked triumphant in his disguise. She didn't have the heart to ease his conscience. She didn't want to tell him that she had already decided to end her friendship with Adam for his own sake.

As she stared stubbornly, she impulsively added, "I don't know where you gathered your information from but let me assure you that money means nothing to me." She wondered what the great Jack Taylor would think if he knew that Jenny's biological father could buy Taylor Corporation ten times over and still not put a dent in his multinational conglomerate wealth. She could have gone to Gianfranco when she found out about her pregnancy and he would have taken care of her and her child forever; she never doubted that. Her child would not have wanted for anything in her lifetime. But that was her secret and she would never divulge that to Jack Taylor.

"I'll admit one thing to you, Mr. Taylor; I would love to stay at home and raise my daughter. Nothing would give me more pleasure than to spend my days with her but, just so we are clear, I'm not willing to sell my soul to do it. I would also like to tell you that your biggest oversight is that I never saw Adam as anything more than a friend. Though, truth be told, you have surely made it tempting to do otherwise."

Jack Taylor gestured for the waiter and watched as he approached them. "Are you ready to order?" he asked, as if the conversation they just shared had never happened. She was astonished at his audacity, though she shouldn't have been so shocked by his behavior.

"No, I won't be staying but don't let me stop you from enjoying your lunch though," she added with distain. The waiter didn't know what to do or say. He offered to give them more time to look at the menus before disappearing. She couldn't help but feel sorry for the young man. He had obviously overheard parts of their conversation and was embarrassed by it. Katelyn couldn't help thinking about Adam. *His father thinks so little of his own son's personal happiness that he would deny his existence before allowing his money to be separated from the rightful blood heirs.*

Just then, a child fell out of her chair while trying to climb up and her mother jumped from her seat to care for the child, who was apparently fine. Katelyn was sure that Adam had never known that kind of love and protection from his own father. Their family dynamic was based on greed.

"In a few days, Miss Donavan, *Glitz* magazine will be taken over by a larger more solvent magazine based here in New York City. *Glitz* may cease to exist as we know it. When the merger is announced many of the jobs at *Glitz* will be eliminated. I'm sure my son's job will be the first one on the chopping block. After all, who wants to keep dead weight around? My son is weak, contrary to what people believe. I can almost guarantee that this takeover will affect his career first and foremost." Pausing for few seconds, not sure if he wanted to divulge too much he added, "This takeover had to have been planned long ago because I had no time to react or to stop it, once the wheels were set in motion. I assure you that it was by the shrewdness of one man who caught us at a weak moment. I've since met this man, Miss Donavan, and I assure you he's not the sort who makes mistakes."

This meeting had suddenly taken on a new twist. Jack Taylor had abruptly gone from being a man who seemed to enjoy playing with other people's lives to a broken and beaten man. She knew plenty of people with money; some had more than others, and none would have behaved as Jack Taylor did today. Her first thoughts were of Gianfranco Broccolini, Jake Lonetree and Brody Calder. All three men were men of means and none of them were without a conscience, like the man who sat across from her.

"You say that this man who outwitted you is ruthless and arrogant; I can't imagine anyone being as cold or as uncaring as you have shown yourself to be today. Good Luck with your plans, Mr. Taylor, and have a good day," she snapped back proudly as she stood up and proceeded to walk toward the exit.

"I'll see that my son is taken care of if you and this child are out of the picture. It will be up to you to decide the fate of my son, Miss Donavan. You have a good day," he echoed dismissively. His words sliced through the air just as he intended and Katelyn knew it was his attempt at getting in the last word but she decided foolishly to one-up him with her Irish temper.

"I think this conversation is over and I'd like to take this opportunity to tell you in person that you can take this job and shove it where the sun doesn't shine. My resignation will be on your desk this afternoon." Katelyn was shaking; she was so angry. It took a few minutes more for her to gain her composure and leave the restaurant. She couldn't get out to the safety of the street fast enough.

As she started to walk along the crowded streets of Manhattan, she realized that what she had just done was stupid and impulsive. Jack Taylor may have aggravated and upset her but he had just openly admitted to a takeover, in a few days time. An announcement was imminent and she had just ruined her chances of staying on after the merger. She should have at least ridden the storm to find out where she stood after all the dust settled. There was the off chance that she would have been asked to stay on. *Why do I always have a problem controlling my stubborn Irish temper?* It was her knee jerk reactions that always got her into trouble.

She finally arrived back at the office to clear out her desk and hopefully make one final call to Kevin. There was nothing stopping her from taking an extended vacation now. She wondered what Adam would have to say when his father shared the news with him over tonight's dinner table. Katelyn was sure his father would put a completely different spin on her hasty withdrawal from the company.

It took all of about fifteen minutes to pack up her desk and box everything. She was repeatedly stopped by other staff members, curious about what she was doing. It didn't take long before the office was buzzing with speculation. Katelyn decided, for Adam's sake, she would say nothing to the office rumormongers. Let them focus their gossip on her for now and leave the worry about their futures and the merger for later.

Katelyn recalled being the focus of gossip once before in her life. She had returned to college, from winter break, barefoot and pregnant. She dealt with that gossip the same way she wanted to deal with this mess. She was going to ignore the whispers and take the high road. These unsuspecting people, who had families to feed and support, had no idea what was about to happen to them. Some coworkers, who she had come to admire, would lose their jobs and the security they had relied upon over the years. It didn't seem fair for her to be privy to this information and not be able to share it with them.

Katelyn left the building feeling like a criminal as she hailed a cab. Jack Taylor had seen to it that she be immediately escorted from the building but not before being searched like a two-bit hoodlum. Her apartment was about a half-hour away by cab and she decided to use the time to call Kevin. His secretary answered promptly and put her call through to him. She smiled when she heard his voice. "For a minute there I didn't think you wanted to talk to me," she teased. She'd telephoned him several times a week which is why she didn't think he'd suspect anything with this particular call.

"How are you, Irish? How's Jenny doing?" he asked lovingly. "You know better than anyone that, other than my wife, your call always takes top priority." He had always called her Irish. It was a nickname given to her years earlier by a close neighbor when they were kids and it stuck. Her neighbor had always thought she wore the map of Ireland on her face. Willie, the neighbor in question, had always called her Irish affectionately and Katelyn didn't seem to mind, not even later when Kevin picked it up as well. "Did your intuition kick in again? I was going to call you later today," Kevin whispered in a teasing on edge voice.

"I'm not sure what you're talking about but I needed to talk to you. I have something important to discuss with you," she added. He'd known when she was troubled before but this time she was worrying him. There was something in the tone of her voice that made him worry. Kevin had been her only family since their parents' accident and they had become very close. He felt her pain when she hurt and her joy when she was happy. It was a special connection they both shared. She could never hide her feelings from him.

After talking about the events of the day, Kevin convinced her that, in this instance, Adam was right. She and Jenny should come out to Montana for as long as it takes to clear her head. "It's not as if I'm a struggling attorney, Kate. If you don't find a job right away, it's no big deal. I could always help out, until you get back on your feet. That's why I'm here, Irish, remember that," he said after her protests; he had already done so much for her, she felt.

"Kevin, I think you have supported Jenny and I long enough. I'm not going down that road again. I need to do this for myself. Things are different now. I'm an adult and I'll find work. Jenny and I will be just fine. However, I will take you up on your offer for a short visit. By the way, we were so busy discussing me and my problems; what news do you have to share?" she asked.

There were a few quiet seconds of hesitation before he spoke and Katelyn knew he was holding back to protect her. "I'm not sure that this is the time to tell you after the news you just shared." he said hesitantly. "Then again, maybe it's the best time. Sylvia and I found out a few months ago that we're expecting a baby." She could feel Kevin's chest bursting with pride even though she wasn't there to witness it. She was so happy for them both. They had waited so long for this joyous event. She remembered Sylvia telling her recently that they had given up hope and were going to be looking into adoption.

"Oh Kevin, I'm so happy for both of you. How were you able to keep this from me for this long?" she asked. She couldn't help the tears as they happily flowed down her cheeks. At least this time they were tears of joy. The cab had finally reached the apartment and she told Kevin she would have to call him back later when Jenny got home from school.

Katelyn walked around the apartment and stopped when she arrived at the door to Jenny's room. She smiled, as she glanced around at all the stuffed animals scattered along the wall. She couldn't wait to become an aunt to Kevin and Sylvia's child and spoil her niece or nephew the same way they had spoiled Jenny. *It must have killed Kevin not to tell me.* She decided to call Sylvia right away and offer her congratulations.

Sylvia was tickled pink to be able to talk about her pregnancy and glad that Kevin had finally told Katelyn. Sylvia explained to Katelyn that it bothered them both not to be able to share their news with her but she wanted to get past that first critical stage of her pregnancy since previous attempts had failed. "I'm due around October 15th. I don't need to tell you how nervous we both are," she reiterated.

Yes, happy and nervous all at the same time. She remembered those feelings and informed Sylvia of the gamut of feelings she would go through, until the baby came. The first emotion she would feel would be excitement. A baby was a gift, a part of two people who loved each other. "You both waited so long for this to happen; nothing will go wrong this time. Besides, you have two angels watching over you." She held the cordless phone in her hand and walked over to her wall of memories. This wall held all the images of her favorite people in frames which she proudly displayed. It was there that she smiled as she touched the outline of the faces of her parents.

"Look out for the baby, Mom," she whispered silently. She missed her parents more than she had ever let on to anyone. The one and only person who knew just how devastated that loss was to her was Kevin. It was another feeling they mutually shared. She continued her conversation with Sylvia, all the while glancing from frame to frame. She had come upon the one of the three musketeers and smiled. It was a picture that Kevin had sent her while away at college, him and his two best friends, Gianfranco Broccolini and Jake Lonetree.

The three men shared a lot of good and bad memories alike during their time together in college. They each had a story to tell as to what led them to Yale and in turn led them to each other. Jake was a very good-looking American Indian and proud of it. He fought his way to the top of his high school class and was offered a scholarship for all his hard work by an unknown donor. While at Yale he was called upon to defend his heritage time and again and it often ended in physical brawls. Gianfranco and Kevin were more than willing to throw a few fists of their own in aiding their friend.

Jake shocked them all when he announced after graduation that he had enlisted in the service and yet they weren't surprised to later hear that he had become part of a Navy Seal elite squad. It was that military training that quieted the restlessness he had always felt. With his Ivy League education in business and his Navy Seal training, Jake became a very wealthy man in civilian life. He was the one person Kevin trusted to keep an eye on Katelyn and Jenny after Kevin accepted a position at a large law firm in Montana.

She and Jake had formed a lasting friendship over the years and spent a lot of time together. Some friends and coworkers alike wondered if there was more to their relationship than friendship.

Then there was the third member of the trio, Gianfranco Broccolini. Unbeknownst to Kevin, he and Katelyn formed a relationship quite different than the one she formed with Jake; that liaison would change Katelyn's life forever. He taught her what it was like to be totally consumed by love and then, afterwards, he tore her heart from her chest and hurt her so badly she thought she would never recover. The only saving grace was that Kevin and Jake never found out about the affair. Had they figured out who had fathered her child, it would have upset and disappointed both men. It was a secret she swore to keep to herself.

Gianfranco Broccolini entered Yale to break away from the presumptuous rich cronies that surrounded him since his grandmother's demise, when he was sixteen. He had no family left to speak of and an education abroad seemed to be the best solution for him until his trust fund was released to his care. He had the grades and the money to pay for his education himself. The lawyers may have had temporary control over his amass fortune but when he turned twenty-five he took over full control of his company, and no one could stop him. He'd doubled his investments and holdings in a short amount of time. It didn't take long before the men and women who hadn't had to answer to him before respected him and were learning from him.

"Sylvia, have you, by any chance, heard from Gianfranco?" she asked as she glared at his picture. She thought she heard her sister-in-law teasingly ask if she could make things move too and wondered what she meant by that.

"Kevin was right; you really do have a sixth sense. We were just talking to Gianfranco yesterday. He flew to the states on business last week and, if I'm not mistaken, he left for New York City yesterday. He told us he's back in the States for good this time. I guess we'll all be seeing a lot more of him. Your brother is thrilled that he's back in the country and I can only imagine that Jake is too. The three musketeers back together again; it's a little scary to think about." Stopping to take a breath, Sylvia laughed before continuing.

"I believe Kevin gave Gianfranco your number and asked him to look in on you. He told him he should hook up with Jake and get a home-cooked meal at your place," she added jokingly. She loved her conversations with Katelyn and when they got on the phone it was as if they lived around the corner and had just spoken, never missing a beat.

"Jake never needed an invitation to come for dinner. He's been known to stop by and check up on us. I'm sure he's following my brother's orders." She loved her brother but sometimes he was a bit overbearing. Kevin thought she needed a man in her life and poor Jake bore the brunt of his over-protective attitude. She was sure Jake passed up many dates to spend time with her and Jenny.

"Jake never minded spending time with you, Kate, and my husband is just a worry wart. Maybe, with a new baby to keep him occupied, he'll leave you alone," Sylvia teased. "By the way, I don't know if I should mention this or not but Jake didn't think Adam was the right guy for you and I'm sure he'll be glad to hear you're done with him; he never told us why he felt that way though."

Katelyn smiled, thinking of all the American Indian tales that Jake had shared with her and Jenny, night after night. "I'm beginning to think that you are all believers in Jake's mumbo jumbo. I love Jake Lonetree with all my heart but I can't say that I believe in tales of rings linking people's lives together, forever. It's hard for me to believe that such a well-educated man like Jake could believe in all that nonsense."

She had great respect for Jake and the work he did with underprivileged Native American youth on his ranch. He had turned his massive ranch into an Indian reservation from the past. If anyone were ever allowed to go beyond the entry gates, they would think that they had stepped back in time. He felt, if he took the youth back to where it all began they could move forward with pride in their heritage. The kids were taught everything about how their ancestors lived in the past. They became excellent marksmen and horseman. They learned to survive living off the land using nothing but knives and a bow and arrow and later the occasional rifle. Jake proved to be quite a success with the kids that he took there. A high percentage of the kids who spent time with Jake on the ranch went on to college and beyond. It was amazing; even those opposed to his project had to applaud him in the end. Jake was able to instill a feeling of hope and pride that many of the children hadn't had before. Talk about paying it forward, Jake took his work with underprivileged youth very seriously and it was paying off.

Katelyn heard the doorbell ringing in the background and assumed it had to be Adam. No one else would expect her to be home at this time of day and she chose to ignore it. She had no wish to rehash the events of her meeting with him or his father. She was surprised that he would come to her apartment, knowing how she felt about that. She had always insisted that they meet at their agreed upon destination. She had no desire to explain her relationship with Adam to her daughter. Jenny was a bright child and sometimes a little too presumptuous; she didn't want Jenny to become little Miss Matchmaker.

Chapter Three

The doorbell was still ringing and, although Katelyn wanted to ignore it, the person on the other side of door had a different idea altogether. She didn't feel up to a confrontation with Adam; she had already been through enough.

"I have to go, Sylvia, someone is at the door and they are being very persistent. Again, congratulations, I'm very happy for you both," she said before replacing the receiver on its cradle.

As she opened the door, the face that greeted her wasn't Adam at all. It was the face that had haunted her thoughts for many years. His eyes were so dark that you couldn't tell where the pupil began or ended. He smiled warmly and asked if she were going to let him in. He acted as though they were two long lost friends who hadn't seen each other, nothing more. Katelyn found it difficult to speak to him as their time together came flooding back to her. Gianfranco stared at her for a brief moment before reaching out and embracing her in a friendly hug.

"Hello, Irish. I wasn't sure whether you would want me to stop by but I took the chance anyway." He still hadn't let her go. It was almost as if he were holding on to a lifeline. "I'm glad I decided to though. I must have walked around your building for twenty minutes before coming up," Gianfranco added without hesitation.

"Don't be ridiculous; I'm always happy to see one of Kevin's friends." She didn't know what had prompted her to be so dismissive but she couldn't take it back, now that it was out there. Once again, her stubborn pride needed to lash out in response to the disappointment she felt. She wanted him to pay for his nonchalance toward the past they shared together.

He smiled but grunted too, "Is that all I am to you, Irish? Am I just your brother's friend?" he queried mysteriously. Katelyn could see that she had stung him with her words. When she tried to make up for it by shaking her head, in response to his question, she thought she felt a slight kiss on her head. It was ever gentle but he had indeed kissed her, just above her ear. She had always wondered what their first meeting would be like after all this time. It was going to happen sooner or later; they were both bound to see each other eventually.

There was no way to describe the effect he was having on her by holding her in his arms for so long. *It is time to break from his embrace.* She stared up into his eyes and willed him to let go of her but she could see his intent was very different. He wanted her to remember. He willed it; he needed her to recall what it felt like to be in his arms. His Italian pride would not allow him to be dismissed by her so easily.

She pulled away just then and made a poor attempt at safer conversation. She would do anything that would help erase the shameless thoughts that his touch evoked. "Kevin tells me you're back in the States for good this time," she stated as she fidgeted with the door behind him. "Come in and sit down. I don't want my neighbors to start speculating about all that banging you were doing," she added. "I don't keep any liquor in the house but there is some beer in the fridge if you would like one. Jake has been known to stop by now and then and I keep some beer cold for him," she rambled, but not before noticing she had triggered another reaction; she couldn't quite figure out why.

"I don't want anything. Thank you for asking though. I should have come by sooner but I didn't know what to say to you," Gianfranco said. He could see that she was uncomfortable in his presence but, instead of feeling compassion, he felt amused. "Am I making you nervous, Irish?" he asked arrogantly. He was sure his close proximity was having an effect on her and he could see that she was struggling to keep herself together. As they continued into the apartment, Katelyn was having trouble relaxing. He could see that and wondered why he affected her so deeply, even now after all this time.

"Don't be silly. Why would you make me nervous? I have a lot on my mind right now and you and your arrogant self aren't high on my list," she added, rushing past him.

She turned slightly to ask another question. "By the way, whatever happened to Italy being in your blood? I recall you said that you wouldn't be happy unless you were there." Katelyn hadn't meant to reveal so much. She could feel his eyes bearing down on her from behind. It was as if he were trying to read her thoughts as they made their way down the narrow hall. She couldn't turn to face him because her eyes would most certainly give her away.

"Be careful, Irish, I might think you memorized our last encounter word for word. I wonder what the experts would consider that to mean. Are there some deeper unresolved thoughts running through that beautiful head of yours? Or, better yet, are you trying to bate me, as you have so expertly done in the past?" he asked conceitedly. He didn't want to scare her but she was hiding something from him, of that he was certain.

Gianfranco had finally come to terms, believing that she had had an affair with another man shortly after leaving his bed. That affair produced a child and he wasn't sure if he could get past that knowledge. He knew that every time he looked at little Jenny, it would remind him of her mother's betrayal. The blame for the betrayal lay with him. He never blamed her. He had taught her all the ways of sensuality and left her.

"Don't be silly. I have nothing to hide. I'm just a little surprised that you came back and maybe a little curious, about why you came back," she blared as she sat down on the sofa. She cursed herself; how easy it was for him to read her thoughts and make her uncomfortable in her own skin. He joined her on the sofa because he knew she was hoping he would opt for the chair across the room. He wasn't about to let this opportunity pass.

"I'm impressed," he said as he looked around. "The apartment is nice. It's small but very warm and cozy." He paused for a moment before continuing. "I came back, Katelyn, because I needed to and, as far as our past is concerned, I said what needed to be said at the time," referring to their time together.

Gianfranco needed to explain himself further. "If I remember correctly, which I assure you I do, you were the one who had plans for a bright future that didn't include me. You were going to California to experience your new independent life. And, by the way, I'm proud of you and all you've accomplished. I know that it's been hard for you over the years." For a man who made multi-million dollar decisions on a daily basis, why was talking to Katelyn increasingly impossible for him. He fumbled with his hands; he was afraid of what would happen if his skin came into contact with hers. He wanted to pick her up at this very moment and take her to the bedroom and make love to her. Make her forget the man who fathered her daughter but that was impossible.

"Would it have mattered if I had decided to stay here instead?" she asked nervously. She wanted and needed to hear his answer. The answer might convince her that she had done the right thing by keeping the secret of their daughter's birth from him.

"That, my sweet *Cara,* is a loaded question. Are you sure you can deal with the answer? It may be the answer you don't want to hear, then what? It would be too late to take back the question, once I have answered it." He glanced around the room once again; this time he commented on how much he admired her taste.

"I could use someone like you to decorate my new place. It doesn't have this warm glow that this place has. It's very cold or so my housekeeper tells me." He noticed how much his Irish had matured. Her breasts were the only obvious physical sign that she had had a child. They were fuller and larger than he remembered them and, yes, he did remember. She seemed less trusting and easy going than in the past.

"You did good Irish, I am amazed by you. Kevin tells me you have done all this without any help." He hesitated but Katelyn could see he had more to say. He wanted to add 'without the help of the father of her child' but he didn't dare.

"I could have helped you, Katelyn, if you had only asked me. You're family to me," he added regretfully, after witnessing her reaction. Katelyn felt sick to her stomach at that analogy. They would never be the kind of family he was portraying. She could never be like a sister to him, not after what they had shared.

26

She glanced over at the clock that hung on the wall and checked the time again. It would be at least another hour before Jenny arrived home. Another hour before the child he shared with her would walk through the door and run right past him. It was ironic, they were family just not in the sense that he thought. Katelyn knew there was no Mrs.Broccolini; Kevin would surely have mentioned it if there had been.

"Am I keeping you from something?" he asked, as he pointed up at the clock she had just been eyeing. "You seem a little preoccupied by it."

"I'm sorry. I don't mean to be rude; it's just that Jenny is due home in an hour and I don't usually have men in my home. Of course, Kevin and Jake are the exception. My daughter would take one look at you and have us married by the end of the week," she said jokingly. He didn't seem to catch on at first because he always assumed that Adam Taylor had been to her apartment before. The information, though given unintentionally, amused him. "Jenny would assume that you're good father material and try to play matchmaker," she added with a smile.

He couldn't let this moment go by. It was so easy to get her goat. "You mean that if your daughter comes home and sees us together, she'll assume mommy was having a little hanky-panky while she was at school?" He moved closer to her on the sofa and started a little playful teasing of his own. "What kind of hanky-panky, has your young child witnessed? I wonder." he asked, flicking her hair from her shoulders. He was certain that Jenny had never witnessed her mother with a man but that didn't stop him from teasing her. He put an arm around her waist and gently used the other to touch her face and silky hair. "Have there been many men, Katelyn?" he asked huskily, not really wanting to hear the answer.

He held her chin in his hand and looked into her eyes as both of them fought emotions that were running rampant; it happened whenever they were near each other. He wondered if his lust for her could ever be sated. When he witnessed her lips quiver with excitement, as he drew nearer, he yanked himself away. It was as though all the fires of hell had just burst through the cavern. He promised himself before he came to her apartment that he wouldn't go down this path with her. He couldn't lose himself to her again because this time there would be no returning from the abyss of his feelings for her. He couldn't break eye contact, though he was trying desperately to do just that. His intention was to drop by, make sure she was alright and leave just as quickly as he came. He promised Kevin he would do that; he owed his friend that courtesy.

What was happening between them was fast becoming something neither of them had bargained for. What he wanted to do to her now was unforgivable. A loud knock on the door broke the trance between them just in time. They both found themselves tense, unsure about what to do next. "I'd better go and get that," she murmured with what little strength she could muster. "I don't know who that could be," Katelyn heard herself say aloud. She realized that she spoke aloud but didn't hear his response; it was low and muffled. She straightened her skirt and proceeded to the door.

The loud knocking for a second time today was probably attracting her elderly neighbor, Annabel. She could hear the old woman moving about next door. Katelyn knew she was probably near the peep hole in the door checking out who was causing all the commotion in the hallway. She rarely had male visitors and Annabel was familiar with Kevin and Jake; seeing two different men at Katelyn's door today would raise her suspicions. "I'm coming, stop banging," she pleaded.

Adam stood there frantically at the doorway. He must have heard she left the office escorted with boxes in hand. "What happened today? I didn't think you were ever coming back from your meeting. I dropped by your desk and everyone told me that you packed up your stuff and left with an escort. What's going on? What happened?" he asked as he waited, hoping to be invited in, although she had never invited him to the apartment before.

"Adam, I'd prefer you not drop by the apartment like this. Jenny will be home soon and I'm still pretty upset after my meeting today with your father. How do you live with someone like that? Do you know he asked me to give up Jenny for you? I don't know why is he under the assumption that we are more than we are. Wherever he got that idea, I don't really care, nor do I want to discuss it. I told you before, Adam, that I don't want that kind of relationship with you. Now, if you would, please leave." she said, gesturing toward the elevators. She was so busy rambling on and on about her disappointment in him and his family that she didn't give Adam a chance to speak or to explain how his father came to the conclusion that he did. Nor did she give a thought to what Adam would say about her guest in the next room.

Adam did speak after finally interrupting her rambling. "I don't know what's happened but if you could just settle down long enough to tell me everything, I'm sure there is a reasonable explanation for whatever my father insinuated." Adam tried to hold Katelyn but she jerked away. "Whatever he said, I'm sure it was simply misconstrued." She became angry as he made excuses for his father's behavior. She didn't want to hurt Adam but he couldn't be this naïve, believing his father incapable of such filthy thoughts or that she was lying about what he said.

"I don't have the energy right now to argue with you. I want you to leave me alone." She went to close the door again, hoping he would leave voluntarily. "I'm telling you to leave," she repeated yet again emphatically.

He turned toward her and begged for a chance to talk things through. "I can't leave things like this. I'm in love with you, Katelyn. I'm not going to let one silly argument with my father ruin what we have going for us. Whatever it is he said to you, know that I don't condone it. We can fix this," he said as he tried to kiss her. He'd never acted so presumptuously before and, for the first time, she caught a glimpse of a very different man than the one she thought she knew.

"Adam, we're friends and nothing more. I wish I could offer you more, but I can't," she said before telling him what was to come. "Your father has seen to it that neither of us have a job come Monday. Did he share that bit of information with you? *Glitz* is being taken over and he has assured me that you and I are not part of that equation. He said the new CEO is arrogant, ruthless and his bottom line is always about the money. Adam, watch your back," she said before trying to close the door again.

It was then that Adam suddenly became angry. He pulled her into his arms and the closer he dragged her, the more dangerous he became and the more uncomfortable she was with the situation. This behavior was out of character for Adam and it frightened her.

It wasn't until she heard the strength of his voice that she recalled the man in the next room. He moved stealthily forward from the shadows and let his presence be known. It was then that Katelyn realized what a true force Gianfranco Broccolini really was. Kevin had always told her that he was in awe of Gianfranco's ability to hold his adversaries at bay. He never seemed to lose control of himself.

It was Adam who looked surprised. Adam left little to the imagination as his eyes cast meanness and cruelty toward her at the sight of the other man in her apartment. This was a very dark side of the man she thought she knew. Yet, as she nervously glanced over at the deep pools of ebony behind her, she witnessed a warning being shot at Adam not to persist. She knew instantly that she was safe.

"I think the lady asked you to leave," he ordered, as he moved closer to Katelyn's side.

"Who the hell is he?" Adam asked as he released Katelyn.

"It doesn't matter who I am. All that should concern you is that I've just about used up all the patience I have for one day. You can do one of two things; either you leave voluntarily or I will gladly remove you myself. Which will it be?" Gianfranco asked as he maneuvered himself directly between Katelyn and Adam. Although it seemed that Adam was angrier at this point, it was Gianfranco who controlled the next few moments.

Adam stood a few inches shorter than Gianfranco and at least thirty pounds lighter, not that Gianfranco was at all heavy, just the opposite, in fact. He had a great body; it was what some women loved most about him besides his beautiful face, his intellect and, of course, his wealth. It had become apparent to Adam that he was going to lose this battle so he turned to Katelyn and bid her farewell before retreating, adding that he would get in touch with her when her Neanderthal friend left.

"Don't bother calling me, Adam. I'm leaving for Montana in the morning. It's all arranged. I'll see you when I get back." He only hesitated for a second before nodding and walking away. She knew he felt humiliated and defeated and she got the distinct impression that he would seek his revenge at a later date.

As Adam disappeared down the hall, Katelyn was left to answer a barrage of questions from her more dominating guest. The main conversation seemed focused on Jack Taylor and their meeting this afternoon. What had prompted her to divulge the exchange between herself and Jack Taylor, she didn't know? Gianfranco seemed to know most of the answers before she spoke the words.

Then his concern switched to the physical exchange that took place between her and Adam. Katelyn thought to herself, *I'm shocked and disappointed by Adam's behavior today and I don't want to discuss it any further, least of all with Gianfranco.*

He, on the other hand, wondered. *Had he not been here, what would have happened? Why did she trust someone like Adam? It was obvious that she didn't know the man as well as she thought.*

"You're being ridiculous. I can tell by that look on your face what you're thinking. I could have handled the situation all by myself. What happened here today is none of your business," she said, picking up some mail from the table and tossing it down again. She was trying her hardest to put some distance between them but it wasn't working. He moved as though he were playing chess, all the while studying her body movements and reactions. He was not going to let the subject drop and she was annoyed at his protective behavior toward her. She didn't need a big brother; she already had one of them and another who acted as if he were.

"If I hadn't been here, Katelyn, what do you think would have happened? He was out of control," he stated angrily as he stood face to face with her.

"This is crazy. If you really want to know what I think, it was you that made him snap. Adam has never acted that way toward me before. He would never hurt me. You bring out the worst in people." She caught her breath because she knew she had just crossed the line. She knew what she had just said was so far from the truth. Gianfranco Broccolini didn't bring out the worst in people. In fact, just the opposite was true. People were at their best because of him, not in spite of him.

He shook his head at first and then ran his fingers through his jet black hair as he always did when frustrated. He was pulling his hair, as if inflicting pain would somehow stop him from lashing out at her with words he would later regret. "Why are you the only person alive who can bate me like this? You push every button and you know just which ones will make me react. Don't you understand? I was just trying to help you. He was going to physically hurt you."

She was sure that he felt a brotherly obligation to protect her and she didn't like it. She didn't need him or anyone else for that matter. The only response she could think of had clearly left her mouth before she had time to think about it. It was the story of her life, her stubborn Irish nature; talk first, worry about the repercussions later.

"How do you know we aren't already lovers? You don't know anything about my private life. You gave up that right years ago," she fumed intently. Once again she looked around the living area for anything that she could use to separate them. A high back wing chair stood in the corner and she set out to stand behind it and use it as a shield. It wasn't that she was afraid of him; she knew he would never hurt her but she couldn't bare another heart-wrenching good bye if he dared to touch her.

He tore off his jacket and threw it aside. Both of them realized that they had unfinished business between them and a chair wasn't going to keep them from confronting the past. He thought she needed to be taught a lesson first; who better than him to teach her? He genuinely set out only to show her what could happen if she provoked him any further. "It's obvious to me that you know just what makes me tick, don't you, Irish?"

"Don't call me that. What did I say that made you so angry? " she asked.

Gianfranco relaxed a little and sucked in his lower lip. "That's a laugh. You intentionally goad me and by the way, there was a time when my calling you Irish made you smile." He moved around the chair so that they stood inches from each other. "Why do you enjoy inciting me?" he asked huskily as he cupped her shoulders with his hands.

Katelyn could feel his fingers burning right through her clothes. She felt limp, all of the sudden, and practically fell into his arms. "Your body is telling a very different tale, Katelyn, whether you're emotionally vested or not. Your mind might have tried to wipe me from its memory but your body…it remembers," he said as he traced the curve of her shoulders and neck with his fingers. With the back of his hand he traced the outline of her breast and watched as her nipple rose to his touch. He was right; he only had to touch her to evoke such torment.

She was crumbling fast and he knew it. Without hesitation, he pulled her into his embrace and seared her lips with a long awaited kiss. He was gentle at first. She reciprocated his soft kiss with a gentle moan and, with that, he was lost. He licked her lower lip which seemed to beg entrance and, once accepted, he deepened the kiss. He was biting her lower lip gently as he provoked an even deeper exchange. This kiss that was only meant to teach her a lesson was now flaming out of control.

He couldn't help his reaction to her any more than he could stop breathing. He never could control himself where Katelyn was concerned, though he tried adamantly. He had always prided himself, always self-controlled, given any situation, but it was always different with her. All the women in his life before her or since didn't seem to have this effect on him. He never had a problem walking away from a woman without any feeling of regret but Katelyn was a constant threat to his well-being. She inspired the best and worst in him. He needed to know if it was as difficult for her. He pulled his lips away from hers in order to look into her emerald eyes; the eyes that held the truth within them.

"For someone who's involved with another man, your response to me is a little questionable to say the least. Are you sure your relationship with Taylor is everything it is supposed to be? Think about that, Katelyn, the next time you let me touch you," he added. "The next time I won't walk away." He said as he pushed away from her and once again walked out of her life. As he left her apartment, she was left feeling empty and alone.

She couldn't move at all as she watched him walk out the door. She was waiting for some explanation to come to mind. What had just transpired between them? Why did he stop? They both acted explosively toward each other sexually and it was obvious what they each wanted.

The exchange between them left her body feeling unfulfilled and long-ing. She glanced over at the clock and realized she had some time before Jenny was due home and the Gianfranco she kept hidden in her draw would have to do, for now. She couldn't go through the rest of the day feeling this way.

She had kept her toy in her nightstand and had aptly named it Gianfranco. If she couldn't have the real man, she would settle for the fantasy.

Chapter Four

After a quick shower, Katelyn pulled herself together and tried to decide what to tell Jenny about their unexpected trip to Montana. They would be leaving in the morning and if she hoped to be ready on time she would need Jenny's full cooperation. It wasn't long before Jenny was bouncing through the door from school. She was more than happy to hear about their upcoming journey. Jenny was excited to be visiting her Uncle Kevin. To her young daughter, this trip meant plenty of fun with her uncle and aunt who loved and spoiled her.

"We need to start packing tonight if we're going to be ready to leave in the morning. What do you say to pizza for dinner tonight after packing?" Katelyn asked while taking Jenny's school bag from her little shoulders. If there was one thing in her life that she had no regrets about it was the birth of her beautiful daughter and the unconditional love she felt for her. For that very reason she was grateful for having had Gianfranco Broccolini in her life.

Although most of their dinner conversation weighed heavily on what Jenny would wear to the airport and what toys she would be allowed to bring aboard the plane, Jenny couldn't contain her excitement about seeing and riding the horses again.

"Sweetheart, this is going to be a short visit. I don't know how many activities we are going to be able to fit in," Katelyn reminded her daughter. But Jenny didn't care; all she knew was that she would get to see her uncle and aunt and get to ride a horse. Jenny also knew that Sylvia would have a surprise for her; she always did when they came for a visit. And her uncle would make sure that there was a tame horse ready for her to ride. It was all Jenny could talk about.

"I'm not sure I'll be able to sleep tonight. I can't wait to leave," Jenny chuckled excitedly.

"I'll draw you a warm bath; then we'll read a story together. You'll be asleep as soon as your head hits the pillow." Katelyn smiled at her daughter. *What could be better than this?* She enjoyed all their private moments together so much.

An hour later, Jenny was fast asleep. Katelyn soaked in the sight of her beautiful sleeping child, thinking, *I was right.* Moments like these were most memorable, watching Jenny as she drifted off into a peaceful slumber. She caught Jenny's little smile every once in awhile and thought angels had to be speaking to her child; at least that was what her mother had always told her in the past and believing it lifted her spirits.

Katelyn stood there, enjoying her daughter, for a few more seconds before reaching for the switch to turn off the light. *Someday, I will have to tell Jenny about her father and it seems as though that day is looming nearer and it's a lot sooner than I expected.* She heard the doorbell ring again and wondered who it could be this time. She was hoping that it wasn't Adam. She couldn't deal with him right now, and, whoever it was they weren't leaving.

"Who is it?" she asked before opening the door.

"Well, it's refreshing to know that you have some sense," the voice said from the other side of the door. "I need to talk to you," Gianfranco stated quietly but firmly.

Katelyn took in a deep discernible breath before opening the door for him and didn't hesitate to tell him what she thought about his un-announced visit. "If I had any sense at all, I'd keep you locked out of my life permanently," she added curtly. She was working the chain on the door when she remembered just what she was wearing but it was a little too late. She didn't have time to be shy; the door was already ajar. She was in her nightgown and getting ready for bed when she'd heard the knock. She knew he noticed her state of undress right away and seemed to enjoy her discomfort. She politely told him she needed to change into something more appropriate and would be back shortly. Before he allowed her to step past him; he held up a bottle of wine and a bag chips and salsa he had in his hands. It was Mexican salsa and chips from her favorite restaurant. It was the only place that made the salsa hot enough for her. It didn't neglect to register with her that he had remembered.

"I come bearing gifts. I know two weaknesses you have and one is very hot salsa." He smiled teasingly, holding up the jar again. "I am your other weakness"…he said under his breath.

"You don't want to send me away now, do you? I've never had to beg for anything in my life; I don't think I would be very good at it," he added knowingly.

Katelyn couldn't help but be amused by his candor. "You win; you can stay for now but after we talk you're out of here. Do we understand each other?" she asked nervously as she waited for a reply.

"I'll agree on one condition…" he said as his eyes moved feverously down the length of her body. It was then that she became flushed from head to toe. "I would love to stay and admire the view, Irish, but you are killing me. I'm not sure I could stand here without touching you." He patted her behind through the silky nightshirt and laughed as she strode annoyingly away. He disappeared into the kitchen but not before she had a chance to shout out what an arrogant, egotistical ass he was.

Katelyn glanced at her reflection in the floor length mirror in the hall on her way to her bedroom and saw what he had for the first time. She realized that her appearance left little to the imagination and with the lighting in the foyer she looked practically naked. She reached into her closet and hastily picked out a white wool sweater to throw over her head and added a pair of blue jeans to complete the toned-down, covered up look.

The table was already set when she joined him in the living room. He had dimmed the lights and added candles. The atmosphere was perfect but for what? Everything screamed of romance, down to the logs she saw burning in the fireplace. She shook her head slightly to dismiss the memories she was conjuring up, memories from another, happier time. She was becoming skittish by what was going on in her mind and she knew he was well aware of her feelings. Yet, he silently challenged her to put a stop to what was occurring between them because he knew better than anyone that she would never back away from this challenge.

"If you're afraid, I can move all this to the kitchen," he said, pointing to the food and the candles. "That is, if you would be more comfortable where it's all lit up and less scary for you. It just seemed a waste not to enjoy the sound of the ocean while we talked," he said as he pretended to gather the food to move the venue. He knew without looking in her direction that she had the courage to face him. But would this new, more mature Katelyn need more time to take the bait? She was one of the few people in his life who wasn't afraid to confront him and he loved that about her.

"Don't be ridiculous; what would I have to be frightened of?" she asked, assembling all her wits to take on the demon in the room.

"Indeed, you have nothing to be afraid of. I pride myself on being the perfect gentleman. I always control my baser instincts…at least around most women," he added unmercifully as he smiled. The Katelyn he knew and loved was present just below the surface and begging to break free.

She laughed at his teasing out of sheer timid desperation. Her nervous laugh must have amused him because he was enjoying himself at her expense. For a long drawn out moment, they stared into each other's eyes; each not knowing what to expect or want from the other. She had changed very little in the past seven years but those emerald eyes that told her story never changed. They spoke a language all their own. At this moment, they were reaching out to him but he didn't dare touch her. This had to be her decision and she had to come to him, willingly.

She was a stubborn little minx back in the day and he had hated to leave her behind. At the time, he didn't believe he had much of a choice. She was eighteen years old with a promising future ahead of her; one he had no right to deprive her of. He knew that, no matter what the cost to him, he would have to let her go and give her time to explore her dream. He wanted her to have all the things she craved; he didn't want to be the one to hold her back. Of course that was then and this was now.

He moved closer to her drawn in by eyes that were willing him to do so. He brushed at the strands of hair that had fallen in front of her eyes and wondered if she had missed him as much as he missed her. It was the connection between them that moved her to reach out and touch his face. At this moment, she invited him into her space. The wall they built between them shattered with just a tiny touch of her hand. No matter what happened now, he knew they were both fighting the same demon; neither had the power to control it. He only hoped that he could make her fear disappear as they answered the need that compelled them.

"I promise I'll stop if that's what you want. All you have to do is say the word," he stated huskily. "You do trust me, don't you?"

"What?" Katelyn asked, barely whispering, as she tried to inhale and make sense of what he was saying to her.

"You don't trust me?" he questioned as though she offended him somehow. He didn't need a response from her; it was written in the expression she wore on her face. "Don't answer that. I'm not sure I want to hear the answer. I came here tonight with good intentions; I mean that. I came to talk about your employment. What made you quit your job at *Glitz*?" he asked attempting to change the mood in the room.

"I'm not sure what business it is of yours but if it'll make you stop pestering me I'll tell you. I'm sure you've already figured it out for yourself that Jack Taylor does not approve of me for his son. It's unfortunate for me though that I'm employed by the man who believes I'm wrong for his son. It never occurred to him to ask how I felt about his son; when I said that my feelings for Adam were purely platonic, I don't think he believed me."

Gianfranco coughed and interrupted her train of thought before she could say another word. "I hear that Jack Taylor no longer owns any part of *Glitz*." He reached over to the back of her neck and instantly she felt tension begin to disappear as he began to massage her there. "I heard somewhere that *Glitz* had recently been acquired in a hostile take-over," he stated factually.

"Jack told me the same thing; but he didn't tell me that it was made public yet. If anything, he warned me against divulging that information," she said in shock as she turned to look at him. "For some reason, I'm not surprised that you know about the takeover." He had her turn her away from him again and she could feel his fingers kneading down either side of her neck softly and methodically.

"He warned me that he would see to it that Adam and I lost our jobs before he'd sit back and watch any relationship between us develop." She felt his body tighten and his hands abruptly stall at her statement. The longer his fingers touched her neck, the more aware of him she became. "Did you say something?" she asked as she turned to face him.

"I said I agree with the old man," he said. *Here, is where you belong*, he wanted to say out loud, but he only thought it. It was the coldness of his remark that Katelyn responded to so negatively. Again he was deciding what was best for her, as if he had the right to do so.

"I didn't solicit your opinion nor do I want it. Jack's reason for disapproving of my relationship with Adam had nothing to do with me and everything to do with Jenny." She flung his arms away and sighed in frustration. "He thought that Jenny was a liability to his family. He didn't want my bastard child to inherit any part of the Taylor fortune or taint their good name. He was kind enough though to offer me a deal. He suggested that I allow Kevin and Sylvia to adopt Jenny. Do you believe that?" she asked as she began to shutter. She couldn't stop the tears or the impulsive convulsing from the ultimate anger at Jack's suggestion. Katelyn saw the look on Gianfranco's face too. He looked totally and utterly disgusted as well and irritated by the man's comments.

Gianfranco took her in his arms and listened intently as she described her meeting with Jack Taylor through her tears. He felt nothing but extreme loathing for both Taylor men. He had no respect for the elder of the two for all the pain he was causing Katelyn and only too happy to take his company from him.

As far as Adam was concerned, he saw him as a complete waste, a man without a purpose, a man with very little regard for women and one who had absolutely no business sense. He was glad that Katelyn had never had to learn that truth about Adam from him. He detested the man and his fetish for cruelty toward women. When the research came across his desk about *Glitz* he was shocked at the skeletons in Adam's closet. The younger of the Taylor men was into some very kinky stuff. He was only too happy to protect and save Katelyn from that man.

Gianfranco continued to listen compassionately but he couldn't help the jealousy he felt at the mention of Jenny's father in their conversation, even if it was indirectly. It was this unknown man's ghost that he would have to fight perpetually if he were to attempt to have a future with Katelyn.

The kiss they shared earlier in the afternoon and her reaction to him told him she wasn't immune to him. He missed her and she felt right in his arms. Was he the only one who recognized that they belonged together? The question for him was whether what they felt for each other was enough to hold the ugly thoughts he was having of Jenny's father at bay. He didn't know if he could look at her beautiful little girl everyday and not be reminded of the man Katelyn betrayed him with. Every time he thought about how quickly she betrayed him, he cringed. How could he promise her and her child a future if he couldn't let go of the past?

Gianfranco wondered for years how Katelyn could have thought so little of what they shared that she went so willingly and so quickly into the arms of another man. It nearly destroyed him to think that he had readied her body for someone else. *Was she as compliant in the other man's arms as she was and continued to be in mine?*

"Are you listening to a word I'm saying?" she asked him as he looked lost in thought. "Gianfranco..." Katelyn repeated before he finally shook out of the trance he was in. *What was he thinking about?*

"I'm sorry, my mind keeps drifting." Their eyes met and it wasn't his imagination this time; he definitely saw her lips quivering, anxiously. She thought he had been ignoring her, that his thoughts were not about her. How wrong she would have been if she were able to read his mind. His thoughts were always of her. He wanted to take her in his arms and brand her, ruin her for any other man. It was taking all his might to

41

keep himself focused and not to think about the man who might steal his future happiness from him. He wanted Katelyn and he wanted to erase any memory of him from her head, once and for all.

"Did you love him so much that you wanted to share a child with him, Katelyn?" he murmured.

"I told you before, I don't love Adam." She knew they weren't talking about Adam anymore. He had meant Jenny's biological father. A subject that was not open for discussion. He was getting too close to the truth and she wasn't ready to deal with that truth herself, not yet. In her state of mind, the slightest slip would be all he needed to put two and two together. Gianfranco was a brilliant man and one mistake on her part and her secret would be revealed.

"As you well know, I meant Jenny's father. Did you love him?" He watched carefully as Katelyn struggled with her answer. He could see the pain the subject caused her. It was written all over her beautiful face. She looked away to avoid eye contact or to avoid talking about him at all. He couldn't decide which.

"I'd rather we not talk about him. But, for the record, I think you know me well enough to know that question does not require an answer. Let's clean up and I'll go get you another drink." Katelyn wanted to change the subject and talk about something a little less threatening so she left the room. She could hear him moving around in the other room as she washed the salsa and chips bowl. It was obvious, from the way his voice carried, that he was now in the hall looking at the pictures hanging on the wall.

"Kevin tells me that you're back in the states for good this time. What prompted you to change your mind?" she asked nervously. She knew he was studying the pictures and the faces in them. She knew as sure as she was breathing that her secret was at risk.

He followed her voice after glimpsing the photos hanging on the wall. There was something about the lack of certain photos that puzzled him. He couldn't quite put his finger on it but something was just not right. He glanced over at them again and studied the various snapshots. There were many pictures of Katelyn with Jenny, along with pictures of her parents, some of Sylvia and Kevin and there was even some of himself and

Jake and a few female friends but not one picture of the mystery man. He surmised that perhaps she might not want Jenny to know who her father was and might have put those aside.

"There's not a lot to tell. I've been planning this move for years. I've been progressively transferring our main hub of GFB Enterprises to the States to make my eventual move here less hectic when the time was right. I'm finally at that point where the majority of my business can be handled directly from our home office based here in New York. I'll still have to travel around the world but not nearly as often. I have excellent staff strategically placed in satellite offices all around the world who can handle things as they come up, just as well as I can myself," Gianfranco stated.

"Sounds like you've been busy. If you've been planning this move for years, why haven't I heard anything before now? I would think Kevin or Jake would have mentioned your return to me?" she asked as she joined him in the living room with fresh drinks. Katelyn placed a drink in his hand and waited for his answer.

He hesitated for a moment and then decided to be frank with her. "I postponed my own personal move because of you…" he answered softly. Her choking sound of disbelief made him laugh. "I'm serious; my company has been changing for years. I personally would have been back here in the States a long time ago but I delayed my return, which is why you hadn't heard anything. I'm sure you've heard of us, GFB Enterprises? I've been known to dabble in many different interests. One of the vast holdings is in publication," he said, knowing she would put the two together within minutes.

He was intrigued by her response. "I guess that look in your eyes means you're a little surprised?" *A little surprised, isn't the word*. His company just took over *Glitz* magazine. The magazine she worked for. Was it a coincidence? Just five years ago, the same company had acquired *Intrigue* Magazine and made it into one of the hottest magazines on the open market. Perhaps, she was jumping to conclusions. Katelyn couldn't understand how he had hidden behind such an obvious corporation for this long.

"I had no idea. I'm not even sure what to say in response," she added, completely shocked.

"You could start by rescinding your notice of resignation to my magazine. I want you to stay. Please?" He moved past her and the scent of his cologne overwhelmed her. She remembered how he had searched for cologne that she could tolerate with her allergies. The smell of his cologne, one he eventually had a designer create, made specifically with her in mind, was still as titillating now as it was years ago. She was surprised that he still wore it. She tried to resist him but he was closer now and drawing circles on her wrists while bringing her hands forward until they rested against his chest. Her breathing was becoming irregular and labored from his touch.

"We shouldn't be having this conversation. I don't need you to protect me, Gianfranco," she whispered, barely audible. She couldn't let him do this to her as she fought to control her breathing. He couldn't be allowed to see just how much she craved his touch, not if she knew what was good for her.

"You mentioned visiting Kevin. Are you still going?" he asked curiously.

She could tell he was up to something, but what? She simply nodded and waited for the next shoe to drop.

"Is Jenny going with you to see Kevin and Sylvia?" he asked.

"Of course, I don't go anywhere without her. How could you ask such a silly question?" The devil himself was no match for Gianfranco Broccolini. It was his smile that affected her most. His smile was electrifying and when he smiled you were hauled into his world, a world in which you had little or no control. She felt that he was up to something; maybe it was paranoia but she couldn't shake the possibility that he was putting things together in his head. He wanted a specific scenario and he was working to assure its execution.

There is more to her story than she is telling me. But rather than push her for the information, he would find out the information himself, his way. There was something she didn't want him to know. If there was one thing he knew for certain, it was that Katelyn; was a terrible liar. *What is she hiding from me?*

"I was thinking about going out to see Kevin again myself. Perhaps we could make the trip together?" he suggested considerately.

Katelyn managed to hide her discomfort. All she could think of was how close he would be to his own child. *If I agree, how will I avoid the inevitable? He will never forgive me if he finds out about Jenny and I will be the target of his wrath, truth be told.* He would never forgive her for keeping his child from him for so many years. She found herself questioning why she had come to make that fateful decision.

"Cancel your reservations if you've already made them. Let's all fly there in my jet. It'll be fun for Jenny and you won't have to deal with airport hassle," he added as an afterthought, as though it would make a difference.

Warily, she scrambled to come up with an excuse, one that he'd believe. "I get very nervous on small planes. Thank you for the offer anyway," she said the only thing that popped into her head.

"You sound more afraid of me than you are of the smaller planes, Katelyn. Besides, my small plane is not so small at all; it's a Boeing 727. I assure you that it's big enough for all three of us," he said wanting to put her at ease, suspecting that her reluctance had little to do with closed quarters and more to do with being alone with him.

Katelyn lightheartedly smiled; she couldn't help seeing images of the three of them on that plane together. *Not even a plane that size would keep his child's eyes from looking back into his own.* "I'm sure you're much too busy to chauffeur us around."

"Katelyn, I didn't make the suggestion out of friendship. I was making the trip myself anyway; I wasn't going out of my way." He glanced past her toward the bedrooms and let out a deep discernible breath. "I don't know much about her and for that, I'm sorry. Is she much like her mother? How old is she?" he added disappointedly. He wanted her to be like her mother. He couldn't take it if she were more like her father. If she looked more like him, then little, innocent Jenny would be a constant reminder of how little Katelyn valued what they shared together.

"Why the twenty questions?" she asked, trying to keep her anxiety under wraps. Suddenly, she realized her anxious response seemed just a little peculiar. "I guess I'm a little overprotective," she added to distract him.

Gianfranco knew something wasn't right about this whole situation. His sharp business sense warned him when someone was trying to put one over on him; he was getting that distinct impression while speaking to her. It was obvious from the way she spoke and if that wasn't enough to convince him, he saw it in her eyes.

Katelyn felt terribly guilty that their child slept only a few feet away. With tears threatening, she moved against the wall for added support. Once he found out the truth, there was no telling what he'd do. She knew one thing for certain and that was that the truth had to come from her first. There might be a very different outcome if he heard it from her. "I have something I need to tell you," she whispered. "I'm not sure where to begin."

"Then don't say a word. I'm not sure I'm ready to hear your admission," he said with dread. She was going to tell him about her child's father; Gianfranco was sure of it and he didn't want to hear it. He wasn't prepared to hear the explanation she would give and needed time to escape quickly before his chest burst open from the pain her confession would cause him. "I'll make all the arrangements for our trip and have Dana, my assistant call you with the details. Are we in agreement?" he asked.

"You don't have to do this," she said offering him a way out.

"I'm doing it. It's already been decided. I'll have my assistant Dana call you with the details tomorrow." He made a mental note to have Dana arrange the trip for two days from now, alert his pilot and when it was set, notify Katelyn with those plans.

This whole situation is utterly and completely mad. Katelyn knew the admission would come eventually but she didn't know if she was ready, just yet. How could two people who wanted each other so much not love each other? She was glad that he was withdrawing, running from what was happening between them because she was frightened as well. She was afraid she would lose herself to him and never be able to pick up the pieces that he would leave behind. But the look on his face pleaded with her to agree to this trip. *What choice do I have?* He would be even more suspicious if she had declined his offer.

Yet, as he retreated, she longed for the touch that had left her so empty for far too long. She fantasized about being held by him, making love to him, the only man she had ever loved. He was the one man who could make her body act as he saw fit. He was the only man who ever made her body cry out with pleasure. Her burning hunger for him could never be extinguished, as much as she wished it could.

Gianfranco shut the door behind him as he left, ensuring that their actions wouldn't affect her daughter, just as Katelyn wanted it. She had to explain to Jenny when she woke up, that there was a change of plans; they wouldn't be leaving today but would be traveling to Montana with Kevin's good friend, Gianfranco Broccolini, on his private jet.

Chapter Five

Katelyn woke from sleep to the sound of her phone in the distance and knew it would probably be Gianfranco's assistant calling with their itinerary. She reached for the phone on her nightstand and was greeted by a young sweet sounding voice.

"Miss Donavan, My name is Dana and I'm calling on behalf of Mr. Broccolini. All the arrangements have been made for your trip to Montana and I've sent the flight information to you by email. Please call the office if you don't receive it. Mr. Broccolini has also arranged car service to pick you and your daughter up as well. If you need any further assistance, don't hesitate to call me here at the office," Dana said.

"Thank you Dana. I'll check my email and if it's not there I'll give a call back today. Thank you for all your help," Katelyn said before hanging up the phone and silently hoping that this trip didn't turn into a total disaster.

Jenny woke earlier than usual that morning and ran into her mother's room as soon as she heard the alarm clock go off. Jenny couldn't contain the enthusiasm she felt about their trip to Montana. Katelyn hated to burst her bubble but she needed to explain that their trip would be postponed until the next day. Jenny couldn't believe what she was hearing. She disliked the fact that the trip would be delayed another day but the news that they were traveling in a private plane excited her more than the disappointed delay and she couldn't wait to share that news with someone else.

"Mommy, Uncle Kevin has a friend with his very own plane?" Jenny asked with unbelievable excitement. "I have to tell Rosa," she screeched lively. Jenny ran to the phone and, with her little fingers, dialed her mom's best friend. She knew the number by heart.

Within minutes Rosa returned the call and asked Katelyn all sorts of questions, grilling her about the mystery man, Gianfranco Broccolini. Who was he and why hadn't she mentioned him to her before? "I want details and leave nothing out," Rosa said. "I have a feeling there's more about this man than you're telling me, since, one, you have never mentioned him to me before and two, you dropped everything to follow him in his private plane. I'll be over at noon and we can talk during lunch," she said before hanging up the phone.

Katelyn had decided last night, while lying in bed, that she would tell Gianfranco the truth; she would do it tonight. She would ask Rosa, when she came for lunch, if she could take Jenny overnight and she would invite him for dinner. She would attempt to tell him the truth and they would decide how best to break the news to their daughter.

Katelyn stared at the phone and sighed. She had never told Rosa about Jenny's father before and this was definitely going to be a lot to take in at one time for her friend. She had never told this to another living soul. It was her secret and it had been well guarded for so long that it finally felt as if a giant weight were being lifted from her shoulders as she prepared herself to tell the truth. It felt good. Finally, she would be able to admit the truth to someone else; who better to tell first than Rosa.

The next hour or two went by quickly, Katelyn barely had time to clean the apartment and catch up on laundry before her friend was due to arrive.

Rosa and a delivery truck from a local florist arrived at the same time. Katelyn smiled as the man handed her a beautiful and unexpected arrangement of red roses. They weren't her favorite flower so she knew they weren't from Gianfranco. "They're not from him, are they?" Rosa asked, she noticed the disappointment in her friend's face. Rosa knew roses were not Katelyn's favorite flower; she also suspected that the mystery man knew that too, by the look on Katelyn's face when she was handed the arrangement. So she assumed the roses had to have come from the only other person in Katelyn's life, Adam. She couldn't put her finger on it; but she just didn't like Adam Taylor. Call it a woman's intuition but she knew that Adam was not the right man for her good friend.

"Why don't you stop seeing Adam? You know, he thinks there's more to your relationship than there is, right?" Rosa questioned. She walked passed Katelyn as her friend filled a vase with water for the flowers. Rosa had been emptying the grocery bag she brought in; she had everything she needed to make her famous chicken salad. She began to heat up the chicken in a frying pan and clean and shred the lettuce as the chicken cooked. She turned to her friend and told her to relax; she would take care of lunch. Katelyn smiled and continued her attempt at small talk while setting the table and opening a chilled bottle of wine. It took only a few moments for Rosa to join her again.

"I'm sorry about that remark in the kitchen. It was uncalled for, regardless of how I feel about Adam," Rosa said as she gently placed the lunch plates on the table. "Your feelings matter to me; and I shouldn't have said that."

"So much has happened in one day that I'm not sure where to begin my narrative. I quit my job yesterday. Jack Taylor requested a private meeting with me yesterday morning. I went to it thinking we were going to discuss the article I just completed when, in fact, he had called the meeting to discuss my relationship with his son. He made me so angry during our meeting that I reacted before I had a chance to think," Katelyn said with regret.

She briefly told her about the events of the previous day and Rosa was a little shocked, to say the least, and she hadn't gotten to the best part yet. Rosa knew Katelyn loved her job and did it well. "Why does Jack Taylor want to jeopardize your career when he was obviously impressed with your work?" Rosa asked.

"Apparently, he finds the thought of Adam involved with someone who has a child to be repulsive. He called my Jenny a bastard and said she would never inherit a dime of his money if he had anything to say about it. He actually said that and then complimented my work in the next breath. He said that if I discontinued my relationship with his son all would be well." Katelyn hated to repeat the revolting words he snarled at her, even to Rosa. "He had no idea during our meeting that I never had intentions of exploring that kind of relationship with Adam." She said as she took a forkful of salad into her mouth.

This latest development was bewildering to Rosa but she was happy to hear that Katelyn still had no interest in exploring a relationship with Adam. Though it seemed to her that Adam's thinking was quite to the contrary.

"Adam and I have been going down two very different paths for some time now. I'm sure you're happy to hear that. He wanted more than I was willing to give," Katelyn teased. The two friends spent so much time together these days they could finish each other's sentences.

"This salad is delicious. I can never seem to get it right when I make it. Anyway, there is just so much I have to tell you but let's finish lunch first. It's too upsetting to repeat while I'm eating."

Katelyn pulled the bag of overflowing garbage from the kitchen pail and told her friend she would run it down to the curb before the garbage men were due for a pick up. The lunch was delicious as always and the conversation enjoyable. Rosa insisted on doing dishes while Katelyn ran the garbage downstairs. She promised to have two fresh glasses of wine poured before she returned.

The incinerator wasn't working and that meant either a trip outside or a garbage pile-up in her apartment. Katelyn could see that it was clear outside but unusually brisk for this time of year. She could almost smell the changing temperature in the air. The flowers were from Adam and that only meant that she would have to face him again at some point and make it clear, once and for all, that she only ever saw him as a friend. It had been obvious to her from the onset, that no other man would make her feel the way Gianfranco Broccolini did, which was proven once again last night.

Mixing business and pleasure was something she had always frowned upon. When you mixed work relationships with personal ones, it always ended badly. She and Adam were certainly no exception to that rule.

She had just dropped the bag in the can outside when she spotted the Taylor limousine approaching. She was a little surprised when it came to a halt next to her and that Jack Taylor stepped out onto the sidewalk. *What more could he possibly have to say to me?* He watched her cautiously, before speaking. It was his body language though that she had noticed first. He seemed like a changed man since yesterday afternoon and she was perplexed. He had the edge right now but she was sure she would learn the nature of this visit soon enough. There had to be a very good reason for him to make this trip to her neighborhood.

"Miss Donavan, I was hoping that we could have a word. Could you spare a minute or two?" he asked properly. Katelyn was a little curious, to say the least. If he had asked that same question yesterday; it would have seemed more like an order but today he was a different.

She stood silently for a moment, studying him, while he barked orders to his driver, Martin, to give them a few minutes alone. This was not the same calm, iron-fisted man she had witnessed yesterday. She didn't like where this was taking her as the pieces began to come together. There was desperation in his voice and she had an idea who might be behind it. Hopefully, it wasn't what she thought at all. Perhaps Adam had talked to him and, if so, that would all have been for naught since their relationship would never be more than platonic. But the longer she thought about it, the stronger she felt her first theory might be correct.

"I'm here to talk about your resignation. I'd like you to reconsider and come back to work at the magazine," he said impatiently. "If it will take offering you more money or an apology to get you back, then it's yours. I'm willing to spend whatever it will take," he stated mysteriously. Something was amiss and she suddenly realized that Gianfranco had his hand in this for Jack to have a change of heart.

"I thought you were glad to see the back of my head," Katelyn stated, knowing full well that the real culprit behind this offer was about to be revealed.

"I want to apologize for the way our meeting went yesterday. It seems I've underestimated you. You're far more dangerous to me than I had given you credit for. Why didn't you tell me that you and Gianfranco Broccolini were friends? You must have been amused when

I confided in you about the takeover?" He paused for a second as if considering what to say next. He must have thought better about what he was going to say and opted not to go down that path. "He did everything but threaten to have me killed for dismissing you and I'm not sure he wouldn't have done precisely that if he could have gotten away with it." He looked up at the building in front of them and let out an exhausted sigh of defeat.

"The mere fact that you never mentioned his name tells me a lot about the person you are. His name alone could've opened a lot of doors for you in the past but I think you know that. I'm more intrigued by you at this moment, than I was before." he stated with real interest.

"I'm not sure where Mr. Broccolini fits into the scheme of things but I assure you that I would never have used his influence to further my career. So whatever has taken place between the two of you since yesterday has nothing to do with me."

The elder Taylor eyed her speculatively and laughed. "I admire your naivety, Miss Donavan; but I must point out just how wrong you are. I'm not sure what kind of hold you have on him but Broccolini has involved himself in your life whether you like it, or not. Truth be told, Miss Donavan, I don't envy what you've gotten yourself into. He's a hard man and not easily crossed. He may pretend to close an eye here or there but, believe me, unlike Adam he's never asleep at the wheel. I learned the hard way that he's not a very forgiving man and he has no problem stepping on anyone or anything that gets in his way."

Jack Taylor seemed a little hesitant to continue discussing his reason for being there but decided that he had little choice. "As I'm sure you've already been made aware, Broccolini robbed my magazine right from under my nose. I blame myself; I trusted Adam to do his job and his lack of business savvy has cost me dearly. Adam's only job was to oversee our investments and to make sure our financial people were doing their jobs. Instead, he thought he could make investments on his own with the company money and that mistake cost me heavily. I was only warned about the risk from our traders who informed me that Adam was told months ago that what he was doing was too risky. Apparently, he was preoccupied at the time and didn't see the need to bother me about what might happen. I now find myself in a bad position; I need this sale to go through in order to survive financially."

"Miss Donavan, you're the only one who stands between me and total ruin. I cannot take back what I said to you yesterday. I can only beg your forgiveness and ask for your pity," Jack added apprehensively.

Jack could see that his confession rendered her speechless. "I find myself in a very awkward situation. On the one hand, I was right about you and Adam," he acknowledged before pausing.

"Neither of you are right for each other," he added as matter of fact. The elder Taylor was under enormous pressure; she could see that and he wasn't comfortable with the foreign feeling. "I'm here today to implore you to reconsider your resignation. Unless you're back at your desk with a signed contract very soon Broccolini has threatened to pull the deal."

Katelyn knew why Gianfranco had done this. She would have been offered a place at the magazine regardless of what happened today. But Gianfranco wanted Jack Taylor to eat some humble pie, to feel what it was like to make someone feel insignificant just as he had enjoyed doing to her the day before. The one thing Gianfranco hadn't counted on was that she wasn't as hard as he was; she felt sorry for the man who stood before her.

"I will talk to Mr. Broccolini and have him withdraw his ultimatum. It wasn't fair that he put you in this situation," she added, trying to give him back what little dignity he had left.

"I think you're wrong in this instance, I'm afraid. He was adamant about his demands and I have too much to lose to gamble that this was some required punishment. It's ironic, isn't it? Adam allowed himself to get lured into a deal with the devil and that deal could cost us everything. He thought that using shares from the magazine as collateral to finance one of his other investments, would be a safe bet. He hadn't anticipated Broccolini waiting in the wings for just that sort of mistake. Now I find myself in bed with the devil, doing his bidding in order to survive."

He was a beaten man and Katelyn couldn't help but feel pity for him. She knew Gianfranco better than anyone and her gut instinct was telling her he had planned this takeover a long time ago and wanted it to happen exactly the way it did. Gianfranco didn't leave things to chance; he made things happen. He might not have planned on making Jack Taylor suffer so publicly; but he would definitely enjoy bringing him to his knees because he messed with him and what he claimed as his.

This whole situation is ridiculous. "I don't like being used as a pawn, by either of you. I'm planning on going out of town, for a couple of weeks. I don't really want, or need, this added pressure on me," she said. She requested that he join his driver, who had just returned from his trip around the block. She watched as he walked in the direction of the waiting vehicle. The self-assuredness and the tough exterior she had witnessed the day before was all but gone.

"If it's any consolation, I'll try to reason with Gianfranco before I leave. What he's doing to you and your family is not fair," she added offering a cryptic smile. Martin had overheard their latest exchange and told her with a glance that she was one classy lady. Jack Taylor didn't deserve this much and she knew Martin was thinking just that.

"Thank you, I know I don't deserve even that much from you," Taylor admitted in defeat. He faltered for a moment then stamped out the cigarette he had lit and turned again toward Martin. Katelyn noticed that Martin had bowed his head a little, a gesture toward her; he smiled before closing the door behind his employer. Jack put the window down and paused again before speaking to her through it. "I probably shouldn't say this much but my son would have been a lucky man to have been married to you, even without the money." He didn't wait for a response as he closed the window and began his drive down the road.

Katelyn tried to process what had just happened as the words echoed over and over in her head; still she couldn't believe it. Gianfranco used his money and power to get what he wanted and he was using that power to control her life. *Maybe it would do him good to have to part with some of that money!* No matter what she accepted from him as support for their child, it would mean mere pennies to him. If he wanted to, he could turn around and use all that money and power to take Jenny away from her. That was a scenario, she didn't want to visit.

Gianfranco could very well convince a judge that he would be the better parent for Jenny. Suddenly, this train of thought wasn't leaving a good taste in her mouth. Her life was spiraling out of control and, once again, the person pushing the buttons was Gianfranco Broccolini. She was still shaking from her own thoughts as she entered the elevator that led to her apartment.

"Sorry that took so long; I had an unexpected visitor downstairs," Katelyn explained to Rosa as she opened the door and tossed her coat on the chair. *What else could possibly go wrong today?*

Rosa smiled warmly, wondering who the unexpected visitor was as she tapped Katelyn gently on the shoulder and handed her a glass of wine. "It can't be all that bad. Once you let it all out you'll feel much better. Who was your visitor?" she asked.

"It was Jack Taylor, I'm afraid this story is so unbelievable that even you will be shocked by its twists and turns; it's funny how one event in your life intertwines with another. I have to tell you, I'm beginning to think this day is a little more than I bargained for." Katelyn took a sip of the wine and plopped down on her favorite chair.

"This should be interesting. You rarely, if ever, drink alcohol and you've already had two drinks and its only 2:00 p.m. Are you sure, you're going to be alright?" Rosa asked her friend. Despite her craving to hear Katelyn's story, Rosa didn't want to see her friend like this. She knew that when Katelyn was ready, she would tell her the story in her own way.

Katelyn didn't know where to begin. Two days ago, she was living a very dull existence and now it was anything but boring. Her life seemed to have taken on a very surreal spin, as if she were taking part in some-one else's life. She was being torn in different directions and that's why the trip to visit Kevin came at the right time and made the most sense. "Yesterday, Jack Taylor warned me that, if I continued my relationship with his son, both he and I would be without employment and Adam would be left penniless. Gianfranco arrived here last night and, after we spoke, he didn't like Mr. Taylor's threats toward me and devised his own plan of retaliation."

Rosa heard the words but couldn't believe what she was hearing. Did this kind of stuff still happen in this day and age? Who was she kidding, of course, it did. Money was money and it did strange things to people. She was even more shocked that someone would suggest to Katelyn, of all people, that she give her child away, as if that were ever something she would ever consider. "I can't imagine you taking the suggestion to give up Jenny without a fight?" she added dumbfounded and with attitude.

"No, of course I didn't. Rosa, by the time our meeting had concluded, I told Jack to take his job and stick it where the sun doesn't shine. That was how angry he had gotten me," she said, before picking up her drink and offering a silent toast. Katelyn thought for a moment or two before continuing her story, not wanting to confuse Rosa with all the twists and turns.

"That's not the worst of it. Do you remember me telling you that I would reveal who Jenny's father was to you when the time was right?" She could see Rosa's eyes perk up over her wine glass. "Well, *Glitz,* was recently taken over and will merge with *Intrigue.* It seems that my boss, Jack Taylor, was in way over his head financially and stands to lose it all if the sale of the magazine falls through for any reason. Merging the two magazines wasn't his intention but apparently he had little choice because a takeover was set in motion; it seems the CEO of GFB Enterprises, who currently owns *Intrigue,* set his sights on *Glitz* and right now is threatening to pull out of the deal, unless I come as part of the package."

Rosa was a little puzzled at first and wondered why Katelyn, of all people, was being used as a pawn in this sale, but she knew it would all make sense soon enough. "Why are you part of the deal? I'm not understanding something," she asked, knowing her friend was about to tell her something important.

"Do you remember the man Jenny mentioned this morning?" Katelyn asked as she watched her friend's eye twinkle with clarity. "Rosa, the man who is taking us to Montana is Gianfranco Broccolini; the sole shareholder of GBF Enterprises. Gianfranco Broccolini is GBF Enterprises." Katelyn added uneasily.

Rosa was shocked and it took a little time for the bulk of the conversation to sink in; but when it did she had no idea what to say. For the first time Rosa was rendered speechless. *Gianfranco and Kevin are good friends; that has to be good thing,* she thought to herself after a few seconds. She almost fell off the chair when Katelyn declared that Gianfranco Broccolini was, in fact, Jenny's biological father. Rosa grew concerned for her friend. Things didn't seem so easy any longer, and, worst of all, she knew her friend was in way over her head. She shuddered, thinking about what was going to happen when the truth was finally revealed to Gianfranco, that he had a child.

Katelyn swallowed another sip of wine and walked over to the terrace doors. She stared out at the ocean waves as they hit the jetty below. The ocean offered some comfort to her even in her darkest hours. "It's a tremendous relief to admit the truth out loud to someone. Rosa, Gianfranco was here last night; he left only because we couldn't keep our hands off each other. I don't know how or when it happened. It was as though we were transported back in time, back to that summer again," she said turning to her friend.

Katelyn sighed as if it was all too much to take. "I don't understand this game he's playing with Jack Taylor. Gianfranco likes to be in control of everything he touches and that kind of scares me when I think about what that will mean when I finally tell him about Jenny." She turned to her friend and watched Rosa's reaction to the information she was being bombarded with.

Both women took a swig from their glasses at the same time and laughed. Rosa put hers down as she reached out to embrace Katelyn. "What do you think he'll say when you tell him about Jenny?" Rosa asked the question but already knew the answer from her friend's demeanor. It was clear that Gianfranco Broccolini was not the type of man to be an absent father. "What happens now?" Rosa asked.

"I'm not sure. After my reaction to him last night, it is obvious that I am like putty in his hands. Which, to tell you the truth, frightens me when it comes to making decisions about the role he will play in Jenny's life. Why do I feel like such an idiot?" She started to pace back and forth in front of the window; that was something she did when she was feeling nervous. "I almost let him make love to me again last night, Rosa. What's worse than anything is the fact that neither of us was thinking clearly, yet again; we almost threw caution to the wind, not thinking about the consequences of another union between us. How stupid is that?" she asked, as tears ran down her cheeks. "I don't think he was carrying any protection on him and I certainly have had no need for it."

Rosa hugged her friend. She knew that Katelyn must really love this guy to be willing to make such a foolish mistake, not only once in her life but almost a second time. Rosa also began to wonder about Gianfranco Broccolini, the man. He had to have feelings for Katelyn too if he was also willing to behave so recklessly. She couldn't imagine that he had gotten where he was by making careless mistakes. Rosa was sure that Gianfranco had been Katelyn's one and only lover and that her friend was still in love with the man. "You'll get through this. Tell me; how did you meet him?" she asked.

Katelyn recalled the memories as though it had happened yesterday. No matter how many years had passed, the memories of that summer were vivid and, honestly, it was that raw rapture that they shared that saw her through some very rough periods of her life.

"The first time I saw him, was at Kevin's wedding. Do you remember me telling you stories about Kevin's college buddies? Gianfranco was one of them," she said smiling, as she recalled the three musketeers. She remembered fondly the nickname they were given all through college and it was a well-deserved metaphor. They were always together, one as rogue as the other. She could see that Rosa realized who Gianfranco was. After all, she had stared at those pictures in the hallway for years. Gianfranco was the third musketeer that, she hadn't yet had the pleasure to meet.

"It was funny that, as fate would have it, Kevin came home from school during the early years of college on many occasions and would bring his friends with him. Gianfranco and Jake would come to our home but, for one reason or another, I wasn't around when Gianfranco was there. I did get to meet Jake on two or three occasions during that time. It was accidental but I think fate had a different kind of meeting in store for us. Our paths crossed, for the very first time, at Kevin's wedding." Katelyn drifted off into her own private memories for a second before continuing her story.

"He was Kevin's best man at the wedding and I was one of Sylvia's bridesmaids. Jake was a groomsman and, actually, my partner. I had arrived just in time to take my place in the wedding procession. I had just flown in from meeting with representatives from Berkley College in California. I had big plans for my future back then. Up until that point, my plans were set in stone and I wasn't going to let anyone or anything derail me until the night I met Gianfranco Broccolini," she said.

Katelyn recalled the dress she wore keenly. She remembered how it made her look older than her eighteen years. It was a very pale sea foam green, long silk flowing gown. The front of the dress draped over the bust giving the illusion of modesty, yet making her look fuller than she actually was. The most dangerous part of the dress was the back; it dipped quite low. She remembered the way Gianfranco made her feel when he stared at her. She could still feel his stare now all these years later.

"I have to admit, the gown that Sylvia picked out for the wedding party was very sexy; it looked great on each and every girl, regardless of size and shape. It was during their vows to each other that I felt eyes on me. He stood right next to Kevin; I looked up and I could feel his eyes burning through my skin. No one else noticed what he was doing because it was ever so subtle. At first glance, I thought that I had imagined it; he was so dangerous, so good-looking. He could have had any woman in the room and, in the end, he wanted me." Rosa was captivated by the story of love and lust and listened intently. She was beginning to like this guy and somehow she knew that the story of Katelyn and Gianfranco wasn't complete. She knew they needed to find a way back to each other again; maybe when they did they would better understand what had kept them from each other this long.

"I tried, time and again during the wedding, to turn my focus away from him but it was almost as if he held me in a trance with those ebony eyes of his. We were in a room full of people and yet to me it was like being trapped in a cocoon that he had created for us. I couldn't believe the way my body was betraying me. He was a complete stranger and I was totally, uncontrollably, wanton-like in his presence. It was terrifying to me and intriguing at the same time. At eighteen, I wasn't ready to deal with someone so sophisticated and worldly but I couldn't back away from the challenge either." Katelyn went on tell Rosa how he had awakened a desire so deep within herself that she thought she would faint with the embarrassment of it all.

"I'll never forget how flushed I became. One of the other brides-maids became concerned for me and thought that I was ill. I don't think I ever believed in soul-mates before that night; but what we shared was bigger than the two of us." She wasn't so sure she believed in soul-mates any longer though. Her feelings were a bit more one-sided these days. She continued to pour out her story; Rosa was shocked and saddened at how naive Katelyn had been in the past. Of course, her age had a lot to do with that. She wondered about Gianfranco; *with all his worldly experience back then, what was he thinking?*

"I was so stubborn and I didn't want to back away from his chal-lenge, no matter who he was. I glanced over at him during the vows and I saw in his eyes that he was accomplishing exactly what he had set out to do. He knew he had awakened wantonness in me that I had never felt before. He also knew that I was questioning what I was feeling. I remember he smiled smugly, as if to say he'd finished what he set out to do and, for the time being, he would leave me alone to bask in my new feelings. At least, that's what I felt," she added.

"Rosa, I had thoughts about him that I had never allowed myself to think about before. It was strange; he had done such a complete job of captivating me, I was surprised he had retreated so hastily. I knew he was dangerous and that I should keep my distance but I was compelled to find out who he was and what he wanted from me that night."

She pushed her drink aside, leaned back on the couch and contin-ued her story, in complete detail. "After the service was over, we went to the reception hall and the bridal party was asked to join in the first dance. Jake and I were partners; he led me out to the dance floor and together, along with the rest of the bridal party, we danced. It was then that I found out that Gianfranco Broccolini was the third musketeer; the one I hadn't met until that moment. The man who had captivated me only moments before in the chapel was about to be introduced to me, by Jake. He introduced us as we were all dancing. Jake said that both he and Kevin were kind of embarrassed that Gianfranco and I hadn't had an opportunity to meet sooner."

Rosa smiled at the innocence of the teenager she had been and thought about how that young girl transformed into the woman she became later. She couldn't help being curious about Gianfranco Broccolini. He had to know that Kevin would be upset if he hurt his sister. Somehow, she chose to believe that there was more to the man and his feelings for her friend than Katelyn was leading her to believe.

"Jake went on and on at the wedding, telling Gianfranco how proud he was of me and all my accomplishments. He told him that I had received a scholarship and was going away to college that fall." Katelyn went on to explain how Jake continued to talk to Gianfranco while dancing with her and when the song ended he hugged her affectionately and said that he was going to leave her because he was on the prowl for a loose woman. Gianfranco saw this as his chance to join her on the dance floor.

"While we danced, he took the opportunity to apologize for not being able to make my parent's funeral and further explained his absence; he'd had urgent business that had kept him out of the country. I told him that Kevin had already explained it to me but he felt the need to explain it again personally."

"While Jake was off flirting with another bridesmaid, he had his eye on earlier, I stayed with Gianfranco and we talked and danced. Later in the afternoon, they made an announcement that the bridal party was needed outside for pictures; this time Gianfranco led the way. He put his hand on the naked flesh of my lower back and his touch awakened a sensual being in me that I hadn't known existed, until that second. I had never in my life wished more fervently that my body were covered with gorilla-like clothing as I had at that moment." Katelyn smiled as she recalled how embarrassed those new feelings were to her.

"Gianfranco must have sensed my unease when he noticed what his touch was doing to me. He offered his jacket to cover what was exposed for everyone to see. I became openly aroused and he enjoyed being the savage who had caused my momentary lapse in judgment."

Rosa was mesmerized, almost choking as she begged her friend to continue. This story was better than a movie and Katelyn's love for this man was evident in the way she spoke about him. "Don't stop now, this is getting interesting. I want to know what happened next," she said as she stood up and offered to put their glasses in the sink. It was then that Rosa remembered this story didn't have a happy ending.

"After the photographer had taken all his pictures, and polite conversing with everyone, we were all ushered back into the reception area. I didn't see much of Gianfranco again until after all the toasts were done and the cake was cut. He came over to me and asked me to dance the final dance with him. Before he had a chance to lead me out to the dance floor, my brother and Jake practically pounced on him. Kevin said something to him in private and Jake seemed to concur with him. When I asked Gianfranco about it, he simply said they told him who I was and warned him not to take advantage of me or hurt me. I remember feeling as though they all knew something I didn't. Kevin thought I needed his protection and that angered me, but, I guess, given what history has uncovered, he might have been right."

Katelyn thought about their first dance together and his thoughtful whispers into her ear as he told her she would always be safe with him. Gianfranco asked her what her plans were for the future and, at the time, she didn't want to seem as if she were inexperienced or unsophisticated so she rattled on about her plans for college and how she wanted to travel the world afterward as a journalist.

"I tried to sound worldly and confident when, in actuality, just the opposite was true. All my life I wanted to have a family and if I could have stayed at home and raised a couple of kids that would have made me happy. My parents were great role models; I wish you'd had a chance to meet them. My mother taught us both to go after your dreams. Don't let anyone tell you that you can't have something or can't do something. She always said that even the impossible was possible. My dream was to have a family of my own. I miss them, I'm glad we had them around during the important years of our development but it doesn't make it easier. Kevin and I were lucky to experience the love they felt for each other and us, even if it ended too soon." Her mood had suddenly become melancholy as she remembered her parents.

"I stretched my story out to impress him and I went on and on about becoming this famous journalist one day and how those plans didn't jive well with having a family. I don't know what possessed me to say that. After all, I was an old fashioned girl and raising a family was high up on my to-do list. I wanted a career, but I also wanted a husband and partner to share it all with me." Katelyn stood and moved around the apartment a bit before continuing.

"Gianfranco held me in his arms and we danced that last dance as if our lives depended on it. It was hard to think of myself in anyone else's arms after that. I wanted more from him but I was afraid; I couldn't imagine what it would be like to be with him, in every way. The heightened pleasure I experienced up to that point was coming just from dancing in his arms."

Rosa was speechless. This was her friend who rarely went out and if she did it was usually with a friend. "This is so insane. It's like I don't really know you."

"The music was still playing when he led me out on to the verandah after our dance. I remember looking up at the stars and silently asking my mother what she thought about him. Somehow, I knew even then that he was going to change my life." Katelyn was silent for a moment as she slipped back in time and let her memories consume her. She could still hear the music in the background as she turned her attention toward the man who was leading her down this path.

Continuing, "He asked me if I was afraid of him and when I told him I wasn't, he said I should be. I can still feel what I felt that day so vividly. My body was experiencing such sensual turmoil and it was all at his hand. To say that I wasn't afraid was an understatement." Katelyn knew that her knowledge of desire had come from Gianfranco because to this day she had never felt it again. She recalled bits and pieces of their conversation.

"I would never hurt you," he said as ran his long, masculine fingers down her arm. *"I've waited so long to touch you."* He hastily pulled his hand away from her body as though it burned to touch her and she could see he was fighting some kind of war within himself. She, at the same time, was trying to make sense of what he had admitted to her.

"What do you mean, you've waited so long? We've only just met tonight," she

65

asked. Katelyn was a little nervous and afraid to trust Gianfranco. What he said was strange but Jake and Kevin had trusted this man with their lives.

"Katelyn, I don't want you to think that I'm some crazy stalker, I'm not. I have heard stories about you for years and, quite frankly, I feel like I've know you forever. I have watched you mature into the woman you are now by looking at all your pictures and listening to all the stories from Kevin. I convinced myself that my curiosity about you was harmless. That was until I saw you standing at the altar today." He kissed her for the very first time; it was gentle at first, he tried with all his might to pull back but she didn't allow it. Katelyn deepened the kiss herself and, before she could blink, she saw that he was watching her, desperate for her to put a stop to what was happening between them but she didn't dare.

"I've never felt this way about another woman in my life," he said deepening their kiss yet again. That night was the beginning of the end for her. Any chance to have a relationship with any other man after him was all but destroyed that night. His words were sweet, but, as Kevin and Jake had told her often enough, Gianfranco had always been and would always be a ladies' man. He was one man who would never settle down, they often teased. Any woman foolish enough to get involved with him would risk getting seriously hurt. *"I've heard about your numerous women, from Kevin and Jake. Why am I any different?"* she asked.

He laughed aloud and kissed the palm of her hand with his lips and proceeded to take one of her fingers into his mouth and devour it. The gesture itself was both erotic and painful to her. She knew what he was doing to her and, if she were smart, she would put a stop to it before it was too late. Gianfranco was dangerous; there was no doubt about it. *"I assure you that there have been other women, not nearly as many as you've dreamt up in that beautiful head of yours. I never lied to any of the women I dated. They knew from the beginning that I had no intentions of committing myself to any of them,"* he had said to her.

"Maybe I want more than just becoming an added notch on your belt," she said, letting her hands rest behind her on the railing for support.

"I'm not interested in getting you into my bed only to have you slip away into the night. What I want from you, I'm willing to wait for. If I have to..." he said surrendering to her before finishing his train of thought.

Rosa could tell that Katelyn had come back from her clandestine thoughts because her eyes seemed more focused and less glazed than minutes before.

"We spent the most wonderful eight weeks together. I never thought that would ever happen to me. As the time drew nearer for me to leave for school, I regretted what I had told him when we first met. I wanted him more than I could ever imagine; in my innocence all I could think about was becoming his wife and having his children. I thought he wanted the same thing." Rosa studied her friend's face and witnessed the pain the memories brought back.

"I'm guessing he didn't feel the same way?" Rosa questioned as she watched Katelyn turn away from her. She didn't answer at first; it hurt too much. Katelyn had convinced herself that, after spending eight glorious weeks with her, he had felt the same way she did. Why he had a change of heart, she didn't know.

She told Rosa how he persuaded her to allow him to take her to California for her college visit. No one was the wiser because Kevin and Sylvia had taken a lengthy two month honeymoon and Jake was away at the summer camp he ran, for at risk youth. None of the people in her inner circle were aware of the relationship developing in their absence.

"Gianfranco came with me to register for classes and I kept hoping that he would whisk me away and take me back to Italy with him. He had ample opportunity to do just that; the last weekend we spent together there were times that I caught him looking as if he wanted nothing more. But there was always something that held him back. I was desperately in love and he was basically telling me, it's been fun, but it's over. He told me he had to go back to Italy and that there was a chance he might never return." Her face felt damp as she relived those awful moments over and over again in her head.

Rosa handed Katelyn a tissue from the table and ordered her to take a sip from the fresh glass of wine she had just handed her. "Sometimes things aren't always as they seem. Maybe he had reasons for leaving you back then. Did you ever ask him why he left?"

She didn't look at Rosa but she felt her friend studying her closely. "I didn't ask. I was too afraid of what his answer would do to me. It was better for me to believe that his leaving had nothing to do with how he felt about me. When I found out that I was pregnant, a few weeks after he left for Italy, I didn't dare tell him. I wanted him to stay with me because he wanted to stay. I didn't want to be that woman, the one who trapped him into a relationship he didn't want and would later regret."

"Is that why you left California and came back to New York, because you were pregnant with Jenny?" Rosa asked.

"Yes, Kevin was really great through that whole phase of my life. He offered to let me move in with him and Sylvia but I didn't want to go to Montana and I couldn't do that to them. They were newly married and I needed to learn to raise my baby on my own. Kevin and I had agreed before I left for college that it would be best to sell our parent's home; we did, just before I left for school. I was shocked when Kevin handed me the proceeds from the sale; he said it would see me through my rough times. He didn't want me to quit school and he didn't want me to struggle. The money from the sale of the house and some other money my parents left me not only paid for school but allowed me the freedom I needed to be a good mother."

Rosa had always known that Katelyn and Kevin had shared a special bond but she had more respect for the man after hearing this story. Kevin Donavan was a great guy in her book and if he weren't already married she would have tried to snag him herself.

"All that time your brother never suspected that Gianfranco was Jenny's father? What about Jake, he was around you all the time; didn't he try pressuring you into telling him about Jenny's father?" In fact, Rosa was surprised that the man she had come to know in Jake hadn't figured it out for himself at some point. Jake was a great guy too, he was around a lot, so Rosa got to know him pretty well. She had always believed that he was hiding some deep secret of his own and told Katelyn as much.

"You seem to be forgetting that they weren't around that summer to know that Gianfranco and I had been seeing each other. As far as they knew, Gianfranco had gone back to Italy directly after the wedding and I had enrolled in summer classes in California. It was easy to keep my secret from them. Kevin and Jake assumed that Jenny's father had to be someone I had met the first few weeks of classes or during my visit to

Berkley over the summer." Katelyn recalled the wounded look on Kevin's face when she told him she was pregnant. "He wanted to go after the guy for money to support the baby but I wouldn't allow it."

"I convinced Kevin that Jenny's father came from a wealthy family and that, if he was told of her existence, I might be forced into a marriage with a man I didn't love. It's ironic that being forced into a marriage with someone who doesn't love me is exactly what I'm most afraid of now." Katelyn was having trouble telling her story through her tears but she could see that Rosa was having an even tougher time listening to the tales of her painful past.

"It must have been hard for you, being alone. With Kevin living in Montana when Jenny was born you must have been lost." Rosa said as she made herself more comfortable.

"Yes, but I was lucky; my mom's best friend still lived in the neighborhood and had just the year before become a widow. She had time to help me out; it helped with her loneliness as well. She became a surrogate mother to me and a grandmother to Jenny. She took care of Jenny for me while I went to class and worked my part time job. After graduation, getting a full time job wasn't all that difficult. I'd gotten excellent grades and I had super referrals. Jake and Kevin were well known in their fields and had their connections and their connections had other connections. One connection of Jake's connections was a friend at *Glitz* magazine and that was how I landed my first interview. I've been with *Glitz* ever since and that is where I first met Adam. He and I have known each other a very long time."

Rosa smirked at the mere mention of Adam name. She joined Katelyn on the couch and she could see what a toll these last few days were taking on her friend. Rosa had told Katelyn about the poor opinion she had of Adam before but she didn't know why. She had kept those feelings to herself because they had no merit to them, none that she could prove. Yet, there was something about Gianfranco Broccolini that didn't make sense to her either. She couldn't put her finger on it but she didn't think that the relationship between Katelyn and Gianfranco Broccolini was over, not in his eyes, anyway. Katelyn wanted to believe they were a thing of the past, but after this week Rosa wasn't so sure.

Rosa watched Katelyn close her eyes and rub either side of her head with her fingers. The stress was getting to her and her probable headache was an apparent sign. Rosa went into the bathroom and grabbed her friend a glass of water and some aspirins. "When are you going to tell Gianfranco about Jenny? You should before this stress takes its toll on you." she added, handing over the glass and the pills.

"I'm not sure. I wanted to tell him everything yesterday but things didn't go the way I wanted them to. I know one thing for sure; I really need to see Kevin. I always feel more confident after a visit with him. My mind is always clearer when I bounce things off him. Whatever happens after my visit with Kevin is anyone's guess." Katelyn knew that, if she were able to spend a few days with Kevin, she would feel more grounded and able to handle whatever came her way.

"Are you going to be able to sit that close to the father of your child on the plane and not tell him? Katelyn, his child will be sitting inches away from him. Aren't you afraid that something about her will seem familiar to him?" Katelyn knew that Rosa was right, besides, trying to hide this secret from him, was turning her into a bundle of nerves.

"You know, all he has to do is ask Jenny when her birthday is and you're sunk. He's not a stupid man; eventually he'll figure it out. He didn't get where he is by being oblivious to what goes on around him. What about Jenny, don't you think she deserves to have him in her life?" Rosa questioned curiously.

Katelyn knew that everything her friend was saying made sense; there was no use denying it. Jenny had a right to have Gianfranco in her life. After all, he was a good man and he most definitely would be an even better father. Katelyn was the problem, not Jenny. Could she stand to have him in their lives when he didn't love her? She didn't doubt the physical attraction between them was still easily ignited with a mere touch but would that be enough to sustain a marriage. She was sure he would insist on making their union legal, for Jenny's sake. The desire they felt for each other was irresistible but was it enough?

More importantly, she wondered if Gianfranco could ever grow to love her. She needed that commitment from him. She glanced at the clock on the wall and winced, seeing how much time had passed. She

needed to call Adam and end things between them officially before she
left for Montana. Leaving their relationship hanging in limbo wasn't fair
to him and she wanted it over.

"I can't make any decisions about Gianfranco right now. I have to
call Adam, apologize for all that has happened and end it, properly." She
reached for the phone as Rosa shook her head, as if to say she was making a mistake.

She felt that if she settled things between herself and Adam, she
could move forward and turn her attention to the most difficult obstacle in her life, the dark Italian whose eyes haunted her since the first day
they met. She knew that telling him about Jenny was going to be hard
and she had doubts about whether or not he would forgive her. There
was also his anger; she would have to face that initially. She did have
one thing going for her and that was his ignorance right now. She could
probably work that to her advantage for a second or two. It was up to
her to decide where and when this conversation would take place.

Katelyn dialed Adam's number and, after much debate with him,
she agreed to meet him at a midtown tavern. It wasn't far from the office and since it had been a favorite meeting place for the staff, she
knew where it was. She had met Jake there on occasion for dinner. She
could see her friend shaking her head in disagreement. Rosa thought
meeting Adam alone was a bad idea. *Could anything positive come of this
meeting?* Rosa pondered.

If Katelyn was insistent on meeting Adam, Rosa would offer some
kindly advice. "If you're going to insist on meeting him, then at least do
me one favor. You know that red dress that he hated on you and you
loved so much? Wear it to your meeting with him. Let him see that
you're declaring your independence from him. It might give you that
extra bit of courage you're going to need." Katelyn hadn't known the
depth of Rosa's dislike for Adam until now. *"Does Rosa know something
about Adam that I didn't share with her?"* She didn't have time to think
about that right now but she would ask Rosa about it in the future.

Katelyn silently contemplated what could be worse; a marriage of
convenience to Gianfranco or a life alone without him in it? "Maybe
you're right; it's time for me to make some changes in my life. I might

have bought that red dress on a whim but why shouldn't I wear it. I love it and that's all that should matter. I'm going to go and meet Adam later on today, say what I have to and leave in the red dress that he told me to never wear," she said aloud, declaring her independence, and, for the first time today, giggling.

Rosa assured her once again that she didn't mind taking care of Jenny, at all. As a matter of fact, she was going to suggest that Jenny spend the night with her so that Katelyn could pack for their trip. "I'll drop by a little earlier to pick her up; that way you'll have plenty of time to get ready," Rosa smirked.

"What would I do without you? I only hope that I don't regret putting off confronting Gianfranco until after I speak to Adam." It was strange but since she hadn't heard from Gianfranco after last night, she couldn't shake her feeling of unease. She worried when she had those feelings because she had learned long ago to trust her instincts.

Katelyn decided she would tell Gianfranco the truth as soon as she finished with Adam. She couldn't help but wonder if Adam would accept that they were only friends and move on. She was uncertain about their meeting, after witnessing the other side of Adam. Frankly, it was a side of him that she didn't want to see repeated. She had a little time to reconsider the dress but after thinking about his behavior toward her she opted to wear it. The dress would make it clear that they were not a couple. It should be safe for her since they were meeting in a very public place and, if nothing else, Adam was always concerned about keeping up appearances.

Rosa grabbed her coat and made Katelyn pledge again to wear the red dress. After Rosa left, Katelyn walked into her bedroom, went to her closet and took out the infamous red dress. She held it up against herself, looked in the mirror and smiled. She'd purchased the dress on a whim after work one night and didn't think she'd ever have the nerve to wear it. It was very expensive but after trying it on and seeing the responses of all the women in the dressing room, she threw caution to the wind and purchased it. It was a simple design but the material was clingy. After trying it on in the store, she knew it would have a better effect if she wore it without a bra.

Chapter Six

Dana watched as her boss moved from the file cabinet that he seemed disinterested in to his desk. *It's amazing that a man who looks as good as he does, has remained single for so long.* It came as no surprise to her when most of the women in his employ flirted with him but got nowhere. They found out immediately that he didn't date the women he worked with. It was great, as far as she was concerned, because working without the pressure of advances from her superior was quite a relief and very unusual for her. Sexual harassment was something she had dealt with in the past; she didn't want to deal with it ever again. She couldn't help the way she looked and tried without success to dress less sexy. Having a boss like Gianfranco was a welcomed bonus.

Gianfranco Broccolini was an enigma all his own. He didn't keep women around for very long; Dana was privy to that information, first hand. He was generous to a fault. His parting gifts to the women he dated often cost him dearly. He didn't mind as long as the female in question left him alone once the relationship had ended. Dana was convinced that there was a woman out there for him somewhere, one who held the key to his frozen heart. She often wondered if that someone, whoever she was, realized the power she held over him. Dana knew instinctively that his heart was broken a long time ago and that the woman was the reason he was dead set against relationships that lasted for any length of time.

One of the many phone lines in the office started to ring and Dana quickly picked it up. After her usual business greeting, she realized that it was Kevin Donavan, Gianfranco's good friend. "Hello, Mr. Donavan, he's in and I'm sure he'll take your call. Hold on, while I connect you," she replied.

"Mr. Broccolini, Kevin Donavan is on line two for you. He's says it's not important. If you don't have time, he can call back later." Dana knew immediately that Kevin Donavan was one of the few people in his life that, no matter how busy Gianfranco was, he would take his call. He told her to put the call through immediately.

"Kevin, miss me already my friend? I was going to call you later myself. Have you spoken to Katelyn yet this morning?" he asked. Gianfranco knew she would have called her brother by now and told him that he had offered to fly her and Jenny out to Montana.

"Actually, that's the reason, I'm calling. I appreciate what you're doing for her. I'm sure your schedule is busy enough with the takeover we talked about last week. You didn't have to do this," Kevin stated appreciatively.

"I wanted to do this for her, Kevin. If I didn't, I wouldn't have offered. That is, of course, if you don't mind seeing me again, so soon," Gianfranco added with a grin. He knew Kevin better than anyone and there was no doubt that his best friend would be glad to hear that he would be delivering both his sister and his niece personally to the ranch. Kevin loved his sister and their relationship was one of the most important relationships in his best friend's life, besides his wife, of course, and Gianfranco envied him for that.

Kevin nearly climbed through the phone at the suggestion that he would not want to see him. "What are you talking about; do I want to see you again? You can visit anytime, no invitation needed. I'm only calling to thank you personally and say again that I appreciate what you're doing," Kevin reiterated.

"I've got the jet on standby for tomorrow night. I had Dana email Katelyn the itinerary. Since she called you, I assume she got it." Gianfranco was interrupted by another call, after taking the brief call he instructed Dana to hold all future calls until after he was finished talking to Kevin.

Kevin and Gianfranco spoke for some time about the takeover and how it was evolving. It didn't take long before the conversation shifted to his kid sister again. "I'm glad Katelyn has agreed to come out here for a visit. The poor kid has been through a lot lately and could use a break. She's had a lot to deal with these past few days," Kevin said dryly.

"If you're talking about her job, Kevin, don't worry about it. The confidential merger I spoke to you about last week was with *Glitz* magazine. I have it on good authority that the CEO is quite a nice guy; he insisted she keep her job. You're a big fan of his, aren't you?" he teased. Though they never talked about the name of the company that he was taking over, Gianfranco was surprised that Kevin never grilled him on it.

Kevin laughed out loud. "At least I don't have to worry about you hurting her. I can't believe what that idiot Taylor said to her about Jenny. By the way, has she dumped that moron of a son yet?" he asked. "Have you had the pleasure of meeting Adam?" a bewildered Kevin asked.

"I can assure you that she will not be seeing Adam Taylor anytime in the near future. I think she knows what a mistake that match would have been," he added proudly. Gianfranco believed he cured her of that lowlife.

"I can't say that I'm not happy to hear that. I'm a little shocked though that she took you into her confidence." Kevin hesitated and wondered if he wanted to continue voicing his thoughts. "If there's something going on Gianfranco, I'm not asking, don't tell me. Do me one favor, don't hurt her. She was hurt once and it took her years to get over it." Kevin couldn't have made it plainer that he was warning his friend that a relationship with Katelyn had to be handled differently than any of his past conquests.

Gianfranco took out the photograph that he had kept hidden in his desk, a photo that only he knew existed. He ran his fingers over the tattered, worn picture. He'd had it for years. He cherished it the same way he cherished her. "Kevin, I promise you, on my life, that I'd never do anything to hurt her. You and I are friends and she's your little sister; I just want to help."

He wanted Kevin to trust him and yet he understood his reluctance. "She's handled everything life has thrown at her with class. Believe me, having me in her life, even temporarily, is a piece of cake for her," Gianfranco added blatantly.

"I hope you're right my friend, because you have no idea the pain she went through before and after she gave birth to Jenny. I know how much she wanted Jenny's father to be part of that process, even though she never mentioned it. I don't think she's ever let her guard down since; with you she'll different. I believe she trusts you because of who you are to me. Don't take advantage of that trust," Kevin added. This conversation felt familiar to Kevin as he remembered having a similar conversation with Gianfranco at his wedding. He assumed Gianfranco had heeded his warning because he didn't believe that anything had ever come of his fascination with Katelyn all these years. He was shocked though that Gianfranco would seek out Katelyn after all this time.

The mere mention of Katelyn's child's father drove Gianfranco mad with jealousy. He was the one who taught her how to love. He was the one who wanted to share the rest of his life with her. He had never, for one second, thought that she would leave his bed for another man so soon after he left. *I have to find a way to control this jealousy or Katelyn will never let me back into her life.*

He took one look at the picture he held in his hand and decided to press Kevin again for some answers to questions that have haunted him for years. "I'm more afraid of what she can do to my state of mind, Kevin, than what I'll do to hers," he stated truthfully.

Kevin said nothing. How could he explain the depth of the pain Katelyn felt to his friend? He hoped that Gianfranco was correct and that, one day, she would find someone who could make her happy. It was Gianfranco's track record with other women that frightened Kevin. He loved his friend like a brother but he was known to be the 'love them and leave them' type and they were talking about Katelyn, his sister. The silence over the phone had become eerie. It was a few long seconds before Kevin finally confided in Gianfranco. Kevin put his feet up on his desk and got comfortable as he continued to speak. It had been a long time since he had spoken about Jenny's father to anyone.

"Katelyn never asked for anything from Jenny's father. She was too proud and thought that if he knew about the baby's existence she would be forced into a loveless marriage. She couldn't accept that situation and, after a long discussion, I reluctantly agreed to support her decision. She'll expect a commitment from you, if you pursue a relationship with her, and, if you can't give her that, end it now before someone gets hurt," Kevin pointed out.

"Do you think that I would ever consider her just another conquest?" Gianfranco asked the question but realized his friend had no reason to believe otherwise. "Don't answer that question; I'm not sure I'd like the answer. I can tell you one thing for certain; I want to pursue a relationship with your sister but I can't promise a fairytale wedding because I'm not sure if it's what Katelyn wants."

Patience, Kevin thought to himself. He knew his sister better than anyone and a ring on her finger is exactly what she wants. The idea that Gianfranco would even mention the word marriage with his name attached was a good sign. He only hoped this endeavor would not turn into a disaster, for all involved, including him.

"What was he like, Jenny's father, I mean?" Gianfranco queried.

"I don't know who he is. Katelyn never told anyone his identity. She thought it best not to. It bothered me for some time but, in the end, does it really matter? The only thing she said at the time was that all she meant to him was a summer fling and she'd rather forget it. It's funny though, everyone always assumed it was someone she met at school over the summer and that was the story she told but I learned a few years later that she never attended the summer classes as she planned. That could only mean that Jenny's father was someone local. I never questioned the contradiction in her story because she was upset and depressed at the time. She was pregnant and I didn't want to push her; I just assumed that when she was ready to talk, she would tell me. Though I'm sure that conversation never happened," he added.

A spark lit, not only in his brain but in his heart as well. Gianfranco felt as if someone had just stepped on his chest and physically ripped it wide open. He needed the answer he craved and he needed it now. "When is Jenny's birthday, Kevin? I'd like to be prepared when I finally do meet Jenny for the first time, I mean," he said with a note of silent sarcasm. He tried to remain calm as not to give anything away.

Kevin didn't seem to catch on to Gianfranco's discomfort so he answered the question without thinking. "As a matter of fact, her birthday is in May. Jenny will be seven on May 19th. You know we got so involved talking about Katelyn that I neglected to tell you my news. Sylvia and I are expecting our own little bundle of joy in October," Kevin said bubbling with pride.

Gianfranco congratulated Kevin and could hear the excitement in his voice but he couldn't concentrate on his friend's good fortune as dates were being tossed around in his head. "Kevin, I can't tell you how happy I am for the both of you. Give my best to Sylvia and you take care of her. You both deserve this." He made a mental note to have Dana send Sylvia flowers and a baby gift. Gianfranco didn't want to believe that Katelyn was capable of this deception but he knew if his math was correct that perhaps he should have been congratulated as well. But the congratulations were seven years too late. He didn't know why but he knew without counting numbers that he was Jenny's father, without a doubt.

He sifted around in his desk for a pen and paper and, after cutting his conversation short with Kevin, began to work out the figures for himself. Based on Jenny's birthday, he went back nine months and added seven days. Wasn't that how Dana, his administrative assistant, figured out the new interns due date. He recalled walking in on them while Dana was doing the calculations. Apparently, things had changed since he had been a young adult; it was normal these days for paternity to be questionable. Gianfranco recalled being disappointed in the young intern since she needed to figure out exact dates because there was a question of paternity. Although, he doubted he could have figured out his parentage this quickly, without that information. So, for that he subconsciously thanked her. He was the father of Katelyn's child.

As he figured out the dates, he realized that conception was on or around August 12th. That made it official; little Jenny Donavan wasn't Jenny Donavan at all; she was Jenny Broccolini. There was absolutely no mistake; she was his daughter. No matter how you figured it, whether you gave two weeks either way, Katelyn had only been with one man during that exact time and that was him. In fact, he was the man who took her virginity that summer and there was no doubt that he was the only man in her life, before she left for school.

Gianfranco stared at the picture of the woman he adored and couldn't believe what he was thinking of her at this moment. How could she keep his child from him? How was she able to keep her lie from all of them, for this long? He had a daughter that he had never so much as laid eyes on. The little girl he was afraid to meet was his own flesh and blood. The little girl he was so jealous of, who would remind him each day of her father, was his own child.

Anger reared its ugly head, as he tried to remain calm. He could never forgive her for what she had done to him, regardless of her excuse. He placed his chair facing the window and sat staring out at the streets below. He tried to decide what he should do next that didn't involve violence of any kind. Could he forgive her and get past this? Was he even rational enough to listen to her reasoning right now, before reacting explosively? He didn't know. He was sure of one thing and that was that nothing was going to keep him from his child any longer.

He thought about it for a long time before pushing the button on the intercom and ordering Dana to ring Jake for him. It took him a few seconds to gain his composure; he felt badly about the way he growled at Dana and apologized for it instantly. Dana felt his wrath on the rare occasion and she also knew that he'd later apologize and make up for it when he came to his senses. She knew that he let his guard down around her because he trusted her. To everyone else, Gianfranco was always cool, calm and collected; his enemies were never aware of his inner thoughts.

Dana was efficient and Jake was on the line in minutes. "Jake, I need to see you right away. Could you spare me an hour at some point today?" Gianfranco asked his friend.

Jake Lonetree, the third musketeer, had no idea what was happening but Gianfranco Broccolini never asked for favors. And he most certainly never sounded out of sorts, which was the only way to describe his friend's behavior at the moment. "I don't have anything on my calendar for this evening, want to meet then?" he asked. "I have to meet with a client in midtown later this afternoon. How about we meet somewhere around there? I know a little tavern, we could talk there, and it doesn't get too crowded. I'll leave the address with Dana before I hang up. This must be something important for you to be calling for a powwow. Is everything alright?" Jake asked with concern.

"I think it's better if I tell you this in person. I'll get all the information from Dana and I'll meet you there." He knew Jake was going to be disappointed in him when he found out that he was the one who fathered Jenny. He also knew his friend would understand why he was upset about Katelyn's decision to keep their child a secret from him.

"You didn't give away the ring did you?" Jake teased. It took a minute for Gianfranco to register what his friend had asked and what he was referring to but he left the question unanswered.

After hanging up the phone, Gianfranco closed his eyes to try to ward off some of the pain and tension he was feeling in his head. It came as a shock to him to feel tears trickling down his face. Tears were foreign to him. He had never let himself get emotionally involved with anyone except Katelyn, and he hadn't since that time.

He had a daughter with the only woman he had ever loved in his life and she let him down by keeping that child a secret from him. Gianfranco sat quietly for awhile and thought about another time. Jake had reminded him of it; the time he and Kevin joined Jake at the Indian Reservation. While there, an elder tribeswoman gave each of them a small block of teakwood and taught them to carve wooden eternity bands from the piece of wood. She told them about an old Indian prophecy regarding the handling of the rings once they completed them.

The elderly woman warned that they should wear them around their necks until they met someone worthy to accept the ring, as long as the offer came from their hearts. *"For the bearer of your ring will also be the bearer of your heart and soul."* She warned that their lives would forever be entwined with the woman who held each of their rings.

Gianfranco remembered the day he gave the ring to Katelyn. He thought she would laugh at him but she found the gesture romantic and endearing. He hadn't thought about that ring until now. He had long ago forgotten about it. *Perhaps the old lady was right.* He pulled himself together again and asked Dana to contact a private detective that he often used for business. "Dana, call Tom Parker and tell him I need to speak to him as soon as possible. Tell him I have an urgent job for him."

He paced the floor waiting for Tom to arrive. Rarely was Gianfranco kept waiting. When Tom arrived, he almost bit his head off for taking so long. Tom was the best private detective money could buy and, though Gianfranco hated the thought of spying on Katelyn, it was the only way he'd know for sure if Jenny was his child without asking her directly. Besides, he thought she gave up her right to privacy the day she decided to lie to him about their child. Gianfranco gave Tom all the information he could supply and what he couldn't; he told him where to find the information that would lead to Jenny's parentage. He knew Katelyn better than anyone and he had all the information he needed about that summer. Unless Jenny was born very prematurely, she was his child.

"The only thing I want you to find out is if Katelyn Donavan could have had another lover during the time her child was conceived." Gianfranco didn't like the look on Tom's face so he set him straight right away. "Look Tom, let me be clear about this. I'm sure this child is mine. I want you to bring me the proof I need to legally acknowledge the fact."

Tom understood his meaning and was shocked that he was trying to prove paternity, rather than disprove it. These rich clients he served were usually on the other side of the fence. He wondered if the mother of this child had any idea who she was dealing with. He almost felt sorry for the woman. Gianfranco Broccolini was a fair man but you didn't cross him because, if you did, you were surely going to pay a high price for doing it.

Katelyn sat at the end of the bar waiting patiently for Adam to arrive. He had never kept her waiting like this before and she was a little uncomfortable sitting at a bar alone. At this moment, her red dress she wore wasn't helping her feel very confident. She wondered if she had made a mistake listening to Rosa in the first place. The dress would have felt empowering under different circumstances but she felt a little awkward, as if she were at the bar looking to pick up a man; judging by the looks she was getting, she could have succeeded. If that had that been the mission.

Finally, the waiter came over to her and said a table had opened up in the corner she had requested. It was a quiet corner where they could talk but Katelyn realized, after sitting down, that it was impossible to see whoever walked through the entrance from that angle. The waiter assured her that he would look out for Adam and show him to her table as soon as he arrived.

Adam finally arrived but not before Katelyn had regrettably added two drinks to the ones she shared earlier that day with Rosa at lunch to calm her nerves. She was not a drinker and the alcohol was beginning to take effect. "Thank you, for showing up," she said to Adam slurring her words. "You were the one who asked for this meeting; the least you could have done was to arrive on time." She knew she sounded annoyed and angry. He had kept her waiting too long.

"Now, don't go getting yourself all worked up," he said dismissively. "I asked for this meeting with you because I think your decision about us was made in haste. I don't understand why you can't take the time that you're spending with Kevin to rethink our situation. Given a chance, Katelyn, we could make it work. I'm asking you to reconsider; don't let my father come between us."

"It's not about your father." She tried to reason with him but he wasn't hearing her. She saw his face suddenly transform in front of her, filling with the same rage she had witnessed back at the apartment. *Why haven't I ever seen this part of his personality before?* As she started to speak again, she noticed a weird expression come over his face. She was tempted to turn around to see what sparked the unkind recognition in his eyes but opted against it. And then, just as quickly, his demeanor changed back and he focused his attention on her again. Perhaps, he had seen an old girlfriend and didn't want to make a scene. She didn't understand anything that was going on with him.

"My father told me what transpired between you both. I didn't want to believe him but I see the way you're dressed tonight and the amount of drinking you're doing. So there must be some merit to his claim. Tell me Katelyn, did Broccolini offer you more than I could offer you?" To her astonishment, he became physical and grabbed her arm and pulled her into his embrace. "Let me have something to remember you by sweetie," he said, as his wet foul mouth came crushing down on hers.

"What the hell has gotten into you?" She tried to wipe his kiss away and was appalled at his behavior. She couldn't help but wonder why she had never seen this side of him before and she fought to free herself from his wicked embrace. If she hadn't been kept waiting and didn't have those added two drinks she would have seen this situation coming and been better prepared to handle it. His kiss was wet, sloppy and un-invited, not at all like the man who could make love to her with his eyes.

Adam lingered for a few minutes before his final bit of payback. "I think you'll have a little difficulty explaining that kiss to lover boy over there. By the look on his face, I'd say he was ready to kill us both, which is my cue to leave. Good luck, you're going to need it," Adam snarled as he let her go and retreated. He escaped out the side door; Katelyn looked toward the direction Adam had indicated and saw Gianfranco standing there.

She might not be able to explain that kiss to him but he had to know that there was a reasonable explanation for what he had just witnessed. She felt that he should, at the very least, be willing to listen. Katelyn stood up abruptly and thought he had no right to be angry, not after what he did, interfering in her career. He was trying to control her life from behind the scenes. She knew she might be naïve as far as men were concerned but she was well in control of her own life. She would tell him that just because he thought his word was law, didn't make it so. She was walking in his direction when she heard a female voice approach nearby.

"Gianfranco, darling, I wasn't aware that you were back in the States. Why didn't you tell me? How could you sneak back into the country, and not call me?" the tall voluptuous red-haired woman, who appeared out of the blue, said for all to hear. Katelyn watched as the woman embraced Gianfranco and kissed him in a way only a woman familiar to him would have kissed. He'd seen her, she was sure of it and yet he allowed this woman to continue to stroke him. She stood there reluctantly, almost in a trance before getting up the courage to run.

When their eyes finally connected, Katelyn thought she saw hate and resentment flare up. He must have regretted the act she had witnessed between him and his lady friend because she thought she saw him try to distance himself from the woman. As she was running out the door, with tears stinging her eyes, she thought she heard Jake call out to her but she couldn't get away fast enough and didn't care to search for his voice. It had hurt her too much to witness the exchange and, lucky for her, there was a taxi at the curb outside dropping off patrons. She was able to escape with what little dignity she had left still intact.

Jake ran out of the tavern after her but Katelyn was nowhere to be seen. He was sure he had just passed her on his way in as she was leaving. He was sure it was her on the other side of the crowd of people who had just walked in. She looked as if she were spooked by something, running from the tavern as fast as she could. He decided to try her on her cell phone as soon as he let Gianfranco know he was there. He would check on that situation with him and call Katelyn. He turned back toward the tavern, strode in toward the bar and spotted Gianfranco pushing a persistent red-head away from him. Jake heard the woman ranting as he got closer; she was saying that Gianfranco went from being hot one minute to cold as ice the next. *What is wrong with everybody today?*

He approached Gianfranco, put an arm around him and noticed that his friend was sucking down shots of whiskey as if he was on a mission; he hadn't seen him do that in years. "Want to tell me what's going on because I'm really getting confused. First, I see Katelyn run out of this place with tears in her eyes and a wounded look on her face, as if someone had just killed her favorite dog, and then I come in here and you're lip-locked with a red-head you obviously could care less about. What's going on, my friend? What am I missing? And whatever you do please tell me, that the two incidents are not related?" Jake asked.

Gianfranco was shocked by his own behavior but Katelyn deserved it. He hadn't meant to push Rita away like that; he only meant to hurt Katelyn the same way she had hurt him. Now that he had time to think about it, it was immature and foolish. He lashed out to get back at her. It wasn't enough that he had to deal with her lies but there she was wearing a dress that cried out 'take me to bed' and she wore it for Adam Taylor. The only consolation was that he knew Katelyn didn't enjoy the kiss Adam had planted on her lips. Under any other circumstances, he would have walked over and punched Adam in his face; but he was still hurting from the whirlwind of lies that were kept from him.

Jake was right, though he'd never lost control before, there was something seriously amiss. He'd kept his reserve in any given situation; no matter under pressure to do otherwise. It was Katelyn; he couldn't control the feelings he had for her or what he felt because of her. He was never in control of his feelings while around her, good, bad, or in-different. She was his Achilles heel, more or less.

"Jake, you have no idea what kind of day I've just had." He paused briefly as he turned to the bartender who was vying for his attention. He was signaling to him that a table had just opened, but before he could reply, his phone began to ring. "Jake, I have to take this. I'll meet you at the table. I have something to tell you privately," he said before moving out to the corridor to answer his call.

It took another five minutes before Gianfranco got back to the table. Jake was busy flirting with the waitress. "I gather the news wasn't good?" Jake inquired, as he hit redial on his phone for the sixth time. "I've been trying to reach Katelyn on her cell but she's not picking up. It keeps going to her voice mail. I'm worried about her. Did you happen to talk to her before she walked out of here?"

Gianfranco nodded in agreement. "She's the reason we're here. I was waiting for that phone call to confirm what I already knew in my heart. Do you remember Kevin's wedding?" he asked before continuing. "There's something I never told you or Kevin. Katelyn and I started an affair that night." After Jake nodded in affirmation, he listened, as Gianfranco continued; suddenly everything began to make sense to Jake and became clearer. "I know you and Kevin warned me off and, believe it or not, I really tried; but I couldn't help myself. God help me, Jake, I fell in love with her."

Jake was astonished, to say the least. *Kevin is going to be destroyed by this news*, as he cracked his knuckles. "I remember Kevin calling me and telling me that Katelyn was pregnant by a guy she met at school," Jake said.

Then Gianfranco remembered the call from Jake that had followed a few months later, as if it were yesterday. He had relived that call in his head almost every day since. Gianfranco had never suspected anything at the time because Jake was totally convincing about her rich boyfriend from California.

Jake interrupted his own thoughts; they were taking him in a direction he didn't want to go. He hoped, with all his heart, that his friend was not about to tell him what he was imagining to be true. "Please, don't tell me that you are Jenny's father?" he asked hoping his friend would deny what Jake knew in his heart to be so.

"I am. But before you punch me in my face, or lecture me about doing the right thing, let me tell you that I never knew that Jenny was mine, until today. When you called with news that Katelyn was pregnant, I assumed, like you that it was someone she met at school. I could ring her neck, Jake. She kept my child from me for seven years. I loved her. I would have done anything for her. I can't tell you how it tore me apart when Kevin told me she had met someone at school." The waitress brought their drinks over and both of them gulped them down so fast that she ran back to the bar to bring the bottle to refill them.

"Are you sure that Jenny is your child? I mean, it's not like Katelyn to keep a secret like that, not from us. She had to know that, even if things between you didn't work out, you would still want Jenny in your life," Jake said as he leaned back in the chair and let out a sigh. This whole situation was perplexing. "I don't need to tell you what this news is going to do to Kevin. He wanted to kill the guy back then. What's going to happen when he finds out the guy he wanted to kill is his best friend?" Jake hesitated but only momentarily. "I wonder why Katelyn never told you the truth. I have no answers, my friend; but I think you should give her a chance to explain herself," Jake reflected as he tried to understand Katelyn.

"There's no acceptable excuse for keeping my kid from me. Think of all the times Katelyn wouldn't accept help from any of us and how my child went without because of it. Jake, I don't need to tell you that my child could have had, and should have had, everything her little heart desired. I would have been there for her; all those years wasted. You know I would have been there." Gianfranco wanted to throw something, anything that could release some of the anger building up inside him.

Jake looked around the bar as the waitress filled their drinks again; he held up his glass to Gianfranco and saluted his fatherhood, hoping to diffuse the situation. "On a lighter note, 'Congratulations, Dad,'" he said before drinking from his glass. "Give Katelyn a chance, go and talk to her. She's the only one who can answer the questions you have."

Jake spotted the woman who had been in a lip-lock with his friend and wondered why he hadn't seen it before. It all made perfect sense now. That show his friend had put on with the woman; it was for Katelyn's benefit. Gianfranco had no interest in the woman at all; he set out to deliberately hurt Katelyn. He had never put it together before but he should have.

Jake tried to remember everything about the wedding and after. He did and didn't know why he hadn't put it all together before now. The way Gianfranco's ears perked up whenever they talked about Katelyn. The wedding, he remembered that night. Both he and Kevin saw that look in Gianfranco's eyes when he spotted Katelyn for the first time. Gianfranco's whole demeanor had been different; he seemed happier and somewhat giddy. But he had always believed the Gianfranco's interest in Katelyn had ended right after the wedding. Yet, he should have put it all together when he announced Katelyn's pregnancy to him. Gianfranco's reaction was a little off for someone who didn't care.

"Let's order a round of coffee. I think we need to get you sobered up completely before you go and see Katelyn. I don't want you regretting anything you say in the morning. If we hang around here and we keep drinking, the two of us are going to have to release some of that built up anger and I'm getting too old to pick fights, like the old days." Jake smiled and then asked the waitress for a round of coffee and the check.

"Do you believe what Katelyn did was wrong?" Gianfranco asked, as he stretched out his legs and sipped his newly arrived coffee. The bar was emptying and, though there were a few strays left, most of the patrons who frequented this place during the day were from the surrounding offices and had probably left for the day. *It's still early enough; I can stop in and talk to Katelyn. Jake is right; I'll give her a chance to explain. I owe her that much.*

"I don't want to play judge and jury. You might just talk to her tonight and make sense of all this. I'm going to give her the benefit of the doubt and I hope you'll do the same." Jake said.

The music on the juke box was getting mellower and the tavern suddenly getting darker, which meant the crowd, would be starting to change. Gianfranco wondered where Katelyn had run off to after she left the tavern and if she'd be home when he got there. "Jake, will you try to her phone again. She must be home by now." Both men were beginning to worry. It was evident that Katelyn was upset when she left.

"If I do reach her, what do you want me to say? Do you want her to know you're going to see her?" Jake queried.

"No, don't call. I want to talk to her but this time we play by my rules. She gets no time to prepare for me. I don't want to give her any length of time to think up anymore lies. I'll call my driver and I'll have him drop you off on the way." The driver was waiting outside for them when they finished. Gianfranco had the driver drop Jake off along the way. He said good bye to Jake and gave the driver directions to Katelyn's apartment.

Belle Harbor was a small beach town not far from Manhattan. It had been a great place to hang out during their college days, when school let out for the summer. When most of their friends were heading to the Hamptons, they headed to Belle Harbor. Kevin and Katelyn were born and raised in Belle Harbor. Their family owned a cute house that overlooked the beach and if you went up to the second floor, you could see the ocean from any room. They were happy there, until the death of their parents. It happened a year after Kevin's graduation from law school. Kevin did what was expected of him and stood by Katelyn. He stayed in New York until she finished high school, in spite of the great offer he had to join a large law firm in Montana. He hadn't accepted their earlier offer because, after the loss of their parents, he didn't want Katelyn uprooted and he wasn't going to leave her behind. He must have impressed the partners because, once Katelyn graduated high school, they came back with a second offer.

Gianfranco glanced out the window during the ride to Katelyn's apartment and thought about all the good times they had here at the beach. He remembered all the bars they frequented and all the trouble they got into. It was a nice place but Jenny could have had so much more. His child could have lived on an estate with horses. He knew from Kevin how much his little girl loved horses. If Katelyn wanted, he would have provided the house on the beach too, for the summer.

Katelyn lived in one of the few high-rise buildings, overlooking the ocean. He liked her apartment, it was quaint. Luck was on his side as the driver pulled up to the entrance of her building. There was usually a guard at the door but there was a woman just leaving the building to walk her dog. Gianfranco dismissed his driver for the night and shouted for the woman to hold the door for him. "I forgot my key," he explained as he reached behind the woman and held the door behind her.

"That's a fancy car you have there. Second one this week I saw here. Do we have someone famous living in this building that I don't know about?" she asked.

"I don't know personally. I had to work late tonight; company policy to send me home in a car." He knew that this was his company's policy so he blurted it out rather than tell the woman too much. He didn't need to alert Katelyn with the buzzer or security because he was already in the building and he knew exactly where Katelyn's apartment was. When he reached her apartment on the 8th floor, he rang her doorbell. The element of surprise was a great weapon. He knew that Jenny had to be asleep by now and he wouldn't be disturbing her.

Katelyn's door stood slightly ajar, with the chain still attached so she could see who might be trying to gain access. After the incident with Adam, she didn't want to take any chances. She wasn't surprised to see Gianfranco as she opened the door a little further. "I thought you were going to be otherwise occupied tonight. Did she turn you down?" she asked curtly.

"I came to talk. Is Jenny asleep; I don't want her to hear what I have to say?" he asked before she allowed him to walk by her and into the apartment.

"He must be under a lot of stress." The shadows under his eyes gave it away. She could tell that whatever it was that he needed to say seemed important enough that it couldn't wait. He had a determined look in his eyes. She was puzzled at first because he led her to believe that what he had to say would lead to a scene of some kind.

"Jenny is staying with a friend tonight. I wasn't sure what time I would get home so my friend kept her overnight. I had some business to take care of," she added as an afterthought.

He raised his brow and she could see his jaw tighten as he turned away from her. "I forgot about Prince Charming, for a second. Do you always dress like that and then go bed-hopping? Or is this a habit, you recently acquired?" He was angry but he couldn't help what she was doing to him. She still had on that dress and it was slowly driving him crazy; now she had no shoes on and her legs and feet were bare. He was sure she was naked under that dress and he wanted to find out if it were true; his thoughts were rampant.

She shook with anger. How dare he think that he could tell her how to dress and think that he could make assumptions, about her sex life? She was seething as she lifted her hand to slap his face in retaliation but she was stopped in mid air. Even with a few drinks in him, he had her at a disadvantage. His strong hands were now around her wrists, as she fought to loosen his grip. He pulled her closer to him and noted, with fascination, as her body tingled from his proximity, her body touching his.

"Why are you doing this to me?" she murmured in barely a whisper as she fought to control what her body betrayed. She was lost in his arms as she felt his athletic body so close to her own. "You made it perfectly clear at the tavern, what I meant to you," she scowled.

"I made nothing clear to you, Katelyn. That woman meant nothing to me and you would have found that out yourself had you stuck around a little longer. The reason I'm here though has nothing to do with what you saw tonight. Why didn't you tell me, Katelyn?" he asked as drew in a breath. He still couldn't believe that the Katelyn he knew would do this to him. "Why didn't you tell me that we had a child together?" he added, as he drank in the scent of her skin next to his face.

There was no use denying it and she would have told him the truth herself soon enough. *How does he know?* She had kept that secret from everyone, even Kevin. "My pregnancy was not your concern," she lashed out. "I found myself pregnant through my own inexperience. I didn't blame you. I should have protected myself," she added, pulling her wrists from his hold. She pushed her hair behind her ear like she did when she was scared.

He noticed her nervous habit and thought perhaps now that she was through running scared; she would begin to settle down and tell the truth. "Your pregnancy had everything to do with me. Jenny is my child too. I should have had some say in her life. Regardless of how you felt about me, I had a right to know my daughter. You had no right to keep her birth a secret from me."

Katelyn couldn't think of any rebuttal because she agreed with him. She had no logical excuse. He still stood close enough to her so that she could feel his breath on her face and, once again, her body was betraying her. *Damn this dress, it was a bad idea.* The material was so thin; her body was on fire as though he were touching the skin beneath it. From head to toe, her body and mind were not acting cohesively. Her brain was trying to concentrate on the conversation but her body wanted nothing to do with it. His eyes softened as he acknowledged the painful lust she was experiencing.

"I could kill you for keeping Jenny from me. I would have been there for you, you know that, Katelyn," he said pulling her into an embrace that only caused more uncertainty between them. The sexual tension between them only added to the stinging grief of what could have been.

She knew he would have been there but his heart would not have been hers and that was where the lie began to take on a life of its own. *Where will we go from here?*

"Tell me, Irish, why is it that when I want you to talk, you say nothing. I find it hard to fathom that my little argumentative vixen has

91

nothing to say. It's not like you to be at a loss for words. You're not going to say anything?" He let one hand move suggestively down the side of her face and, as he did, he saw her breasts rise as if commanded, begging to be touched. He watched her as she struggled to catch her breath. She was his and he wanted her to admit it. His body wanted hers as badly as she needed his. They were each other's weakness as much as each other's strength.

His gaze lingered on her lips; they both knew he was going to kiss her, he had little choice. He did, and, as his tongue moved longingly, tracing her lips, her legs weakened. He tasted all the secret places of her mouth that only he had known. "I've been cursed by the memory of you for far too long," he drawled as he took her into his abyss.

He nipped and teased and suckled until she surrendered to him completely. He could bring her to the point of submission each and every time they were together and he reveled in that knowledge. Most men dreamt of having that kind of power over their lover but not him. This knowledge only proved their weakness for each other.

"Gianfranco," she whimpered. "Please stop, I can't let you do this to me again," she quivered. "You can't barge into my life and take over. Whenever you're around me, it's like, I can't think for myself anymore." Katelyn could barely speak as she put some distance between them.

"That's the first logical thing you've said today. I'm making the decisions about us from now on. You are no longer in a position to call the shots. I'm not marrying you for the sake of some hidden undying love and devotion. No Katelyn, you and I are getting married as soon as possible because we are forever bound to each other by our child. I will not be separated from her for one minute more. I do realize that you are part of the package and I'll live with that but, be warned, I will not tolerate any more lies." He was still angry as he reached for something, anything to lash out at. He would never physically hurt her but he did find a crystal vase to take his anger out on.

Katelyn stood horrified as he flung the vase across the room. It shattered into hundreds of little pieces. She was glad Jenny wasn't here to witness him lose it. Somehow she knew by the look on his face that he had regretted his lapse of control and was finding it difficult to apologize for it.

He had spent the better part of the evening keeping his anger in check. He glanced down at her coffee table and saw the face of his daughter, Jennifer Elizabeth Donavan, who was, in fact, Jennifer Elizabeth Broccolini, staring back at him. He looked at Katelyn differently than he had before. She was no longer the innocent who found herself in a tough situation; she was now the conniving selfish woman who had kept his child from him on purpose. And yet, he didn't want to hurt her, he wanted what he'd always wanted, to love and protect her and have her in his life and in his bed.

As his eyes swept over her body, once again, his pupils flared with need for her. "Why?" he asked. He leaned against the wall for support and tilted his head toward the ceiling. It was then that he noticed all the pictures that held the memories of his daughter's life.

He clenched his fists as he took in each shot of her. There were dozens of photos of her through the years; years that were lost to him. He moved from the beginning to the end, taking in each snapshot of another time lost. Katelyn watched in horror as the tears fell from his eyes. There were pictures of her first bath, her first step, even one of her after saying her first word. Katelyn had added a blurb on one picture in a cloud, Jenny said 'dada'. He hoped that each time Jenny said the word 'daddy', that Katelyn felt the pain, as he did at this very second.

Katelyn was remembering and she wanted to tell him that her heart broke every time their daughter called out to a man she had never met. With tears still streaming down his face, he turned to her and drew in a deep, needed breath before speaking. "My attorney will be in touch with you in the morning. He'll have all the papers drawn up for you to sign, naming me as Jenny's father. The papers are necessary if I'm to be named on the birth certificate legally. He'll also let you know when and where the wedding will take place." He sniffled and Katelyn could tell he was slowly regaining control.

"Don't push me on this, Katelyn. I'll make sure the attorney is here before my car arrives to take you both to the airport," he informed her, in no uncertain terms.

"I'm not marrying you. This is ludicrous." She saw his body stiffen. "We don't have to get married; I won't keep her from you."

"How magnanimous you are, not to keep my daughter from me any longer. But, as I've warned you, you don't get to call the shots any longer. All the arrangements will be made; all you have to do is show up. Katelyn, do let me warn you though, we play by my rules this time and if you give me any trouble at all, I'll take her from you. Don't think for a second that I won't or that I can't," he added abruptly.

"That's just insane. What judge would let you take her from me and the only home she has ever known?" she sputtered nervously. If Gianfranco lived up to his reputation, she knew he was capable of just what he threatened.

"Don't underestimate me or the power I have. I have plenty of money and a lot of friends; don't make me use either of them. Don't you think that a judge would have a hard time justifying your reasons for keeping her from me? I would have given anything to be in her life and you would have been my best witness on the stand. Even you wouldn't deny that I would be a good father." The venom in his voice only added to her fear of him and all he threatened to do to her.

"Why are you doing this to me?" she asked meekly, as if all the life were drained out of her.

"I'm not the one who should be answering that question. Why did you do this to me?" he asked in a voice that didn't hide the sorrow he felt in his heart. "Are we in agreement?" he added staring down into her eyes.

She saw that she had less than zero options and tentatively agreed to his terms with a slight nod. "Was that so hard?" "Anyone watching this would think that you were just sentenced to a life of poverty and pain. Instead, what I offer is a life of luxury for both you and our child, a life most women would love to have; you act as if I've just stolen your life from you."

Her stomach was still churning as he issued his ultimatums about her future. The irony was that there was nothing she wanted more than to become his wife but she knew she would pay a price. Was having him in her life permanently this way worth the sacrifices it would cost? Their union would bring his child into his life but he'd be stuck in a marriage that meant little or nothing to him, or so she thought.

"I'm not going to be joining you and Jenny in the morning but your plans to visit Kevin were confirmed. I'll try to join you both later in the week, if I can. My assistant will handle all the announcements for the newspapers." He stared at her for what seemed like forever, waiting for some sort of rebuttal, but there was none. Instead, all he saw was her expression of rampant fear and rejection. "People will expect an announcement if we get married and I want everything to be above board. It would raise eyebrows if we didn't do this," he added, explaining his reasons for a public announcement.

She was overwhelmed at the extent to which he was making plans. "You're not planning on announcing that Jenny is your child, are you?"

The room was full of emotions that ran from hostility, to regret and she could see he was trying very hard to keep his emotions in check. He took a couple of steps closer to her, thinking that, if he moved forward, she would somehow stop defying him. "I'm going to recognize Jenny as my own no matter how you feel about it. I want everyone to know that I'm her father. I'd love to shout it from the rooftops but I won't do that until we explain to her where I've been all this time."

There was awkward tension in the air. She was afraid to say anything to him. If he went back on his word and made the announcement before giving her time to explain it to Jenny, she would never forgive him. It was as if he could read her mind because he walked over to her and gently lifted her chin so she could see into his eyes. "I promise you that until we have both sat her down and explained everything to her, nothing will be made public. Besides, I still have to deal with Kevin. He's never going to forgive me for this. You know that, don't you," he added disappointingly.

The note of his concern for Kevin's feelings didn't surprise her. Gianfranco could care less about her feelings but he couldn't fathom the idea of hurting Kevin. She wondered what Kevin would say. He would probably feel let down by them both but she knew her brother well enough to know he'd forgive his friend. Gianfranco circled once again and then, as if he could take no more of her, he strode out to the hallway that led outside and dialed a number on his phone before leaving.

Katelyn was left in the apartment alone with plenty of sleepless hours to think about all that had transpired between them. She was glad that the truth had finally come out and maybe now she could give her daughter what she wanted most in the world, a father. She never did find out from Gianfranco how he figured it out but she was sure that no one else had yet. Her cell phone began to ring and Katelyn wondered who it could be and whether or not they knew the identity of Jenny's father. She saw that she had multiple missed calls from Jake. Her caller identification told her that it was Jake, calling again. "Hi Jake, why are you calling so late?" she asked, knowing it had something to do with her exit from the tavern.

"Are you alright, Katelyn? Did Gianfranco make it there?" he asked.

"Yes, I guess, I have a lot of explaining to do, don't I? Does Kevin know anything yet?" she asked. Jake wanted her to know that he wasn't calling for any reason other than to check in on her and make sure she was alright.

Chapter Seven

Katelyn and Jenny arrived at Kennedy Airport precisely at six p.m. and because they were flying in Gianfranco's personal plane, they didn't have the hassle of security. They were escorted to an awaiting Boeing 727, sitting on the tarmac. Katelyn felt like a celebrity with all the fuss being made over them. The surprises kept coming; the pilot and co-pilot were on hand to greet them, as well as their private steward and stewardess. It seemed a bit over the top but who was she to complain. Jenny was really excited about all the attention she was getting and didn't want the day to end. Neither of them had ever been on a private plane before and both were looking forward to the tour promised them by the stewardess when they boarded.

Katelyn watched her child thoroughly enjoying herself and didn't want anything to disturb her daughter's enthusiasm. She, on the other hand, couldn't think about anything else. Her life was about to take some drastic detours and she was afraid of what the future held in store for them. The first obstacle she had to deal with would be telling Kevin the truth about Gianfranco.

"Mom, I don't think anyone else is getting on this plane." Jenny said, looking around the plane and then looking out the window. She didn't see anyone else boarding and turned to her mom. "Is Uncle Kevin's friend, Mr. Broccoli, that rich?" she asked struggling with his last name. Katelyn realized that in a few short weeks it would be their name as well. Somehow she had to prepare Jenny for that reality.

Katelyn took another look around the plane and it wasn't at all what she had expected. In the first compartment, there were buckled seats but they were captain's chairs that swiveled as well as reclined. It looked a whole lot more comfortable than any first class section that she had seen before. As they walked down the aisle, the next compartment they came to was a sort of den or library-type room. She didn't dare go any further than that without permission but she couldn't contain her curiosity. Jake had told her that he often slept in one of the bedroom areas during long flights so she assumed there was a lot more to see.

I'm afraid, we're not in Kansas anymore, silently to herself, mocking the children's story. *Is this, what we can look forward to in the future?* Katelyn still held Jenny's hand, looked down at her little girl and smiled nervously. "It is nice, isn't it?"

Jenny turned her attention to the unexplored area and jumped, as the stewardess came up from behind. She hadn't meant to frighten them and apologized for sneaking up on them. The stewardess had come to offer her services. "Mr. Broccolini has left strict instructions that you are to be made as comfortable as possible."

"I'll take you both on a tour of the plane once we are airborne; there is little that you could possibly need that we can't offer. The aircraft has every comfort of home and then some. Believe me ladies, you're in for a treat if this section of the plane is impressive to you," she stated with a grin. The takeoff was smooth and without incident; before long the seat belt sign was off and they were free to move about.

The stewardess walked over to them and requested they follow her toward the tail end of the plane to begin their tour. "There are sleeping quarters, a dining area, as well as a personal board room and an office. Mr. Broccolini left explicit instructions that the areas normally off limits to his guests are to be made available to you and little Miss Jenny here," she said smiling at Katelyn's little girl.

"Thank you for all this but I'm not sure Mr. Broccolini wants us to have access to his private quarters," Katelyn stated as a matter of fact.

She couldn't get over the luxury in which Gianfranco traveled. Anyone could see that he was a man of impeccable taste, and, if this aircraft was anything to go by, he was used to getting what he wanted, when he wanted it. Jenny was grinning from ear to ear as she followed the stewardess; then she caught sight of the clouds as she looked out the window. Jenny couldn't get over how high they were flying, looking out at the clouds in the sky.

She stared at her daughter incredulously. *It must be great to be a child.* They were offered food and beverages fairly early in the trip which Jenny accepted rather quickly since they were her favorites. It seemed as though Gianfranco made sure that anything his daughter would ask for was aboard the plane. She couldn't believe the extremes he had gone to making sure that Jenny's trip, was a memorable one. He had left instructions that they have available all the food and drinks and games a seven-year old would want. After finishing a second portion of dessert, Jenny was tired and fell asleep.

The stewardess offered to show Katelyn their temporary bedroom. Katelyn picked her sleeping child up and followed the woman to the rear of the plane. As they proceeded to the back of the plane, she was mesmerized by each of the compartments they passed. It was a shame that there were people who lived in the street while others lived like this. As they reached the master suite, the stewardess had to assure Katelyn that it would be alright to put Jenny on the large bed that dominated the room.

"I'll leave you here to rest with your daughter; if you need me push that button over there. You can speak to me from there, without my having to disturb you." She went over to the intercom system and showed Katelyn how to work it and then left, but not before wishing them a pleasurable rest.

With Jenny fast asleep, she could explore the bedroom that her future husband spent time in on his long journeys. With the exception of a delicately carved silver picture frame on a nightstand opposite Jenny, the rest of the room was tastefully masculine. Katelyn stepped closer to get a better look at the picture but, before she could, the stewardess reappeared. She told her not to feel uncomfortable about using anything in the room; it was what Mr. Broccolini wanted. She thanked her again and, as much as she could, she tried to put him out of her mind but she felt his presence everywhere she looked.

"I don't mean to pry but are you, by any chance, going to visit his friend, Kevin Donavan? I know that he and Mr. Broccolini are friends and when we were ordered to fly there, I assumed as much. The Donavan ranch is often his destination," the stewardess stated clearly but friendly.

"As a matter of fact, I'm Kevin's sister and that little minx is his niece," she said smiling. "Do you go there often? I mean, does Gianfranco go there often?"

Katelyn asked the stewardess to join her at the table in the corner of the room. It would be nice to have company while Jenny slept. "By the way, my name is Katelyn Donavan." She said offering a handshake as introduction.

"Mary Alice Duggan, I've been flying with Gianfranco for years. We spent most of our time in Europe but we always knew that he had every intention of moving his holdings here to the States and eventually we'd be coming home. I've met your brother on numerous occasions, as well as Jake Lonetree. They're some team, the three of them. Once in awhile, Brody Calder would join them. Do you know Brody?" she asked with peaked interest.

Katelyn knew Brody well. He was Kevin's law partner these days and good friend. He and Brody began their own firm when Kevin left the larger firm that had first recruited him to Montana. Mary Alice seemed overly interested in Brody and rather shy when she spoke about him. It had been a long time since she had seen Brody. She had very fond memories of him and the times they shared together on the ranch. He had once offered to marry her to give Jenny the father everyone thought she needed. He was convinced that a marriage between them would have been beneficial to them both. Katelyn had declined the offer, even though, at the time, it was a tempting one. "I know Brody well. He and Kevin are law partners as well as neighboring ranchers. He's a great guy."

As they sat and chatted about Brody and Mary Alice's secret desire to meet him, Katelyn felt, for the first time since yesterday, that she could forget the problems that were lying ahead for her. Mary Alice was proving to be a genuinely caring person and a nice diversion from her own problems. Katelyn felt compelled to help her out, if she could. She decided that she would do just that when she reached Montana. If Brody was interested, she would set them up on a date.

She was also a bit curious about something Mary Alice had said in passing. She had mentioned that Gianfranco seemed out of reach to all the women that passed through his life since she had known him. She said he had many women who showed more than casual interest but he was never interested in more than a passing fling with any of them.

"I've always believed that there was someone from his past who had hurt him, but, until now, I never knew who it was. He never spoke of you but I know it was you," she said.

Before Katelyn could question her any further, it was time to land; she had to get Jenny back to their seats to buckle up. She buckled Jenny in first and then herself and once again contemplated what their future held for them. The plane landed without incident; Katelyn thanked everyone for their wonderful hospitality and readied Jenny to disembark.

As they descended the aircraft stairs, she spotted Kevin standing about fifty feet away. She couldn't wait to hug him. The terror attack of 9/11 had made everyone more aware of how important it was to keep family close and let them know how much you loved them, as often as possible. Jenny ran to her uncle's waiting arms and, without a care in the world, jumped into them. She wasn't satisfied until she wrapped her legs around his stomach and her arms tightly around his neck. Katelyn could see Kevin was enjoying every second of it. He smiled to Katelyn, kissed her cheek and asked if she was doing alright.

"It's been too long, Irish. I've missed you guys," he whispered in the dark, as he reached over with one finger and wiped the tears he knew would be there.

"I'm glad, I came too. It's been rough, not having you around," she stated as she guided Jenny's hair gently away from her face. They reached the car, buckled Jenny in and, within minutes, she was fast asleep again.

Kevin listened intently as Katelyn filled him in on her life since they had spoken last. Of course, Katelyn left out the bit about Gianfranco, for now. Every once in a while she would turn around to check on Jenny, who was fighting sleep so that Kevin could talk to her too. Of course, Jenny would remember to tell her uncle all about Gianfranco's visit and his plane. It would be out of the mouths of babes that Katelyn would suffer her embarrassing moment.

"Did you know, Uncle Kevin, that Mr. Broccoli owns his own plane?" she asked her uncle. Kevin didn't miss a beat. He laughed at her pronunciation of Gianfranco's last name.

"You must be tired my little munchkin," he said as he pulled his truck out of the airport.

"You should have seen the plane, Uncle Kevin. It has couches and a bed and a shower too. You could live up there in the sky. There was a kitchen, too." Jenny rambled on and on until all the excitement finally wore her out. It would take a little longer to reach the ranch but Katelyn loved having Kevin to herself, even if it was for a short time.

"Don't read anything into that, Kevin. Gianfranco checked in on us, for you. He and I are friends." Katelyn lowered her eyelids and knew, without a doubt, that Kevin could tell she wasn't telling him the whole truth. "I can't wait to see Sylvia. I'm so happy for the both of you. It will be nice having another child around."

"Wait until you see how much work we've done to the nursery; we still have months to go before this baby arrives. My wife is so excited that I didn't have the heart to stop her."

Katelyn was aware Kevin had allowed the change of subject and she appreciated it. She knew he worried about her and, no matter how old she was, that didn't seem to change. Without looking in his direction, she could feel his eyes glance her way every once in the while. It was as though he were waiting for her to fall apart from all the stress but knew better than to expect it. They arrived at the ranch to a welcoming committee. Sylvia was there as well as some of the familiar ranch hands. Mrs. Footy, the cook, had also come to welcome them. It was then that she spotted Brody, standing next to a tree in the front yard. Brody was Kevin's law partner and over the years had become one of Kevin's closest friends.

"He came especially to see you," Kevin said looking at Brody. "He wanted to welcome you, without getting in the way. I invited him to dinner tomorrow night but now I'm not so sure that was a good idea."

"Don't be silly, Kevin. Brody and I are friends and it's always good to see him. We are civilized toward each other; it's not as if any hearts were broken between us." Kevin smiled at his sister's insistence to avoid talking about Gianfranco. She knew that he hadn't been talking about Brody at all but she was doing everything to avoid talking about Gianfranco.

It was good to be back; she hugged and kissed everyone before going inside to join Kevin, who had already begun taking in the luggage. Mrs. Footy prepared a light snack for them to eat before putting Jenny up to bed for the night.

Sylvia couldn't wait to talk to Katelyn about the baby and all the work she had done to the nursery. "I couldn't wait for you to arrive. I'm so excited about having this baby and giving Jenny a cousin. It's all I think about. I drive Kevin crazy. Tomorrow I'll give you a tour of the nursery. How was your trip?" she asked.

"Not bad, I never traveled that way before and believe me, I could get used to it. Jenny, on the other hand, doesn't want to travel any other way now," she said laughing. "I'm going to get even with Gianfranco for creating this monster in my daughter."

Jenny was thrilled to be getting a cousin finally and, before kissing everybody good night, told Sylvia that. She also touched Sylvia's stomach and told her aunt that the baby was safe and sound.

With all the commotion of the evening and Jenny finally being put soundly to bed, Kevin and Sylvia bid Katelyn good night as well. Everyone else had already left and now it was just her and Brody. They were happy to see each other again and he gently pulled her into his arms and hugged her. It was the intimacy that they shared as friends although some people had hoped differently. Katelyn drew herself out of his embrace, even though it felt good and safe for a change. She hadn't had that feeling since Gianfranco had stormed into her life days before. She learned all too quickly from that experience that he didn't feel the same way about her anymore and that their future was a big question mark.

"What do you say you and I take a ride? I bet you haven't been on a horse since the last time you were here?" He chuckled when he realized how right he was. "I want to show you my new foal. I think Jenny might enjoy her."

Brody pointed toward his horse that stood tall near the oak tree. *Sure, why not?* Brody placed Katelyn up on the horse and jumped up behind her with ease. Without saying a word, he pulled on the reins and they galloped away. Having him close like this didn't feel right anymore. It was a bit inhibiting, to say the least. The whole situation felt wrong because she was with the wrong man.

They rode for a long time before reaching Brody's barn. It was dark as he led her into the stall that held the foal. Katelyn was awestruck by the beauty of the new foal. "She's beautiful, Brody. You should be proud of her." The foal was midnight black without another hint of-color anywhere on her body. "You should call her Ebony," she added quite freely.

"If that's what you think Jenny would want to call her, then that's what she'll be called." Brody took off his cowboy hat and brushed it against his leg. The barn had suddenly become a very enclosed place. She didn't want Brody to get the wrong idea about them and there was no way that she would allow Jenny to accept a horse as a gift.

"I can't allow that; you know that more than anyone. I love you Brody but that would be too much. I haven't told anyone this yet, not even Kevin, but I'm getting married soon. I'd appreciate you not telling Kevin though. I haven't figured out when to tell him, yet." She didn't want to hurt Brody but he deserved to know now that there would be no future together for them.

"Who's the lucky guy?" he asked, breaking the short moment of silence. "I hope it's not that Taylor fellow?" Brody watched her as she struggled to tell him. He didn't mind that she was marrying someone else; he had never loved Katelyn in that way but he did respect her.

"I'm marrying Jenny's father," she said hesitantly. Brody leaned closer so their foreheads were touching and told her he was happy for her.

"I'm happy for you. I know how much you loved him. For the record, we would've made a great team, you and me. Not that we would have had the whole passion thing going on," he said waving his hands in front of him. "But we are good friends and it would have worked, don't you agree?" he muttered softly.

"You know it. Of course, I still have to decline the horse. You know that, don't you? What would I do with a horse in New York City, anyway?" she asked slapping him teasingly on the arm.

"Tell me about him, this fiancé of yours. I always wondered about the man you lost your heart to," he added solemnly.

"For one thing, he's Jenny's father and he loves her and that's important. We'll finally be able to give Jenny the family she deserves to have." She avoided saying the one thing he knew, from experience, that she was hiding. She loved this guy more than anything and didn't believe he felt the same. Perhaps they were not so different after all; they both loved, without having that love reciprocated.

"Well, that answers a lot of my questions and the doubts I've had about myself. I don't think that you would have settled for anyone but him. I can see it in your eyes. Did anyone ever tell you that your eyes are the windows to your soul? No matter what you say, I just look into your eyes and I know what you know." She had been told that before many times. It hurt her to let him down but she was sure there was someone out there for Brody.

They had spent a lot of time together on the ranch and the last time she was here Brody delved deep into her soul and touched on the secrets she had kept hidden there for so long. He knew that she loved Jenny's father, although he never knew who he was. When she turned down his proposal for the first time, Brody knew it was because she hoped that she and Jenny's father would find their way back to each other.

"He's a lucky guy. I wonder if he appreciates what you're offering him. I want you to know one thing and I promise not to mention it again. We both know that our marriage would have been one of companionship rather than anything else. Neither of us will be pining for the other after today but I want you to know, if it doesn't work out with Jenny's father, my offer still stands." She kissed his cheek and thanked him.

Someday he would meet the woman he was destined to be with and then he would appreciate her refusal. She was convinced that Brody hadn't gotten married because he was so intent to settle on a fate that hadn't been his. She believed that he had his own secrets. To ease the conversation between them, Katelyn started teasing him about Mary Alice, the stewardess who had a soft spot in her heart for him.

"I almost forgot about Mary Alice. I think she was quite taken by you and she is very beautiful. I took her number and promised to deliver it to you. Perhaps fate is knocking and the only thing you have to do is answer the door. Or are you going to wait until it mows you down?" she teased.

They returned to the ranch, but, this time, in a safer manner. They took his pickup truck and she was happy that they did. She knew horseback was Brody's favorite past time but living in the Big Apple had left her a little rusty and her backside was killing her. The truck came to a halt in Kevin's driveway and, as he put it in park, she caught sight of a shadowy figure on the front porch. At first, she thought it might be one of the ranch hands but a little voice told her it was Kevin.

Kevin was sitting with his legs crossed at the ankle when she appeared. His hands folded in his lap and his eyes were full of questions. "You want to tell me, what's going on?" he asked, as he dangled Jenny's necklace in his hand.

"I'm not sure what you're getting at. Could you be a little clearer with your question?" she announced unsteadily.

Kevin was annoyed with her as the coloring on his face faded. "I don't want to beat around the bush, Kate. I'm a little confused and I need you to be honest with me. Where did you get this?" he asked, once again holding the necklace up in the air as if it were the answer to all his questions.

In his hand he held the teakwood ring dangling on a chain that she had worn everyday for years beneath her clothes. Gianfranco had given her that ring when she was eighteen years old, right after he had made love to her for the very first time. She remembered that night with clarity. She often wrote about it in her journal so she could cherish the feeling forever. She wanted to capture the moment and never forget it. She wasn't ready to share it with Kevin. She thought about her journal...

August 2004

I didn't believe in love at first sight before now. Yet, these past weeks spent with Gianfranco have taught me so much. I'm in love with Gianfranco Broccolini with all my heart and soul. I wish for the world what I have with him. Who would have thought that I would want to share the rest of my life with one of Kevin's best friends? But then, who better? I can't share this wonderful news with Kevin; it's too soon. He would absolutely freak if he knew that Gianfranco had made love to me. It would make the situation very uncomfortable for all of us. I'll tell him but only if Gianfranco proposes to me and the time is right. I think then, that Kevin would forgive us for keeping this secret from him and for postponing my trip to California, for now.

That was an innocent time for Katelyn. She knew now that nothing was as it seemed. She reached over and took the ring from Kevin, shaking her head and trying to make light of it. "It's only a ring, Kevin. I gave it to Jenny years ago and I'm not even sure where I got it," she answered fastidiously.

Kevin knew she was lying to him; for now, he'd let it go. He touched the ring she held in her hand again and studied Katelyn's expression. He didn't think for a minute that she understood the significance of the ring or that he understood its meaning. From the look on her face, he had no doubt in his mind that she never realized the meaning behind Gianfranco giving her that ring. He knew it was Gianfranco's ring, he had seen Jake's hanging around his neck often enough.

Katelyn watched Kevin as he played his father role, the one he played so well. She wished she could tell him the truth but he'd never understand. He wouldn't understand the marriage of convenience that she was about to embark on either. From his perspective, it had to look as if she had lost control of her life. First, there was Adam, then Brody, and now Gianfranco. She wondered what he must think of her. "*He must think I'm crazy.*"

"I want you to know that I hate keeping secrets from you. I know it seems crazy right now but I promise, Kevin, this will all make sense soon enough." She sat down next to him, reached out and took his hand in hers.

"I have one question and then I'll leave you alone," he said glimpsing into her eyes. He knew he had to stop seeing the young girl she used to be. She was a grown woman and he had to stop treating her like his little sister. He had always felt the need to protect her because she had no one else to do that for her, until now. "Did Gianfranco give you that ring?"

There must have been something he saw in her eyes long before she said the words because he didn't seem surprised to hear her answer. It was barely a whisper but she answered his question. "Yes," she said.

He reached over to her, hugged her tightly and then said good night. It was as simple as that, as though the answer to that one question answered so many others.

"You should get some sleep. It's been a long day and you need to rest." Kevin said. "I'm glad you guys are here. I've missed you."

"Ditto big brother. Ditto," she said as he tagged along behind her. She had often used the word 'ditto', so she wouldn't have to say she loved him when she was younger in front of her friends. Every once in a while she would loving remind him of their earlier days by saying it again.

After showering and checking in on Jenny, Katelyn grabbed her journal and began to write. She had kept a journal ever since she was a young girl; it helped her to work through the events of her life. She had a lot to write about today and she was looking forward to putting it all on paper so that she could read it back tomorrow and try to make sense of it all. She wrote for an hour before putting the pen down and turning out the light. Tomorrow, she hoped that a new day would bring new beginnings.

Kevin didn't mention Gianfranco's name again over the next few days and that suited her just fine. The longer she put off thinking about him, the less explaining she'd have to do and the better off she'd be. She enjoyed the break from all the stress and she was finally beginning to feel like a whole person again and Jenny loved having her around full time. She loved all the attention she was receiving. For now, it seemed as though everyone was happy and content.

Chapter Eight

After four days in beautiful Montana, Katelyn woke early feeling more refreshed than ever. She got out of bed and gazed at the reflection staring back at her from the mirror. The dark rings, that had only days ago surrounded her eyes, were all but gone. She lifted her hand to her face and pushed away the strands of hair that had fallen in her eyes. She'd made the right choice coming to Montana and only hoped that everything else would fall into place too.

She stood at the top of the stairs and her chest tightened at the sight of Kevin and Sylvia in the foyer below. He held her in his arms and, gazing down, as her throat tightened up, she witnessed the loving intimacy they shared. Katelyn had always hoped that one day she and Gianfranco would share that kind of love but it wasn't meant to be. He was offering her a loveless marriage; a marriage that would be based on lies and infidelity. The only thing she could rely on would be the money and security she would have from their union.

Kevin realized Katelyn was standing at the top of the landing and smiled up at her. He and Sylvia looked as though they were sharing some wonderful secret and had no intention of including anyone else. "I'm trying to have my way with my wife before I leave for the office but she's not having it," he said, tossing his jacket over his arm, as Katelyn walked down the stairs to join them.

"I'll be in court most of the day but I'll try to be home as early as I can. Maybe tonight, you and I could talk," he said directing his conversation to Katelyn. He opened the front door and walked down to the Land Rover parked in the driveway. Katelyn followed behind. He tossed his jacket and briefcase in the backseat of the truck, hopped in the front.

He rolled down his window as Katelyn approached. "I hope you don't mind, Brody came by this morning and I told him it would be alright to take Jenny to see the new foal and take her riding, was that okay? You were sleeping, Jenny really wanted to go." He said before starting engine. Kevin assured her that Jenny would be fine at Brody's ranch and that Patrick, Rosalina and their son were there too.

"That's fine; I'm sure Jenny was thrilled that Julio would be there. Patrick's son must be what, about eight now, right? I remember that he and Jenny are close in age." Katelyn had met Patrick and Rosalina on many occasions at Brody's ranch. The couple and their son lived on the large, sprawling ranch. Rosalina was the housekeeper and cook and Patrick oversaw the ranch for Brody.

"Brody said that Jenny's arrival was all Julio talked about. She's in good hands and you need to take some time to relax. Enjoy your day, spoil yourself. We'll talk when I get home." Kevin knew his sister well and she was doing everything to avoid talking about Gianfranco and, although he wanted to have the conversation, he wanted her to try to relax a little and enjoy her time with them. The conversation could wait.

Kevin pulled away and she watched as his car disappeared down the long driveway. She wished her mother and father could see what a success he had made of his life. They would have been so proud of him and all he'd accomplished. She was so deep in thought that she hadn't noticed Sylvia come up from behind. "You're off in your own little world; what are you thinking about?"

Sylvia was exactly the type of woman she would have chosen for Kevin, if she had any say. Sylvia and Kevin's relationship allowed Katelyn brief glimpses into what a happy marriage should look like.

"I was just thinking about Mom and Dad and how proud they would be of Kevin. Mom would be so happy for you guys. She would have loved to have been a grandmother." Her voice cracked with emotion as she thought about her mother.

"I know they would. I'm glad you're here, Katelyn. Kevin wanted so much to share his excitement with you. I originally thought that our moving here might damage the relationship you two share, and, to tell you the truth, it really scared me. Kevin would never forgive himself if he felt estranged from you and Jenny." Katelyn grinned at Sylvia and promised her that could never happen. Together they walked back into the house and she followed Sylvia who had walked into the family room. As she pulled back the heavy drapes it let the sun shine deeply into the room, Sylvia dropped a bomb.

"I don't suppose your brother happened to mention the charity ball on Friday night?" Sylvia asked, knowing full well her husband would choose to neglect telling Katelyn, on purpose. She put one hand on her hip, smiled and sighed slightly in disgust.

Katelyn's lips twisted into an unmistakable grin. "Of course, he didn't tell me. If he had, he knew I would have put the trip off another week. My brother is very manipulative. He knew what he was doing. Now, what am I going to do? I don't have anything to wear."

"It's formal and, though the men complain about the dress code, it's our biggest charity fundraiser. The proceeds this year are going towards the building of the new children's hospital just outside of town. Kevin and Brody chair the ball every year; and a few of us women end up doing all the work. I have a lot to do today but Brody already said he'd be glad to run you into town to buy a dress. He rearranged his schedule when he heard you were coming to town. Kevin wanted to take some time off too but he was due in court this week and couldn't postpone the trial date."

The two women went into the kitchen and Sylvia handed Katelyn a mug of coffee. Two minutes later, the door swung open but Katelyn didn't turn to see who it was. She had assumed it was Mrs. Footy, instead Brody stood there. Sylvia passed him a cup for coffee, told him to help himself and announced that they had been just talking about him. "I just told Katelyn, that you agreed to take her into town to find a dress."

Katelyn watched as he filled his coffee cup. "I'm sorry about this, Brody. My brother seems to volunteer you whenever he's unavailable. I do have a license, I can take myself," Katelyn assured him.

"Don't be silly, it wasn't his idea, it was mine. I thought it would be good for you to spend some time in town pampering yourself a bit, and then, on a more selfish level, I thought we'd take in dinner and a movie. No strings, just two friends out for a little fun, I promise."

Her body was somewhat relaxed but she still felt uneasy about spending so much time alone with Brody. It just didn't feel right with everything that was going on with her and Gianfranco. She also had this feeling of forewarning that something bad was going to happen and she wasn't sure why. She was once again becoming spooked by her feelings. Maybe Brody was right, dinner and a movie with a friend; what harm could come of that?

"I'll have to go and get Jenny so I can tell her that I'm leaving. Are you sure about this, Sylvia? You said you had errands of your own. Wouldn't Jenny be in your way?" she asked, not wanting to take advantage of Sylvia with all she had on her own plate.

"Mrs. Footy said she would take care of Jenny while I did what I had to do; I'll spend the rest of my day with her, once my chores are done. It's all worked out already. Jenny is a dream to be with, I love spending time with her. She's a little angel. I only hope her disposition runs in the family," Sylvia said as she patted her stomach. "Besides, you're too far away for us to offer to babysit, so let us make up for it tonight," she said reassuring Katelyn.

"Katelyn, go out with Brody and have a great time. This will be good practice for us. You have my permission to charge your gown to your brother's account, since he didn't tell you about the ball in the first place," Sylvia said, glancing over her shoulder at Brody. With a glance, Sylvia told him to be sure that Katelyn did just that. "Now go, the two of you. Have a great time and don't worry about Jenny; she's in good hands. She'll be fine."

Brody looked at Katelyn, waited for instructions and, without too much of a struggle, she finally agreed. They were right; she didn't have to worry about Jenny and she did need a dress for the charity ball. Katelyn made one request, that they make a stop at Brody's ranch before heading into town.

Once they got there, Katelyn saw that Jenny was having a great time. She and Julio were riding the horses around the corral. It seemed she had made a friend in Julio. In fact, Jenny encouraged her to leave so that she could go riding again with Patrick and his son.

Rosalina tried to assure them both that Jenny was in good hands and having a great time. "Brody, the kids are having a great time with Patrick. I can drop Jenny off later on after they've had their fun and I've given them some lunch. There's no need for Miss Sylvia to have to rush out and get her." Rosalina enjoyed watching the kids play. Julio didn't get a lot of interaction with other kids, living so far away from other homes. With Jenny taken care of, she and Brody agreed and left to head into town.

Katelyn and Brody drove for miles without saying anything of importance. He turned to Katelyn and looked at her with guarded appraisal. "What's going on inside that head of yours?" he asked.

She fidgeted with the purse on her lap for a few seconds and thought about what to say before looking directly at him. She let the words spill. "I'm a little puzzled about something that's been bugging me." She paused as she bit her bottom lip. "You're a very attractive man, not to mention that you have a great career. Why are you still single? I just don't get it. I believe that part of the problem could be that you present such a hard exterior. But those of us who know you get to see the softer, gentler Brody. Why is that?"

Brody beat his fingers on the steering wheel to the music playing on the radio and snickered. It was all he could do to keep from laughing. She had struggled to get those words out. Had they come from anyone else, he would have asked him or her politely to mind their own business, but not Katelyn. She didn't have an agenda, she was just curious, for curiosity's sake. "I guess you think I should have been scoffed up years ago?" he asked. "I'm going to tell you something I've never told anyone before. I was married once. It was a long time ago. I haven't seen my ex-wife since we divorced and, frankly, I hope I never see her again. We were both young and foolish when we ran away and eloped. We each started off with big dreams and a promise of a great future but in the end none of that mattered. One of us took the vows we made to each other seriously and the other didn't."

What a pair we are. We both have a track record for keeping secrets and holding on to lost love. "I'm curious about something. Tell me, why it is that you never shared that secret with anyone else, before now, I mean?" she asked.

"I could ask you the same question. In my case, it was easier not to talk about it; then I wouldn't have to explain it, like I'm doing now." Brody shut down after his revelation and Katelyn didn't push him, even though she was taken aback by his confession. She had to respect his privacy as he had hers. Brody hadn't bothered to ask her to explain the situation with Gianfranco and she wasn't volunteering information either. She had been very careful to be discreet and willingly withheld his name.

"Point taken, my question dear sir, I humbly withdraw," she added jokingly. Brody didn't respond, though he was amused.

'The town seems small and quaint but it isn't hard to see why people love living here,' she thought, as they continued to drive along the main street. She was looking forward to visiting the shop that Sylvia had mentioned. Sylvia professed that the small shop could give New York City boutiques a run for their money and Katelyn was curious. The proprietor, she was told, was friendly and well-versed in fashion dos and don'ts. Sylvia was quite impressed with Sheer Designs. She and the majority of her wealthy friends frequented the shop. The designs and the quality of the merchandise were supposed to be par with anything Sylvia had seen in fashion houses in New York, Paris and Milan.

As they arrived downtown, it was Brody who first commented on the size of the town. "It's a far cry from what you're used to but I love it here." What he didn't know was that Katelyn found the quaintness of the town to be its major allure. Brody came around the side of the truck to help her out. He raised one arm in the air with a flourish. "My town is your town, my lady," he teased.

"I don't know but this city girl is pretty pleased with your town. I happen to like small and intimate," she added before jumping out of the truck, something she'd never get used to. Why anyone owned these trucks, she didn't know. They were hard to get in and out of for someone of her stature. On the other hand, the weather changed here on a dime and a truck would probably make the most sense, especially during the snowy season.

Brody pointed to a shop across the way. She turned to see what he was pointing at and she saw the exquisitely decorated storefront. The shop stood out on the main street but not in a bad way. It was different, but tastefully so. She couldn't wait to go inside and take a peak.

"You're on your own from here. I' don't do ladies fashion, ever." He closed the door behind her and smiled lovingly down at her face before locking the doors. "I hear that the woman, I think her name is Nellie or something close to that, knows her craft. I'm sure she'll take good care of you. Be nice to the old lady, her establishment is relatively new and we'd like to keep main street thriving. She probably heard you were from New York City and is scared to death to have you in her shop." Brody was kidding with her. He knew better than anyone that Katelyn was far from stuck-up or fashionable. "I'll give you a couple of hours on your own and, while you're shopping, I'll go and see how Kevin made out in court this morning. I'll swing by later and meet you for dinner at the restaurant, Captain's Table," pointing down the block to a large green overhang that jutted out from the rest of the buildings surrounding it. "You can't miss it, that's the Captain's Table. If you're running late, no need to worry, I'll wait at the bar. We don't need reservations on a week night so take as long as you want."

He saw a glint of girlish excitement in her eye as she began to cross over to the shop. As Brody walked away, Katelyn couldn't help but notice a woman staring at them from the shop window. The woman was peeking from behind the curtain, looking in their direction. Maybe it was Brody she was looking at because any interest in her would make no sense. The woman disappeared when Brody came closer to the shop. Katelyn decided she wasn't going to waste time trying to figure it out. She had to find a dress for this charity affair, time was running out. She would put aside the thoughts about all the men in her life and concentrate on the dress. Today was going to be all about her.

Leave it to Katelyn to coerce me into rehashing the secret I kept buried. He had thought he had put Eleanor behind him, and now, after all this time, he was thinking about her again. Brody walked a couple of blocks in the opposite direction and headed for his office. There was a good possibility that Kevin could still be in court; if that were the case, he'd just go ahead and start on his case load for Monday. *Anything rather than think about Eleanor Mulaney Calder.*

The little bell on the door above her head sounded as she walked into the shop. During those first few seconds, Katelyn was totally alone. She wasn't sure if she was in the right place; it looked more like she was in someone's living room rather than a dress shop. She glanced around the room until she heard a woman's voice call out from behind the curtain.

Katelyn sat down on the sofa and wondered what to do next. It was obvious that this wasn't a buy off-the-rack sort of place. The woman called out to her, "Have some tea and cookies while you wait. If you like, you could skim through the albums on the table." The albums were lying on the coffee table; she helped herself as she skimmed through the pages one by one. The designs were magnificent; they were made for all different shapes and sizes and the colors and styles were breathtaking. Katelyn was no expert but Nellie, whoever she was, belonged in New York City or Paris.

Katelyn skipped to the section marked wedding dresses and it was there that she saw it, the dress she had always dreamed about wearing when she married Gianfranco. She tried to describe it to a New York seamstress many years ago when she thought for sure he was going to propose. It was just as well that the designer never understood her vision because the proposal never came. Katelyn stared long and hard at the dress as she pictured herself in it. It was perfect for her. Maybe she was meant to walk into this shop after all.

Nellie watched from behind the curtain as the stranger stared at the pale pink dress she had designed so long ago, wondering whether she was going to purchase it and, in conjunction, break her heart. The dress itself was so pale it looked more, white than the pink it actually was. It was a strapless gown with a delicate piece of expensive antique lace wrapped around the top of the dress, while the rest of the silky material flowed down toward the ankle. It was beautiful and Katelyn couldn't stop admiring it.

She knew that this dress was everything she had ever dreamed of wearing on her wedding day. The more she thought about it, the more she convinced herself to throw caution to the wind and purchase it. She was getting married, after all. She could, at the very least, have the dress she wanted, since it looked very unlikely that she'd get the loving husband to go with that fantasy.

"I'm sorry, I've kept you waiting. I didn't mean to take so long but I was putting the finishing touches on a dress. With this charity event coming up, I'm getting backlogged." Nellie held out her hand to introduce herself and Katelyn graciously accepted the hand offered.

Nellie wasn't the old lady Brody thought her to be; she was young and as beautiful as the clothes she designed. She looked vaguely familiar though Katelyn couldn't remember where she'd seen her before. Since she wasn't one to follow the fashion scene, it hadn't surprised her that her memory was lacking on the subject. The woman was dressed impeccably and the clothes she wore were obviously of her own design, one of a kind. Katelyn picked up the album from the table and smiled as she opened the book. "I have to tell you, I'm really impressed with your designs. Are they all yours?" she asked.

"Yes, I'm proud of them. Was there anything in particular that you're interested in?" Nellie hoped that the wedding dress from the portfolio hadn't intrigued her new customer because she had witnessed for herself the way Brody had looked at the woman and it might mean that he had moved on. She regretted adding that particular dress to the portfolio this morning.

"I work for a magazine in New York and I have to tell you these dresses are better than some of the designs that I've seen on our ad pages. I'm no expert but these look great. Have you ever tried marketing your designs on a grander scale?" Katelyn asked curiously.

"I had a dream once to launch my designs all over the international world of fashion and, for a while, I did quite well but it wasn't what I wanted in the end. You know what they say, be careful what you wish for. Sometimes you get everything you wanted and find out it wasn't what you expected after all," Nellie responded with a note of regret in her voice.

Nellie is turning out to be a mystery as well. What is it with me that everyone who surrounds me these days has a secret to tell? It doesn't take a super genius to figure out that Nellie gave up something near and dear to chase a dream only to find out it cost too much in the end. Katelyn also felt that, for whatever reason, Nellie wasn't taking a liking to her.

"I was admiring this dress and I was wondering if I could try it on? I'm getting married soon and I haven't had a chance to look for a dress. Oh, I'll also need a dress for the charity event. I hate to cause you so much trouble but my brother neglected to tell me about the charity ball until after I arrived from New York." Katelyn could see that Nellie's reaction to the news of her impending wedding was upsetting, for some unknown reason. She couldn't, for the life of her, figure out why.

She began to wonder if there was any way that Nellie knew Gianfranco. She guessed it was a possibility and the way her luck ran these days, it was very probable. But until two minutes ago, they had never met, so Nellie wouldn't be aware of Gianfranco. Although she wasn't sure she was ready for the answer, she asked the question that seemed to be suffocating them both. "My fiancé will be arriving from New York in another day or two and I'd like to surprise him by telling him that I've found a dress. I don't suppose you could put a rush order on the alterations and hope for the best?" she asked, hoping Nellie would ask for the name of her fiancé.

Nellie's demeanor mysteriously changed; she looked confused but definitely happier about something she heard her say. "Your fiancé is not in town?" she quizzed.

Katelyn realized that she had been right with her first assumption and started to put two and two together. It was Brody that Nellie was looking at as they crossed the street and it was Brody she was interested in. Katelyn wondered if Brody was even aware that he was being admired from afar.

"My future husband, I'm afraid, is tied up in New York on business. I don't think you would know him but you might have met him in passing; he's been here on occasion to visit my brother, Kevin Donavan. My fiancé is Gianfranco Broccolini." Nellie almost choked when she heard his name.

"Gianfranco Broccolini is getting married? I'm very happy for you both. Don't get me wrong but I have to tell you I'm shocked by your news. I actually met Gianfranco in Milan years ago. He was at my first fashion show. I believe he, indirectly, helped to launch my international brand. He was there with a friend and let me tell you, he was very generous. I think his investment in my clothes for that woman created a whirlwind of speculation from buyers all over the world. They wanted what he wanted and he wanted plenty." Nellie exclaimed with excitement.

In her enthusiasm she hadn't realized she hurt Katelyn by her revelation. "I didn't mean any disrespect when I said I was shocked that he was settling down. I'm sure he was waiting for the right woman." Nellie led Katelyn to a room at the back of the store where she could try on the dresses she selected.

There were dresses everywhere and Nellie had a story for every piece she created. She stopped at a rack of dresses in the center of the room and found what she had been searching for. The sound of the zipper startled Katelyn, from her own thoughts. She couldn't help but wonder who the mystery friend was who accompanied Gianfranco to the fashion show. Nellie took the dress out of its protective carrier and showed it to Katelyn. *This is the dress.* She couldn't believe her eyes; it was exactly as she had pictured it in her dreams. The attention to detail was amazing. She took the gown from Nellie and held it against her body. As she looked at her reflection, she was almost brought to tears.

Nellie looked pleased with herself. Nothing made her more excited than one of her designs on the right body and she knew Katelyn was meant to wear this dress. "The dressing room is right over there." Nellie said pointing to the room behind them.

Without hesitation, Katelyn went and tried it on. As she slid the gown down over her body, she stared shockingly at her reflection. The gown was everything she'd hoped it would be. The neckline of the gown showed cleavage that she only acquired after becoming a mother. Fortunately, she had retained her some of her fuller breasts after giving birth.

Nellie joined her in the fitting room and saw the tears in Katelyn's eyes. They both stood silently staring at the image in the mirror and it was Nellie that broke the silence first. "It was made for you. When I designed that dress, I had no idea it would look as beautiful as it does on you. You were meant to wear it," she added with compassion.

For a brief and wonderful moment, Katelyn fantasized about a very happy and willing Gianfranco, waiting at the altar. He would be smiling, looking only at her and everyone would see for themselves that the infamous Gianfranco Broccolini had fallen deeply in love. This was her dream, after all.

"The alterations I have to do on this dress are minimal; so I could have it ready whenever you need it. I also have an ideal choice for the other dress you need. Another dress, I think, will wow you. Gianfranco will take one look at you in it and it will be an image that will be burned into his memory forever. I'm still working on it but it will definitely be ready by the time you need it. Do you like the color red?" she asked as she moved to another rack of dresses in the corner of the room.

Katelyn loved the color red and, other than the dress that she had worn to shock Adam the other night, she hadn't owned anything red before. She thought the color would draw attention to her, and, up until now, she wanted to be invisible. She had avoided the color red at all costs because of the attention she might've received. *Rosa is right, it's time for me to come out of my shell and start living again. If the color red pops on me and brings attention, so be it.* Her husband was going to have to learn to deal with the sudden competition.

Once again, Katelyn was moved by Nellie's ability to design. When she tried on the red gown, she saw that it was tightly gathered around the middle to emphasize her small waist. The shoulders were bare; she had no doubt that her bare neck was enough to give her an edge over Gianfranco, should he decide to come to the charity event at all. She knew if he saw her in this dress that he would have a very hard time controlling his desire. It was a perfect fit and as Nellie had said it was almost complete. Katelyn could see how much attention Nellie paid to detail because the dress looked perfect as it was to her untrained eye.

Nellie went over to her workbench and came back with two long strips of fabric that had tiny silver beads hand-sewn into the fabric; she took one strip and pinned it around the top of the dress and the other around her waist. Katelyn couldn't believe what she was seeing. The silver beads were reflecting the red color of the dress. That small detail completed the dress, making the dress even more alluring than before.

"You're amazing Nellie, the dress is beautiful. Tell me something, I don't mean to pry, but is there something going on between you and Brody?" She asked.

Nellie didn't say anything at first. It was as though she were weighing whether she should share her past with Katelyn at all. For whatever reason, the two of them seemed to have connected more in their short visit than Nellie had with anyone else since returning to Montana and so Nellie chose to confide in her. Katelyn couldn't believe how close to the truth her hypothesis had been. Nellie was, in fact, the well-known fashion designer, Eleanor Mulaney, who had disappeared a year earlier.

It was a big story a year ago. Eleanor Mulaney had disappeared the year before at the peak of her professional career. It was as though she had clawed her way to the top in no time at all and then disappeared just as quickly. However, Nellie must have left Brody long before then because Kevin and Sylvia were never aware of Brody having a wife. Nellie told Katelyn that she had lived in Montana years ago with Brody. They had dated all through college and later when Brody went on to law school. It wasn't until they eloped that things changed between them. Brody wanted a family and she wanted to pursue her career. She loved designing clothes and she thought that he would support the career she trained so hard to achieve, just as she supported him with law school. When her work required her to travel more and more, he gave her an ultimatum, their marriage or her career.

He wanted her to come home and raise a family but she wouldn't leave Milan until she achieved what she had set out to do. At that time, Nellie thought she had made the right decision but she found out the hard way that the life she had with Brody was the path she should have chosen. Still, she had no regrets for achieving what she did but she had always hoped that Brody would have supported her career.

"No matter how rich and famous I became, it was never enough. I wasn't happy. It took years to figure out what was missing. It was because Brody was no longer a part of my life. It didn't matter if that life was in Paris, New York or Milan; without Brody in my life, I was pretty lonely. My career was no longer filling the void left by Brody."

"I must have changed a lot over the years or Brody's rich friends simply never cared about me at all because I realized when I came back that I wasn't recognized by his wealthy friends. Brody was the popular jock back in the day, dating the girl from the other side of the tracks. Women I had met in previous years through Brody would come into the shop and not know who I was. I thought if none of them recognized me that I could keep my presence hidden from Brody as well. I came up with this silly idea of how to approach him again. I wanted to finish a dress design that Brody had helped me with years ago. I thought that if Brody saw me in this perfect dress, it would be the best way to win my husband back. Is that silly?" she asked as she opened another wardrobe bag hanging on the mobile rack.

When Nellie opened the wardrobe bag, Katelyn was awestruck once again. There were definitely two sides of Nellie Mulaney. This dress was white and very plain, at first glance, but when Nellie slipped it on the mannequin and turned it around, Katelyn saw what she was hoping Brody would see and admire. The deep plunging line of the dress reached all the way down the back and just barely tapped the derriere of its wearer. *Brody would have to be dead not to react.* She grinned as she gave her approval.

Nellie smiled and turned her mannequin around. "Just like its intended, there are two sides to the dress, a contrast between the front and the back and innocence and sex," she said.

"How long did this take you?" Katelyn asked as she once again admired the dress up close.

"I think I've been working on this design for years. Subconsciously, I knew that without Brody in my life, I could never finish it," Nellie added with a soft smirk.

"I'm meeting Brody for dinner in a few minutes, would you like to go instead of me?" Katelyn asked.

"No, you go, Katelyn, and have a good time. I need to stick to my original plan. Brody will never believe that I'm back to stay unless I prove to him publicly that I have always loved him. When he sees me for the first time, and I'm wearing this dress, he'll know I came back for him. The ball will be in his court then and if I have to wait a little longer, I'll wait. He's waited a long time for me. Besides, I feel better knowing you're with him; I don't have to worry about another woman in his life," she added hopefully.

Brody was waiting, as promised, at the bar at the Captain's Table when she arrived. He smiled when he saw her and, for the first time, Katelyn understood the pain she had always suspected lingered just beneath the surface. There were good reasons for his aloofness and now she knew the secret that he had kept hidden from all the people closest to him. It was easy for him to keep the secret from Kevin and Sylvia; they had moved to town after Eleanor and Brody split up.

Brody waited to order while Katelyn rambled on and on about her purchases. She rattled on for so long about what a great designer Nellie was and how worthy her designs were of the international fashion seen. "Sylvia was right. Nellie is that good." Katelyn couldn't resist teasing Brody as she told him about the plunging necklines and bare shoulders and deep dipping backs of the dresses. Brody, out of shear embarrassment, stopped her from talking and, in doing so, helped to contain her enthusiasm.

She was sure that somewhere in this conversation with Brody, he admitted, quite innocently, to being involved with a designer once. He confessed that they were very young when they were together and he remembered a dress that she had started to design while they were dating. That dress was cut provocatively low in the back, just like the one you were describing. In fact, my ex had designed it so it barely hid a tattoo on her buttock. The tattoo was one that coupled with mine in the same place on our bodies. We got them after a night of too much drinking. It was a young foolish gesture, meant to symbolize our unending love for each other." He admitted while laughing at what he just confessed to.

"I'm afraid now you know all my secrets," Brody teased. He then apologized for bringing up his past, almost wishing he hadn't because remembering the lonely years without Eleanor in his life was painful to him.

"What kind of tattoo?" she teased unmercifully. Brody continued to eat and, in between bites, he tried to change the direction of the conversation.

"I'm afraid I have to draw the line there. You would have found out had you agreed to marry me though," he added triumphantly. When they finished dinner, Brody signaled for the waiter and paid the check. They took their coats and headed for the door and were greeted by a cold brisk wind.

The Montana sky was already beginning to change and a storm was moving in. The temperature had dipped dramatically from the time they entered the restaurant. On the trip home, Katelyn was sure Brody's silence had little to do with his recollection of the past and more to do with the quickly changing weather. They had decided not to go to the movies as planned because the weather didn't look promising. When they arrived at the ranch, it was quiet and looked as though everyone had already gone to bed for the night. There was a porch light on which she was sure was left for her convenience. Brody, being the gentleman that he was, helped Katelyn from the truck again but not before she dropped her purse on the floor in front of him, hoping he would bend over and reveal a hidden tattoo.

"Don't think for a minute that I'd fall for that one. You were going to check out my derriere, weren't you?" he teased. "How you were going to accomplish that with my coat on is another question?" They both laughed; it felt good to laugh for a change.

It was disturbingly quiet and there was a strange car parked in the driveway she hadn't noticed before she left. Brody gently and innocently kissed her good night and she found out who the owner of the mystery car was; he had been lurking in the shadows on the porch. Katelyn saw his figure first as he emerged from the darkness. He stepped into the light and she saw the anger he was experiencing in his eyes.

Brody could sense that Gianfranco Broccolini was indeed the mystery man Katelyn had kept secret from everyone. He didn't know what to do at this point and it was definitely an uncomfortable situation for all. Gianfranco looked as if he were ready to kill someone. Brody had a hard time believing that he was the same man he had come to know and admire. He had met Gianfranco on numerous occasions and knew him to be a man that kept his cool under dire circumstances. Yet, he also knew from experience what the other sex was capable of making men do.

Brody knew that no matter how angry Gianfranco was, no physical harm would come to Katelyn. He couldn't get over it. Gianfranco Broccolini was the man who had stolen her heart. He wondered if he knew how lucky he was. Brody thought that it was time for him to leave and he bid them both farewell and decided to exit, but not before asking Katelyn if she'd be alright.

"I'm fine; you don't have to worry about me. I guess our secrets are out now for the both of us," she whispered, knowing Brody knew what she was talking about. Brody walked to the other side of the truck, got in and drove away. It was no wonder people feared Gianfranco; at this moment, from the look in his eyes, he feared him. He was capable of emanating a sense of power so ruthless that he made you fear for your life without muttering a word.

Every nerve in Katelyn's body was alive when she was in his presence. Her own body was betraying her. He on the other hand was ready to explode and she was his target. She had to give him a little time to gain control of the emotions he was saturated with. He thought that something was going on between her and Brody. She'd be damned if, after his recent display with that woman at the restaurant, she would explain the error he had made. *Let him feel what I felt, only days ago.* Before Brody had reached the end of the drive, Gianfranco pulled her into his arms and punished her with a deep assault of kisses. He wanted to be sure Brody understood and witnessed his branding of her in his rear view mirror.

Katelyn was relieved, when she was finally able to put some distance between them. In another second, her true feelings would have been revealed to him. The relief was only temporary because he cupped her face in his hands and kissed her once again. This time, he was gentler and more loving with his kisses. It didn't take long for him to regret what he'd done and he pulled back. He was annoyed with himself as he leaned back against the rail post he let out an audible sigh of disgust.

"Every part of me is on fire with want for you right now. Whether you choose to admit it or not, you want the same thing I do. Would you deny that?" he asked with a deep husky drawl.

"No. You're wrong, I don't want you, and what's more, I hate your Neanderthal tactics. I seem to be the lone recipient of your bad behavior," she shouted. "I am not your wife, Gianfranco, nor am I your sex slave and I don't intend on being either," she stated sternly. *He makes me so angry, I could spit!*

Gianfranco ran his fingers along the edge of her mouth ever so gently, barely touching her lips, until he thought she could take no more. Of course, he affected her. She could lie all she wanted to but she was his. She belonged to him. His hands reached into her coat and traced the hollow of her throat. She let out a whimpering sigh as he moved his other hand down her back until he touched the bottom of her spine. He then pressed her body into his, close enough so that she could feel his erection through their clothes.

"I can prove how much you want me, right here, or there on the porch, if you want me to. But I'd rather have this discussion somewhere more private, perhaps in the warmth of the house. Which will it be, Katelyn?" he asked rather thickly, his voice was barely able to hide the intenseness of his plight.

"I'll go inside with you but this particular discussion is over. You are not going to control me, Gianfranco. I will choose my own friends and you won't be telling me how to behave when I'm with them," she said grounding out how angry she was with him.

"How to behave…you have got to be kidding. I arrive here to find out that my future wife was out on a date. Then, when you finally do show up, I have to witness you practically mauling another man in public," he added angrily.

"I did no such thing," she spat out, wishing she could slap his face. *How could he think so little of me?* "Furthermore, it is none of your business what I do. You are such a barbarian." Katelyn turned and stomped angrily inside. She was feeling really perturbed and she could see that his feelings matched her own. Neither of them could hide the displeasure they felt for each other at the moment.

As they each became angrier, the more absurd the situation seemed and the more she wanted to laugh at the hideousness of it all. *What a pair we make.*

"Our daughter is lying in a bed upstairs; she cannot witness the two of us behaving like juveniles," she added to avoid her nervous laughter from showing its ugly head.

At the mere mention of Jenny, Gianfranco became incensed. "Let me emphasize two things, Katelyn. First, I would never do anything to hurt Jenny in anyway and that includes my behavior toward her mother. Secondly, you are now bound to me whether you like it or not. The addition of a ring on your finger means very little to me. Whatever Brody may or may not mean to you; that cozy little display I just witnessed is over. Do I make myself clear?" It was a question that he didn't require her to answer. It was more of a demand and she would have little choice but to agree to it.

Katelyn was furious with him and the way he was treating her. She stood before him and said nothing in defiance. It was better to ignore him than get riled up by him and dragged into a screaming match of his own making.

She closed her eyes and briefly shut him out. She didn't want to be tempted by him and show her weakness, for which there was no cure. She wondered why he reacted the way he did toward her when clearly his feelings for her were superficial. It was Jenny he wanted in his life and, unfortunately, she came as part of the deal.

He was getting frustrated and angry; he bitterly chose his next words with care. "In three weeks' time, you'll be my wife and nothing you say or do is going to stop that reality from happening. In the meantime, I expect your loyalty and if that includes severing your ties with Brody Calder and Adam Taylor, then so be it. They may have had the pleasure of knowing your body once, but they'll never know your body again." He came to a halt and stood before her, his eyes burning with desire, as he willed her to look at him. He held her shoulders and stilled her from pacing. "You belong to me now," he said before crushing her lips to his.

There were no concessions made as he staked his claim. This was not the future she had envisioned for herself and Jenny but she was being left without options. She tried with all her might not to react to his kiss but he was right; she belonged to him, body and soul. There was no hiding the fact that she wanted him and he knew it. She couldn't deny him what her body gave to him so freely. It was as if her body and brain were separate entities and both acted without the will of the other.

"We should go inside; I want to let you know that Kevin had the foresight to put me in the room adjoining yours. There's only a door between us; be forewarned that a locked door will not keep me from you if I should desire to come to you."

Katelyn tried to ignore the effect he had on her. She tried with every stitch of strength she had not to give in to the craving she found impossible to resist. She stood silently and thought about what he was saying. She found it amusing that he would think he'd have to break down a door to get to her. *It is much easier than that. I've practically given you the key to my heart and my body.*

His gaze flickered briefly from anger to compassion and then to understanding, if only for a moment. "I know what I'm asking of you isn't easy. Think of Jenny. Are these two men so important to you that our daughter's happiness should be jeopardized?" He didn't wait for a reply because he couldn't bear to hear it. He locked the front door behind him and turned to help her with her coat. It only took a brief second but it was just enough for her to collect her thoughts and regroup.

There were tears in her eyes and she couldn't stop them from rolling down her cheeks. She could feel his regret as he tried to keep his feelings hidden from her. *Does he blame me for his unhappiness; for forcing him into a marriage he doesn't want? Is there another woman? Perhaps the woman in the silver picture frame that he had kept near his bed on the plane, is she the woman of his dreams?* Katelyn regretted that she hadn't taken the time to check who the woman in picture was. Their eyes met for a fraction of a second and, in that time, he gently pulled her into his arms. He wiped the tears from her eyes and apologized to her for all the sadness he had brought to her life.

"I think it's time we get you to bed," he said with tenderness as he led her to her bedroom. He stalled for a moment at the door, filled with regret as he fought to remain gallant. He didn't like seeing Katelyn like this. He knew she felt defeated and hopeless, a rare feeling for her. Her tears were more than he could handle and his gaze lingered on her emerald eyes for longer than he should have allowed.

"I'm not pleased with the tactics I had to use to make you my wife but I didn't know what else to do. I thought I was doing what was best for our daughter and now I'm not so sure," he said, trying to muster up the courage it would take to walk out the door. "We can make this work. I've been to hell and back these past couple of days and the only thing I'm sure of is that you and I belong together. I want you in my life, Katelyn. I want my daughter in my life and I need to get to know her. I need to make up for all the time I've missed," he said.

As he soaked in her beauty, he crossed the room and put his hand on the doorknob that would separate them for the night. He hesitated and turned to her with the image of how comfortable she was with Brody still burning in his head. He couldn't help but feel hurt. Her response to him was just the opposite. He was also appalled when he found out that she hadn't shared the news of their upcoming wedding with Kevin or Sylvia. They were both shocked when he asked them how they felt about the news.

"Why didn't you tell Kevin about us?" he asked hesitating at the door. The pain was evident in his voice as he spoke. She wanted to explain her reasons for holding back the information and to hold him in her arms so she could console him from the betrayal he once again felt at her expense but her body wouldn't and couldn't move.

"I wanted to give you time to reconsider," she whispered into the darkness.

He didn't react at first; he stood silently and pondered for a minute. "I want you and Jenny in my life, no matter what the cost," he said caustically. "Would it be so terrible for you to be married to me?" he said in a broken voice.

There was pain hidden in those feelings as his eyes locked on hers. It was obvious that he believed she detested the thought of marrying him. *He is so far from the truth.* Really, she couldn't remember a time when she didn't love him. It was as though fate had played a sick joke on the two of them, bringing them together at a time when it couldn't have worked.

"Is this what you really want, Gianfranco? I don't think I could bare it if your heart wasn't in it," she said swallowing down the tears that flowed so freely.

He let go of the doorknob as his eyes lingered on her for what seemed an eternity. It wasn't until he was sure of what he saw in those emerald eyes that he made his move. "I want to make love to you but I have to know that it's me you want. I need to hear my name on your lips when I make love to you. I have to know you're sure this time because after tonight there will be no turning back. I promise you that," he enunciated as he waited for her response. She nodded in agreement but he needed to hear her to say it out loud.

"Are you sure?" he asked.

"Yes," she whispered faintly. He lifted her into his arms and didn't stop until he reached the bed. He paused briefly as he went to the door and turned the lock. He walked back to her and started undressing himself and had her watch. She watched from the bed with curiosity as he pulled his black sweater over his head and threw it to the floor and then his crisp white tee shirt too. Seeing his chest bare, she could hardly breathe. His shoes disappeared under the bed, as well as his socks. He knew she was mesmerized, enjoying the striptease she was witnessing.

He maneuvered his way between her legs and, just as quickly, he unbuckled his pants, almost unzipping at the same time. He pulled her up off the bed and began to slowly and methodically undress her. He reached down and undid the two buttons holding her shirt together and then threw the shirt to the floor, quickly followed by her pants. As her pants fell to the floor he directed his attention to her body and what she had on beneath her sweater. The nude and black teddy she wore was barely visible and he gasped at the sight of her breasts as they peaked out of the flimsy material.

"Lie to me if you have to but tell me you wore this for me," he begged.

"I knew that you would show up sooner or later and I dressed accordingly," she uttered softly and truthfully.

He cradled her face in his hands adoringly as he kissed her slowly and deeply. He then brushed the straps of her teddy off her shoulders and let it fall down to her waist, exposing the breasts he loved and needed. He ran his tongue over them and suckled the erect buds that had been crying out to him from under the thin fabric covering them. As he stood up, no longer kneeling between her legs, Katelyn could feel his erection as he removed the last of the barriers that stood between them. Gianfranco gently laid her down on the bed and rejoined her as he buried his face in her neck and took in the sweet nectar of her scent. He spread her legs apart with his knee so that she could feel his need at the juncture of her being.

He held her and made love to her for hours, no longer holding his emotions and needs at bay. *My appetite for her will never be satisfied.* He held her in the crook of his arms hours later, while she slept. She didn't move until she heard a faint knock on the door. She lifted her head from the pillow and realized that she was alone, hugging the pillow that still held his scent. She wondered where he had gone so early.

"Katelyn...are you awake?" Sylvia asked as she opened the bedroom door slightly. She saw that Katelyn was awake, just beginning to get up. "Kevin and I are going to a doctor's appointment and I didn't want you to come downstairs and find the house totally deserted."

"Where is everyone?" Katelyn asked.

"Gianfranco took Jenny into town to go shopping. He told us the news last night when he arrived. He felt bad that he blew your surprise. He didn't know you were waiting for him to arrive to share your news with us. I don't know how you kept the secret. I can't believe how embarrassed I feel, trying to set you up with Brody. Kevin is beside himself, Katelyn. He is so happy for you and Jenny. Boy, you should have heard Jenny's reaction when Gianfranco told her. Mind you, I don't think he intended to tell her but she overheard us talking, I'm afraid. You better watch out for that little girl of yours; he's already like putty in her hands."

Her heart was beating so fast; she thought Sylvia could hear it as well. Her first reaction was to fling her feet over the side of the bed but she stopped herself when she thought about her current state of dress. She had no clothes on beneath the blankets. She couldn't believe her little girl was being told all this information and she wasn't there to explain the decisions she had made and the reasons why she had made them all those years ago. Everything was happening way too fast. She wasn't prepared for this.

"I'm sorry I didn't tell you both myself. I wanted to but I thought I should wait until Gianfranco arrived and we told you together."

"I still can't get over it. Here I am thinking like a fool that maybe you and Brody could hook up and live happily ever after." Sylvia paused for a moment as if she were thinking about something. "I can't get over how you got Gianfranco Broccolini to settle down. I'm so happy for you both. There are no two people more deserving. I honestly didn't think that man would ever settle down," Sylvia said, stretching out her arms, giving Katelyn a hug.

"I can just imagine what the headlines will read when this news gets out. '*One of the top sexiest richest men calls it quits'.*" Sylvia voiced as if reading from a headline already. She sat down on the edge of the bed and continued to tease Katelyn. "The papers will be after you, too. All the crazy single women will want to know how you did it. Don't worry, you'll have us plain folk to protect you from the media, for a little while anyway."

"Oh come on, what makes Gianfranco so special?" She tried to hide her tears; they were just below the surface but it wouldn't be long before they were flowing. They were tears of fear, fear of the future. She wanted this marriage to work more than anything but she had her doubts. It seemed there was only one place where they were in total sync and that was in bed. She couldn't keep him in bed forever, though it would fun to try.

Sylvia apologized again for having to leave her alone before she left the bedroom and added that she wasn't sure if she and Kevin would be back for dinner or if they would grab something in town. Katelyn assured her that she and Gianfranco could handle things without them. After Sylvia left, she got up and looked at her body, a body that had been made love to all night. Then she took a long hot shower before putting on fresh clothes. She ended up wearing thong underwear and jeans and a black sweater without a bra. She was going for comfort since she would spend most of the day alone.

Katelyn went into the kitchen and made a pot of tea while she waited for everyone to return home. As the hours passed she was beginning to think that no one was ever going to return home so she picked up a magazine to keep her company. Ironically, she picked up a copy of *Glitz*. She turned to the story she did on Charles Matlin and was happy to see that Mr. Taylor had decided not to change anything after all. Her story was good and she knew that if he had changed even a small piece of the story, it would have lost its effect. The story had plenty to offer its readership violence, sex and corruption in today's politics. Yet, leaving out any of the details she uncovered and the readers would've been left without closure.

There was also an announcement about the merger in the magazine. It gave a very brief but upbeat scenario about hiring more people to accommodate future expansion. She hoped that the story was accurate and that Gianfranco had planned on the expansion of the magazine because there were a lot of talented people who would probably lose their jobs if he decided to downsize at all.

She laid the magazine down on the table and wondered where Gianfranco could be. *Where did he take Jenny and what are they talking about?* It galled her to no end that he hadn't thought to include her in this important decision. Despite her obvious misgivings about their upcoming marriage, she knew there was no turning back. It was going to happen now, no matter what the cost or to whom.

It was almost lunchtime and she hoped that Gianfranco, where ever he was, would be feeding their child, although she was sure Jenny would tell him if she were hungry. She stood by the large window and looked out at the sprawling acres of Kevin's ranch. It looked cold and damp outside. She thought for a second about Nellie and how much they had in common, two women in love with two men who didn't seem to want to love them back.

Katelyn made a note to call Nellie, also known as Eleanor, and set up a lunch date. There was no reason to wallow in their unhappiness alone when they had each other. *We were fools, fools for love.* Both of their men had the ability to hurt them beyond their wildest dreams and both were probably unaware of the power they each held. She went to the couch and decided to watch a little television to take her mind off things. Surely they wouldn't be much longer?

Chapter Nine

Gianfranco walked hand in hand with his daughter down main-
street; beaming with pride as they held onto each other. He held
her little hand in his and prayed that there would be many more days
like this ahead for the two of them. He stared down into the ebony eyes
he recognized as his own mirror image and smiled with proud arro-
gance. He remembered fantasizing about what a child of a union
between him and the young woman he called Irish would look like. The
answer to the question was standing right next to him. She was a beauty, his daughter, and smart too. He grinned from ear to ear as it dawned
on him how quickly he was falling in love with his little girl.

"I don't think my mom is going to be happy with you. She doesn't
like it when Uncle Kevin or Uncle Jake try to spoil me and you bought
me way more than they ever do. Santa Claus doesn't even bring me this
much and he spoils me," Jenny said with the innocence of a child.

"I think, this one time, your mother will forgive me. After all, it isn't
everyday you get married, is it?" he asked gingerly as he continued to
stroll down the street. This was his child and he had missed out on sev-
en years of her life; he wasn't about to miss another second of it. She
was everything he could have asked for in a child. Katelyn did a great
job raising her so far but she deserved two parents. He saw how reluctant Jenny was to believe that the two of them wouldn't be in any
trouble with her mom; he assured her that her mom would understand.

What Katelyn thought about the gifts was not important to him. Since she had no qualms about lying to him about his child's existence, he'd spoil Jenny if he wanted to; there was nothing Katelyn could do about it. He was determined not to miss another second of the time they would have together.

"I'm having fun with you. I'm glad you're marrying my mom," Jenny stated shyly. He effortlessly scooped her into his arms and hugged her tightly.

"I'm having a great time too. I'm glad we're going to be a family," he added.

Gianfranco kissed her forehead after placing her on the ground again. He could tell by the way she looked at him that she had a question for him but was afraid to ask. *She'll ask me when she's ready and I won't push her away.* He didn't want to make any mistakes with Jenny and if it meant delaying their conversation because she wasn't ready to hear the truth, then he would wait.

"How about you and I find a restaurant somewhere and get something to eat? You must be hungry from all this shopping?" he asked, swinging their hands up into the air as they were locked together. He found a place a couple of doors down as they walked along Main Street and he requested a seat in the center of the room so that anyone who saw them would presume that this was his daughter. It was his silent way of acknowledging her.

"Do you think I could get hot chocolate?" she asked.

"You can have whatever you want," he said as he motioned for a waitress. The woman took their order and Jenny suddenly stood up and made an announcement to the unsuspecting waitress.

"This is my Dad." She stated proudly. The waitress seemed a bit puzzled but smiled at the little girl and said she'd get her a couple of hot chocolates right away. As the waitress walked away from the table, Gianfranco couldn't hide the emotions he felt by Jenny's admission. He was bursting with pride at Jenny's sudden announcement and wished that someone familiar was there to witness it. The waitress returned with their drinks and handed Gianfranco a piece of paper. He glanced at it and saw that it had her name and phone number on it. The note alluded to her interest in him since he wasn't wearing a wedding ring.

"Do you like her?" Jenny asked innocently.

"Do you mean the waitress?" he asked as she nodded back at him. "I think she seems like a nice person but I don't know her. If you're asking me if I would want to date her, I'd have to say no. Why would I be interested in her when I have the two most beautiful women in the world in my life right now? Jenny, I want you to know that I loved your mother since the very first time I saw her. Does that answer your question?" he asked trying to reassure her. He loved watching her expressions; she was so much like Katelyn in that sense. Her insecurity was written all over her face. She didn't want to lose the potential father she saw in him and he wished he could make it clear that he wasn't going anywhere.

"I do have a question, but I'm afraid to ask you," she said. He wondered what it was that frightened her so but not enough to stop her from asking. She opted to continue in spite of the fear she felt. "My momma once told me that my real father lived in another country. She said that if he knew about me, he would have been the best father in the world. She said that it was our secret." She paused a second before continuing, "When you hugged me outside, I saw the mark on your neck; my momma said that my dad had that same mark. That's the same mark I have." She pulled her long hair over to the side and Gianfranco saw that they indeed shared the same heart shaped birthmark. People who passed through his life had always assumed it was a tattoo. How could he not tell her the truth when she came right out and asked him?

"Are you my daddy?" she asked timidly, as she waited for his answer.

He wanted Katelyn to be there with him when it came time to have this discussion with Jenny. He couldn't lie to her when she came right out and asked, so he just nodded his head; his eyes welled up. The silence lasted a few seconds but felt like a lifetime. It was the most agonizing few minutes of his life. His face was strained from the anticipation of her response. He knew he had to be the adult in this situation and explain to her, in words she would understand, why he had been absent in her life. For now, he would let her digest what he had just revealed to her and wait for her to say something to him.

Jenny got up from her seat, at first Gianfranco second-guessed whether he had made the correct choice. He thought she was going to run from the restaurant and he'd have to chase after her but she didn't. Instead, she walked slowly over to his chair, looked up into his face with those big ebony eyes and smiled. "I'm glad you're my Daddy," she said, before hugging him tightly around his neck. He thought she held on so tight that he would choke but he loved every second of it.

Putting her on his lap, he said, "Jenny, I promise you, from now on, I'll be there for you. I don't ever want you to doubt for one minute that I didn't want you in my life. If I had known I had a little girl, I would have come back a long time ago. Do you believe me?" he asked still holding her.

She smiled and nodded and hugged him again. "I'm glad you're here now and that you're staying." She jumped off his lap and returned to her seat. "In my school, they have a father and daughter day. Now, I have a dad to bring. Momma's friend Adam said that he would take me but I don't like him," she said smirking.

Gianfranco laughed. *Out of the mouths of babes*, he thought. "You want to know something? I don't like him either. We should finish up our lunch and then stop at the jewelry store before we head home. We need to buy you and your mother wedding rings."

"You want to buy me a wedding ring? I thought only big people wore them," she said, confused.

He wanted to spoil his child. He wanted to enjoy every second he had with her. "You're right, of course, but I want to buy you a promise ring. I want you to have a ring that will remind you that I love you and I'll always be here for you."

He signed the restaurant check that was given to him by the waitress, and after retrieving the note from his pocket with the waitress's number on it, he left both pieces of paper on the table. Jenny was pleased that he did and took her father's hand proudly as they walked from the restaurant together. The walk was a little bit longer to the jewelry store but neither of them seemed to mind; that was more time they got to spend together.

It was a quiet store and the shop owner seemed pleased to see them. After consulting with the jeweler and picking out two beautiful rings for his girls, he asked Jenny to help him pick out another gift for her mom. He told her he wanted to surprise her with a gift that would be very special. Jenny scrunched up her little nose, as if deep in thought, looking as though she had thought of some brilliant idea; he knew, no matter what the cost, they were going to find it and purchase it.

"I thought of something great. I remember my momma telling me a story that her father told her when she was my age. He used to take momma for walks on the beach and they would hunt for treasures and one time she found a starfish on the sand. My grandpa told her that when more than one person shared a wish on a stranded starfish and tossed it very carefully back into the ocean, their wish would come true. He said because you offered the starfish another chance at life, your wish would be granted!" his little girl shouted excitedly.

He enjoyed watching the excitement on her face as she spoke and rehashed one of her favorite stories. She was so much more like Katelyn than he had realized. It was apparent that she had a gift for words and expressions. For a second or two she stood there and seemed deep in thought again. She didn't seem to be fazed or interested in anything going on around her.

"I once found a starfish on the beach with when momma and her friend Adam took me there for a walk; I wished as hard as I could. I didn't think I would ever get my wish but I did. I wanted you to find me, Daddy," she added with a smile.

He didn't care what Katelyn thought about a marriage between the two of them because he knew for certain that Jenny needed them to be a family and that was all that mattered to him. She needed him in her life and she was going to have him. He promised her that they would be a family and there were some promises that were meant to be kept forever. "I'm never going anywhere, Jenny. I'm going to marry your momma and we're going to be a family. I promise, Adam is gone forever," he said as he gently brushed the straggling pieces of curls back from her face. "You don't have to go and spend time with him and your mom anymore."

He questioned Jenny a little bit about her fear of Adam and realized that Adam had very little direct contact with his daughter but he knew Jenny was uneasy around him. He would make sure that she didn't have to spend another minute with him again. Gianfranco turned his attention back to the salesperson and asked what he could do about finding a starfish pendant for his wife. The salesperson assured him that, although they didn't carry anything like that, he would get on the phone and see if he could locate one for him. While they waited, father and daughter got better acquainted; Gianfranco couldn't help but ask questions about Katelyn.

What little he did find out, without badgering his daughter, he liked. Apparently, his future wife didn't get out much. He already suspected as much, knowing that other than Kevin and Jake, no other men had been invited to the apartment. He smiled because he knew it was what his jealous mind needed to hear. It was so unlike him to be jealous but for some reason all the emotions he felt around Katelyn were different.

The salesman came out from the back room with a smile etched across his face. It seemed that he had found a pendant after consulting with a store in the next town. The shopkeeper said he could have it sent by courier to wherever Gianfranco requested by morning. However, he thought there might be a problem since it was very expensive. "I'm afraid it's an original design and very expensive. It's made up of all diamonds and emeralds inlaid in platinum. The store is faxing over a picture for you to inspect," the salesperson said.

The elderly salesman seemed delighted to see the exchange between father and daughter. The stranger and his child had spent more money in the last ten minutes than his regular customers spent in a month combined and this was a wealthy location. He was definitely happy that this customer had decided to walk into his shop. After showing the picture of the pendant to Gianfranco and getting his approval, he gave the address to the other shop so that they could have it sent to him at the ranch. He added up the price for the pendant and the two wedding rings, along with an exquisite engagement ring, and handed the bill to Gianfranco.

He handed over his titanium charge card and asked if he could have the child's ring now and box everything else. He knew Jenny didn't want to wait to wear it. She wanted the ring on her finger and he wanted to be the one to put it there. Gianfranco took Jenny's little ring in his hand and got down on one knee and promised Jenny that he would be there for her forever and placed the ring on her little finger before standing and kissing her forehead.

"Someday Jenny, this ring will be replaced by another promise ring and I'll be replaced in your heart by a boy we haven't met yet. You know, when he comes along I'm going to hate him on sight. But for now, this ring is meant to remind you that I love you and I'm proud to be your dad," he said with tears in his eyes as he touched the ring on her finger.

"Daddy, don't be silly. I would never pick a boy over you. That's totally gross." He couldn't help but laugh. It was apparent that fatherhood was having an interesting effect on him. He couldn't get enough of her and wondered how Katelyn would feel about having a whole houseful of children. "I love my new ring, Daddy. The only other ring I have is this one and it's too big for me so I wear it on a chain. Momma gave it to me," she said lifting a gold chain from underneath her shirt.

Gianfranco stared in disbelief at the chain that hung around her small neck and at the ring that hung from the chain. He had to blink to see if his eyes were deceiving him. It was the teakwood ring that he had given Katelyn all those years before when he promised her that he would love her forever. *She had kept it; could this mean something?* The thought, no matter how ridiculous, quickly left his brain as he recalled seeing her embrace Brody the night before.

He couldn't help himself, remembering the night he gave her that ring. He became swept up in a cascade of visions and memories from the past. The ring had meant so much to him. It was his way of showing her how committed he was to her. He could have given her diamonds, rubies, emeralds, anything money could buy, but that teakwood ring was his way of showing her that she was his lifeline. She was his reason for pushing himself so much professionally. He had been waiting all these years for her.

Gianfranco called to mind the time the elder Indian woman gave the three of them the blocks of wood. Kevin didn't know what to make of it but they took everything the Indian woman said to heart. Gianfranco took his vow seriously when he gave the ring to Katelyn; he wanted to be bound to her and as he looked into the eyes of his little girl, he knew he would be. He was still dumbstruck as he released the teakwood ring from his grasp and let it fall to Jenny's chest. *There is indeed truth to that legend.*

With purchases in hand, they made their way to the rental truck. The skies looked grey and gloomy all of the sudden. There was a promise of bad weather coming their way; he decided not to take any chances with Jenny and head home now. He should have paid better attention to the changing weather; it was unlike him to be this irresponsible.

"I think we're going to be in a lot of trouble with Momma. I'm glad you're going to be with me when she sees all this stuff," Jenny said placing her little hand on her lap after strapping her seatbelt. "I think she may forgive you though when you give her that big diamond ring," she added mischievously.

Once again he found such humor in the little things she said to him. He wondered if women in general learned how to scheme from each other or were they born with that ability. "I'm sure she'll understand," he said as he jumped in the front seat and adjusted his own seatbelt.

As soon as he buckled his seatbelt, it started to rain. It didn't take long though before Jenny was fast asleep; he was glad because he knew that she felt safe with him. The road was slick from the rain and it was still pouring as he made his way up the long driveway toward the ranch. He tried his cell phone but there was no service; he assumed it had to do with the mountainous terrain. Gianfranco knew that Katelyn must be frantic with worry and he wanted to bring Jenny home safely without incident. Her little nose kept twitching when he glanced back at her. He could see what the problem was. She had a little curl dangling in her face and when he reached behind him and removed it, she smiled in her sleep.

He had spent the last seven years engrossed in his business. It wasn't because he was ruthless and determined as people assumed he was because of his success. It was more to hide from the loneliness of missing the relationship he had with Katelyn that he kept himself so immersed in work. There were other women in his life but all those affairs were empty and void of emotional ties. None of the women he spent time with could ever erase the memory of the green-eyed vixen he loved with all his heart. He couldn't help but compare each and every woman he met with her and, in the end, they never stood up.

He should have been in Jenny's life all this time and he felt slighted. He should have been there for all the wondrous beginnings that Katelyn witnessed alone. It pained him to think about it and, the more he did, the irritated he became. *Will I ever be able to let go of this anger and forgive Katelyn?* The future remained unwritten and a mystery.

Chapter Ten

Katelyn glared up at the sky and knew she should have listened to the ranch hands; they warned her that this was a bad idea. They told her taking the horse out when rain was imminent for an inexperienced rider was foolish. She thought she would take a quick ride on Diamond while the weather was clear and crisp and then head back to the ranch once her head was cleared before the rain. It was a stupid idea and as she rode Diamond back toward the ranch, she realized just how stupid. Her clothes were soaking wet and, although the ride felt exhilarating, it was easy to get lost. She had originally set out with clear markers embedded in her head to find her way back without incident but, after arguing with herself she finally admitted that she was lost and going in circles.

"Well Diamond, I really did it this time, didn't I? I don't blame you one bit for being mad at me girl," she said, rubbing the side of the horse's head. Katelyn could feel the rain coming down heavier now. "I know it's my fault you're stranded out here. I think I should listen next time one of the hands tells me it's going to rain. You think I'm crazy too, don't you girl?" she asked, not expecting an answer from the animal but receiving a short snort which; Katelyn wondered if Diamond had understood after all.

It started to let up a little bit as she road in circles but Katelyn wasn't all that confident that she would be able to find her way home any longer. She stopped the horse when she spotted the pond. Sighting the pond, she realized that she was at the farthest point due west from the ranch. She decided, since she knew where they were, she would give the horse a rest before heading out again. She jumped off Diamond and walked a little, taking in the serene breathtaking views. Even in the rain the views were magnificent.

Katelyn was so involved in her own thoughts that she hadn't notice the sound of an approaching horse or the speed at which he was traveling. It wasn't until the rider and the horse were directly upon her that she realized who it was. Gianfranco was riding on pure adrenalin and his eyes were dark and full of fearful rage. "This is one of the stupidest things you have done yet. What the hell were you thinking? Juan warned you that the weather was changing. You, being your normal stubborn self, didn't listen to reason," he said in a commanding voice, echoing his fury. "If this was your idea of running from me, Katelyn, forget it. I'll never let you go, never," he stated flatly.

He continued his rambling for a long time and she didn't get the chance to respond before he jumped from the horse and crushed her body to his. She could feel his fingers digging into her coat, knowing full well he wanted it to be her flesh. He was kissing her intensely as if he wanted to punish her for something, what, she didn't know. "I ought to take you over my knee for this. You act like a child sometimes. I'm not going to let you keep us apart if that was part of your stupid plan."

His voice was curiously foreign. It was as though he were jealous and worried for her safety but that couldn't be. She could almost swear he was doing all he could to mask his own anxiety. When he mounted the horse again, he sat straight with his shoulders back and commanded her to mount her own horse. Never before had she taken orders from him, or any other man, but she decided to cut him some slack, at least for time being.

"I have no idea why you're in such a mood but I will not allow you to speak to me like this," she bit back, knowing full well that her remarks would make the situation worse. They were both soaking wet and this badgering back and forth was not helping the situation. He stared at her for several seconds before again jumping down from his horse and joining her on the ground. She had no idea what was going on or what he intended to do until she saw him tie the reigns from her horse onto the back of the saddle of his own. He then mounted his horse again and, without any effort on his part, reached down, lifted her up, and placed her in front of him.

Never before had she felt such humiliation, anger and wanton hunger all at the same time. She hated the way he was treating her, as if he owned her, yet she couldn't deny what her body felt in response to him any more than he could. She mumbled profanities in anger and moved around on the horse, as she did she felt him grab her waist and lift her up and over the horse so that she faced him directly. She went from sitting forward to sitting face to face in front of him in seconds. This was not a position she wanted to be in. He stared into her green eyes and willed her to look deep into his burning soul.

She hadn't comprehended how close they were until she felt the stab of his erection as it screamed out to be taken into the warmth that resonated from the core of her womanhood. She followed his gaze and knew it was her sweater he was looking at because her jacket had come undone. She'd worn this sweater for him and it was obviously having the desired effect. He could see there was no bra separating them and he took full advantage of that knowledge.

He stopped the horse and dismounted, bringing her with him. He strapped the two horses to a nearby tree and turned his full attention to Katelyn. He positioned her against another tree, pulled her into his arms and thoroughly kissed her. His hands found their way to her coat and he shrugged the jacket off her shoulders and let it slip to the ground. The sweater, which so loosely covered her breasts, fell to her waist and he reached out and touched her naked wet skin. He worshiped her body and with each touch of his hands, she begged for more. His mouth reached down and replaced his hands on her swollen breast. It wasn't long before he had her begging him to take her. He undid her pants and pulled her thong panties aside; he let his fingers delve into the moist heat that awaited him there. As her breathing continued to become raspier, he unbuckled his own pants, and entered her and took his future wife right there out in the open Montana landscape as their bodies became drenched in rain.

"I'll never let you go Katelyn, not now, not ever," he drawled as he buried himself deeper and deeper inside of her. His fingers tightened on her buttocks as he kneaded her skin beneath him. His breathing became harder, more labored as he rode her with pleasure until they each released a storm of orgasms.

Neither one of them could speak as they readjusted their clothing. There was nothing either of them could say to one another. This is what always happened whenever they were together. They each knew how to ignite the flame in the other and only the other could extinguish it. She detested that look of disgusted disappointment in himself that he felt each and every time they made love. She recognized that he was resentful that she had had this carnal control over him.

Katelyn suspected that he preferred the obedient wife, one that he could control. She wasn't about to be that person, for him or any other man. "How dare you? You have no right to treat me like this," she said coldly.

Gianfranco only laughed at her sudden game of laying blame for what transpired between them. "I dare, alright Katelyn. I'm going to be your husband so get used to it. Come hell or high water, we're in this for the long haul, whether either of us like it or not," he stated. "I won't let you take the easy way out. Do you understand me?"

She couldn't believe what her ears had just heard. *Does he actually think that I was out here in this weather because I wanted to do harm to myself?* She lifted her hands in the air, frustrated that he could think such a thing.

"It's me you'll come to when you need a man, Katelyn. Don't think I'll sit by when you're sexually frustrated and allow another man to take my place."

She couldn't hide her frustration. "I never want to have sex with you again. I wouldn't care if you're the last man on Earth," she lashed back angrily. He hadn't been worried about her safety at all. He just wanted to make sure she wasn't with Brody.

His eyes locked onto hers and, as if she had amused him in some way once again, he set out to prove how easy it was for him to take her. Erotically, he traced her lips with his fingers and held her eyes in a trance, willing her to do his bidding. He watched hypnotically as she drew his finger deeper into her mouth. "Don't make me prove what a liar you are," he said mockingly as he took his finger from her mouth into his own in mocking triumph.

Frustration, madness, whatever it was, Gianfranco Broccolini brought out the worst in her and he enjoyed having that power. He made her do things that she would be embarrassed to admit to anyone else and she did it willingly. She stood there in the mud, wishing she didn't feel for him what she did. He watched and waited patiently for her to come over and mount the horse. She vowed that she would never slip up like this again. She would fight these carnal feelings for him and make sure they would not defeat her again.

They arrived at the ranch together and in one piece, or so everyone thought. Sylvia had been on the porch to greet them when they arrived. She looked a little shaken up and worried but happier now that she knew that Katelyn was safe. Sylvia turned to Katelyn and whispered, "Juan mentioned your expedition to Gianfranco when he got back to the ranch. He couldn't believe that you had gone out riding in this weather and hadn't returned so he immediately left in search of you."

"Juan told Patrick the same thing, who in turn, warned Kevin. Juan said that he had warned you that the weather was changing but you said it was going to be a short ride. He knew you must have gotten lost, after so much time had passed. He would have gone looking for you himself but Gianfranco pulled into the drive just as he was about to leave. I can't tell you how worried we all were. I'm glad it's over and that you're safe and sound," Sylvia stated calmly.

"Even Brody was worried. Kevin called over there to see if you had ridden to see him. He offered to double back but Gianfranco asked that everyone give him a little time to find you himself before sending anyone out."

"I'm fine, just a little wet and embarrassed. I didn't mean to make anyone worry. I thought I could remember all the markers, I'm sorry. Maybe I should call Brody and tell him I'm fine." Out of the corner of her eye, she could see Gianfranco leaning against the doorframe drying his face with a hand towel, all the while watching her as she dialed Brody's number. She could tell from his ice cold glare that he didn't approve of what she was doing. *To hell with him,* Brody didn't deserve his wrath; he'd done nothing wrong.

She dialed his number and when Brody answered she knew he had been worried. She took her time convincing him that she was a big girl and everything turned out fine. Gianfranco didn't flinch but she knew he was not excusing himself until this conversation was terminated. She wasn't sure when but she was sure he would make her pay for this little indiscretion of hers.

"I should go take a hot shower and change. Sylvia, if you wait I'll help you with dinner after I'm cleaned up. I just thought of something; weren't you two supposed to go to dinner?" Katelyn asked with curiosity as she tried to forget the man leaning against the doorframe.

"Kevin decided it was best to come home, in case the rain got any worse. The roads are more hazardous going up and down the mountain in rain. Did you have any luck finding a dress today?" her sister in law asked as she walked across the room. Sylvia couldn't help but take notice that Gianfranco wasn't budging from where he stood. She didn't want to guess at what was going on between them.

"As a matter of fact, I did. Nellie is very talented. You were right about her. I found a gown that is quite an eye-opener. It's simple, but sexy. I can't wait for you to see it on me," she added, knowing Gianfranco was listening to every word she uttered. She wondered what he would think if he knew that Nellie was, in fact, the famous designer that he helped to establish, Eleanor Mulaney. She couldn't help but recall what Nellie had confided in her. She was curious about his past and his female date at the fashion show.

Sylvia was pleased that Katelyn had found a dress and was planning to attend the charity ball. If she could convince Gianfranco to rearrange his schedule, she knew Gianfranco and Katelyn would have a great time together. She could see that there was something very strange going on between them and she thought it might be better if she excused herself and left them alone to talk.

Katelyn couldn't believe how cruel fate was as she stared at the love of her life. This was a confusing time for her. In just two days, she had three marriage proposals, one by a man who thought he loved her, another from a man who wanted a friend and yet another from the man she loved with all her heart but he couldn't or wouldn't love her back.

"I think I should go and check on Jenny. I'm sure she'll want to fill me in on your adventures today," Katelyn said, trying to walk past him. He held her arm gently as she moved toward the exit and blocked any advance she was hoping to make to get past him.

"I think we should talk before you go and see Jenny. She knows about us, Katelyn. I told her everything. She suspected the truth and when she came right out and asked me if I was her father, I couldn't lie to her. I know you would have preferred to have been there but I assure you I was careful about what I told her." He saw how disappointed she was and he knew what she was thinking. *She thinks I told Jenny the truth to get back at her.* "I would never hurt her or use her as a pawn against you. I only told her because she asked me," he said waiting for a reaction.

Katelyn didn't doubt him or his intentions, regardless of what he believed she thought of him. If there was one thing she was sure of, it was that Gianfranco was a good man and she knew he wanted to be a good father to their daughter. The only person Gianfranco Broccolini seemed to have issue with was her. They decided that they would talk to Jenny again and this time they would do so together. From now on, they agreed that whenever they were in Jenny's presence they would present the happy family she deserved. It was the only way this situation was going to work.

"I guess we should go and talk to her together. I'm sure she'll have a lot of questions for me," Katelyn said.

"One more thing before you go, actually two more things. I don't want our daughter, or anyone else, to ever have reason to think that this marriage is a farce. I want you to at least pretend that you are happy. You can start by not fighting me on the second request I have," he said handing her a jeweler's box. "Put this on."

Katelyn opened the ring box he handed her and had it not been for the cold way in which he presented it, she would have been jubilant. *He wants me to pretend to be happy but what about him?* If this was any indication of the life they were going to share outside the bedroom, she was not looking forward to this volatile existence. He took the ring from the box, placed it on her left ring finger and then kissed it and then gently kissed her on her lips. Katelyn didn't understand his contradictions; how he ran so hot and cold, but soon reality sunk in when she looked behind her and saw Jenny standing there.

"Daddy got me a ring too, Momma. Isn't it beautiful?" she asked displaying the little gold ring on her finger.

"Oh honey, it's the most beautiful ring I've ever seen," Katelyn said, kneeling down so she could be at eye level with her daughter as they spoke. "I want you to understand that I didn't keep your father from you on purpose. I wanted to wait and make sure he wanted to be with me; that was a foolish decision on my part. You see, if he knew about you, he would have come home to us a long time ago."

I know Mommy, Daddy already told me. He said it doesn't matter anymore because we're together now. Daddy said we'd be together forever from now on. Right, Daddy?" she asked looking up at her father with eyes that worshiped him. Still star-struck and in awe of her father, she waited for him to assure her that he would keep his promise.

Katelyn couldn't say she was surprised to witness the camaraderie between father and daughter. Their relationship was one that she knew would be fast developing and solid. They both had the same determination to be in each other's lives and his stubbornness would assure it happened. She only wondered where she would fit in the scheme of things.

Gianfranco lifted his little girl into his arms; sensing her mother feeling left out, he pulled her into their embrace as well. He could never get enough of his daughter calling him Daddy. He gleamed with pride every time he heard the word. "Jenny and I did a little shopping today and I don't want you to be angry at us but I might have gone a little overboard," he said, winking at his little girl.

He led them all into the other room and she saw that there were packages strewn everywhere. *What has he done?* She turned to him as if preparing to say something, then thought better of it when she saw the look in his eyes. It was obvious Jenny and her father had bonded today and who was she to spoil their fun. She owed him that much, she thought, but this would be the last time, her eyes warned him.

He nodded in agreement and told her he couldn't help himself. They both watched as Jenny took an exquisitely delicate porcelain doll from one of the boxes in the corner and went to show it to her Aunt Sylvia who was in the other room with Kevin. Something about that doll reminded Katelyn about her Nana Julia. Nana Higgins had always loved collecting dolls and this one would have been a welcome addition to her collection. Katelyn couldn't help wondering about her parents and grandparents who had passed on. *"Mom and Nana watch over us as we go through this difficult time,"* she said softly, hoping that they could hear her request.

Everyone gathered in the living room after dinner and talked about the events of the day. When it was time to put Jenny to bed, Katelyn excused them both and she and Jenny went upstairs. Jenny took her bath and Katelyn read her a short story before Jenny finally fell into a deep slumber. So much had happened in her life today and yet there was nothing but contentment on her face as she slept, Katelyn noticed. She turned Jenny's light off and walked down to her own room to change into her nightgown.

Katelyn sat, looking in the mirror and brushing her hair as she recalled her afternoon with Gianfranco and glanced down at the ring he had given her. She hadn't thought about it up until now. It was huge and beautiful and she was sure he'd paid a fortune for it. She couldn't help but think of all that had happened this afternoon and wish that this ring meant something significant. Sylvia came into the room, interrupting the sensual thoughts she was having about her afternoon of lovemaking. Sylvia took the brush from Katelyn's hand and continued to brush her sister-in-law's hair, talking as she did.

"I would never have believed it if I didn't see it with my own eyes. Who could believe that the mighty Gianfranco Broccolini would be pining with jealousy? It was actually amusing to witness him being bitten by the love bug," she said with a hint of amusement.

Katelyn got up from the chair and walked over to the window and hugged herself as she looked out at the night sky. What would Sylvia think of me if she found out that our upcoming marriage isn't as it appeared? She knew she had to keep up a front; she promised Gianfranco she would but she didn't get a chance to do that. She heard his voice and listened intently as he built their story for Sylvia.

"That's because I was bitten a long time ago," he said. "It happened at your wedding the first time I saw her. I haven't been the same since. Every kiss, every touch, every word from any other woman in my life was held up to and compared to Katelyn," he said as he held Katelyn's gaze. He strolled masterfully over to his future wife and gently, but erotically, kissed the side of her neck from behind. "By the way Sylvia, I am trying to rearrange my schedule so I can attend your ball. I wouldn't want my lovely fiancé all dressed up and without a dance partner," he said holding Katelyn in his arms while talking to Sylvia.

Sylvia took notice of his advances toward Katelyn and very politely excused herself, before bidding them a good night. He didn't let go of Katelyn as Sylvia left the room but turned her around and made polite conversation. He asked about her dress, what it looked like and if she had a good time shopping. Katelyn didn't know what he was after but she knew him; he was fishing for something. She had almost let her guard down when, suddenly without warning he went in for the kill.

"Tell me, did you purchase your simple, but sexy dress for Brody?" he asked, sulking like a little boy. He was trying to reach down into her private thoughts for answers to his questions. *My feelings don't really count. He's just trying to protect a future investment.* Their eyes met and he saw the resentment she felt at his interrogation. To him her silence only meant her guilt, or so he believed.

"I think this is where I take you into my arms and make you forget him or I put you over my knee. I can't decide which. I could ring your bloody neck for what you do to me," he said, with resigned discomfort.

"Which should I expect from you?" she asked, scrunching up her nose at him. *Let him be jealous of Brody; he will find out soon enough how unfounded his accusations are.* She knew she was provoking him and she also knew where it would lead. He studied the look on her face as he contemplated how he wanted to approach the next step.

Gianfranco's piercing brown eyes devoured her as he processed her statement. He knew what she wanted because he could taste it himself. He watched her as her tongue slipped from her mouth nervously and ran across her lips. He gave in just like every other time his body hungered for hers. He responded to her with a soft sigh of surrender as he crossed the room. "Come to me, Katelyn..." he pleaded in a slightly chauvinistic undertone.

She didn't know whether she should give into him or not but after trying to avoid her surrender to him she couldn't help herself. Nervously, she went into his arms and admitted defeat. She couldn't fight him anymore and she wasn't capable of winning that battle, she knew that. His long dark hands wrenched her forward as his arms circled around her waist and held her in place as he tried to stay in control. His face touched hers; he whispered her name over and over in her ear.

"What did you think my reaction would be when you called Brody on the phone? Did you want this to happen? I want you to break your ties with him and this time I mean it. This is never going to work if you keep flaunting your relationship with him in front of me. I don't think I'm asking too much of you," he demanded as he loosened her robe and let it fall to the floor.

"Don't do this, I don't want us to make love every time you're angry with me," she begged. "Brody is a friend, nothing more. I won't have you turn our friendship into something ugly. I know that's what you want. You want me to hate him but I can't," she added miserably.

All of the sudden, without provocation, it was as though he were possessed animal. It seemed that every time they moved two steps forward, they would take four steps back. She tried to close her eyes to avoid looking into his but again she could not stop what her body was compelled to do. He tore her nightgown from her body as though it were a scrap of paper; seeing her thong underwear, his body ached and it became his undoing. He drank in the sight of her practically naked body before lifting her off the floor.

As he hastened toward the bed, she could see that his jealousy had been replaced by a fierce yearning to bury himself inside of her, a desire so strong that it pained him to know that she held that kind of power over him. Gianfranco lifted her into his arms and wrapped her legs around his stomach. He gently nipped at her breasts, before he buried his head in her neck and soaked in the scent of her. He continued to covet the pleasure of loving her as he let her body slide down the length of his. He wanted her to know exactly what she did to him, how deep his need was for her.

Katelyn couldn't switch off her burning desire for him no matter how hard she tried. She couldn't disguise her wantonness for him or the feelings he evoked when he touched her. She wanted to hate him for making her want him this way but she couldn't. This was the life she was fated to lead. The need for him was just as powerful as his physical desire for her. It was a predestined need they shared. She let her hands take the journey they longed for as she began to undress him.

One by one she undid the top few buttons slowly until he reached up and tore his own shirt hastily from his body. Buttons flew everywhere until he finally he threw what was left of the shirt to the floor. It joined the nightgown that was just as carelessly discarded. Katelyn undid his belt to his pants as she ran her other hand up over his bare chest before returning to unzip his pants. There was no end to the strong connection they felt for each other. She loved to touch his naked body and did so until they fell onto the bed together. They continued to make love with their tongues until Gianfranco put a stop to their lovemaking.

He yanked on the back of hair softly until she was forced to look up at his eyes. He spoke to her as if it hurt him to speak. "This is not what I would consider anger, would you?" he asked hoarsely. He was laughing at her and what hurt most was that he was absolutely correct. He ignited sparks in her that no other man could satisfy and he knew it. It would be easy for him to take her anytime and anyplace he chose. Neither of them could control this outcome; they were on a collision course of a carnal bliss of their own making.

"I want to make love to you more than anything right now but I won't. I won't make love to you unless I have your word that you'll sever your relationship with Brody. I want a family, Katelyn that includes you; I don't want Brody to get in the way. You and I and Jenny are a family unit now. If I have to keep you far away from Brody to accomplish the harmonious household I crave then that's what I'll do. If you won't do it for me, do it for Jenny," he said breathing as evenly as he could, given the situation they were in.

Katelyn reluctantly agreed, promising she would have no contact with Brody unless Kevin invited him to the ranch. He nodded quickly and left her on the bed, alone. He shut the door behind him as he left the room, her pain bared for no one. She threw herself across the pillow and cried. She wasn't sure her tears were tears of the love she longed for or the disgust she felt for herself, having given in to him so quickly. She stared down at the torn shirt on the floor, picking it up to cradle in her embrace. With each breath she took in his scent. The smell of his cologne lingered on his shirt as she inhaled his scent and fell asleep and in her dream she relived the happier moments of their time together.

Their brief affair that summer came back to her in her dreams. Their souls connected and longed for each other. The four weeks they spent together turned into an idyllic eight. She was aware, even then, that he battled with himself over the desire he felt for her. No other man had made her feel what he did. He took special care with her that first week and tried very hard not to succumb to the feelings that were yearning for them to move to the next level. That was the plan until fate decided to intervene. He had taken her to dinner and a movie one night and afterwards; they decided to walk home, only to be caught in a downpour.

The rain came out of nowhere, a summer storm. They laughed all the way home as the rain soaked through their clothes. She had been wearing an all-white a halter style dress and they barely made it to the porch before the lightening and thunderstruck. She could see herself the way he did as she stared down at her body. He looked intently at her body through her drenched dress, closed his eyes and prayed for the strength to walk away. He didn't want to do this; it wasn't part of the plan. Kevin was his friend and this was his sister, the woman he was quickly falling in love with. He knew that taking her now would be a mistake. He had to let her go. She needed to grow up and experience what life had to offer and college life would do that for her. He wouldn't steal that time of her life from her.

Yet when he opened his eyes and looked into her pleading eyes, he snapped. He reached out to her and kissed her. His mouth was both teasing and tormenting at the same time. He was awakening the sensual being inside of her and he knew she had never felt this way before. In some ways, it warmed him to know he'd be her first and, if he had any say at all, he'd be her last as well. They entered the bedroom together and he tried to ease any of the fear of the unknown she felt by holding her tight.

He stared lovingly at her as she reached for the zipper of her then soaked dress. He watched as she peeled the clinging dress from her body; he didn't need to guess what she was trying to do. He knew she was trying to prove to him how mature up she was. It was difficult for her, he knew, but that didn't stop him from enjoying the risk she was taking for his benefit. He decided to make it easier on her and reached out to take over from there. He pulled down her panties and discarded them, without hesitation. He tore his own wet clothes from his body just as feverishly.

He wanted this night to be perfect for her in every way. He wanted to make sure that the first time they made love, would be burnt into her memory forever. He wanted to ruin her for any other man. He wanted and needed her for himself. Slowly, he ran his tongue teasingly across her lips; he was barely touching her skin with his hands as he watched her buck to his touch. He felt her moving uninhibitedly beneath his expert touch. She wanted more; she had grown hungry for him and him alone. He moved slowly because he wanted her to be ready for him.

It felt more right with her than with any woman he had ever been with and, at this point, there had been many. He was enamored by her and she him. He gently nipped at her breasts until she was crying out in lust, wanting more. She had had an orgasm from his touch to her breasts. He hungrily covered her quivering lips with his own as his fingers delved into her most aching need. She cried out again, only this time louder, and he again covered her mouth with his own and this time rode her sweet orgasm with her.

Over and over she cried out his name and he knew that although she had never experienced anything like this before, she was reacting to him as no other woman ever had. She was ready for the final surrender; part of him wanted to do the right thing and stop but, God help him, he couldn't. He lowered his body onto hers and entered her as gently as he could. After the initial pain, he felt her body start to relax and begin to come alive again. She matched his movements, thrust for thrust, until they were surrounded by a whirlwind of erotica.

All during that night and the many nights that followed, he continued to teach her sexual positions that she had only read about before in books. She knew nothing about real sex and he was pleased to be her tutor. Moments after their lovemaking, Katelyn collapsed, soaked and exhausted in bliss. There was nothing that could describe what she felt for him.

"I never thought it would be like this," she whispered. Gianfranco smiled back at her and promised there was more to come after they rested.

"If I can promise you one thing, Irish, it will be that you will never want this, from any other man," he whispered to the sleeping Katelyn.

"Do you love me?" she asked innocently, as if it made all the difference.

"If I say no, will you make me leave? If I say yes, that I fell in love with you long before we ever met, would you run from me? You see, I'm afraid to answer your question and right now I think it's best if we table this discussion for now. Ask me again after we've dated properly. Neither one of us is having much luck controlling what we feel right now," he added as an afterthought.

She looked at him bewildered. *Does he feel the same way that I do?* Katelyn would gladly give up her plans for college and a career if she could spend the rest of her life with him raising a family together. She wanted to ask but she was afraid of the answer he would give her. Her concerns were warranted when he asked coldly if she had been on birth control.

"I'm on the pill. My doctor put me on them to regulate my period," she admitted with regret.

Gianfranco studied her as the silence between them lengthened. He couldn't put his finger on it but he was sure that she was hiding something from him. He felt guilty that he had hoped he had made her pregnant. He knew if she were pregnant that she would agree to marry him, fair or not, it was what he wanted more than anything. He didn't want to send her away.

When Katelyn felt the sun's warmth on her face, she glanced up and was met with the ebony eyes she had just been dreaming about. "I guess this is one of those awkward moments when you're not sure what to say. If you want to know whether or not, I regret anything that happened between us, the answer is no, in case you were wondering," she added.

He smirked and laughed at the same time. "I have absolutely no regrets either. In fact, last night was a wonderful surprise and I hope a promise of more to come."

Katelyn reached for her bag and took out a photo that she had kept hidden in a special compartment. It was taken on the night that he gave her the ring from the reservation. She stared at it, thinking. *Just like before, he walked out leaving her feeling unfulfilled. I can see how much that ring meant to him. I fantasized that it meant forever for us. I had always believed that it meant more to him than he shared with me, but I was wrong.*

She remembered that night as she reached up to his neck to touch the chain he wore there. It was a gold chain with a wooden ring dangling from it. She knew it had to have some kind of significance to him because it was an odd thing to have hanging on a chain. She was afraid to ask about it in case it was from a former lover, a lover he hadn't been able to forget. Gianfranco caught her by the wrist and kissed the palm of her hand gently, rapturously.

"Do you remember Kevin ever talking about his trip to an Indian reservation with Jake and me?" he asked. As she nodded, he proceeded to tell her a story about an elderly Indian woman who had given them blocks of teakwood to carve the rings from and warned them of the significance of each of the rings. Gianfranco told her that they had to wear the rings close to their hearts until they each met the right woman and gave their ring to her. He undid the clasp, reached toward her neck and placed the chain and the teakwood ring around her neck, its rightful home.

"This is where this ring belongs. I promise you, that when you've finished college, I'll come back for you. If you still want me, we'll talk about our future then," he said as he leaned up on one elbow. Those last weeks were the most memorable of her young life.

Gianfranco fought long and hard with himself about how to end their relationship. It was becoming more and more apparent that she grew more infatuated with him as each day passed and he was becoming dangerously guilty of committing crimes against her emotional youth. She'd reached the age of consent but was not nearly ready for the kind of commitment he wanted from her. She needed time to become the woman she needed to be before he had the right to ask her to take a vow of forever with him. It would take everything he had within himself to offer that time to her and he knew he had no choice. He loved her enough to let her go, hoping that she'd come back to him.

Gianfranco Broccolini thought about the large painting he had hanging in his office and other than himself no one was aware of its meaning to him. It was of a tree with a large nest in it with a single beautiful bird. In the distance was another singular bird, flying in the air, away and free. There was an inscription on the bottom of the painting which read, *'If you love something set it free. If it comes back it was and always will be yours. If it never returns it was never yours to begin with.'* He bought the expensive painting because he thought of Katelyn each and every time he looked at it. He had almost given up hope that she would come back to him. He wondered if it was going to work between them since he had all but blackmailed her into this marriage.

Chapter Eleven

A soft knock on the door brought Katelyn back to reality. It had to be Jenny. She carefully pulled herself together and threw on a robe. "Momma, are you awake?" Jenny asked. "I can't sleep," the little voice called out.

Katelyn ran to the door at the sound of her child's distress. "Honey, what's wrong? When I left your room you were sound asleep." She didn't notice him standing there at first but he had obviously heard their child cry out too. He didn't speak at all; he was letting Katelyn handle the situation but, true to his word, he wanted to portray a united front. He would be there to offer his support regardless of what Katelyn thought. "Momma, promise me that Daddy is not going away again. I had a dream that he went far away and he never came back to us," she stated as little tears streamed down her pouting face.

Gianfranco sprang into action, lifting her little body up into his arms, carrying her to Katelyn's bed. He reassured her over and over again that they were a family now and nothing would ever come between them again. He had Katelyn lie down next to them to reaffirm what he had already said. It didn't take long for Jenny to fall back to sleep and Katelyn hoped that it was for the night. His silence was worse than anything he could ever possibly say to her. He sat watching Jenny sleep for a long time without saying anything. He seemed to be thinking of just the right words.

"I want to apologize for what happened before. What I did and what I said to you was wrong. I promise I won't let it happen again. I can't explain my behavior toward you or why it happens. I do know that when I'm around you, I lose all control of my emotions, good, bad or indifferent." He stood up and took her with him. He guided her over to the window and held her silently in a loving embrace as they stared out at the mountains together.

"I still think that Brody is going to be a thorn in this marriage if you continue to see him but I'm not going to forbid it. More than anything, I will try to control my jealousy. I know you won't believe this but I've never had this problem with any other woman. I've never been the jealous type. If anything, I've been known to be just the opposite." He kissed the side of her neck as she rested her body against his own. Being so close to him this way felt right. "Why can't it be like this all the time between us?" he asked enjoying the intimacy. Katelyn turned to him and gazed up at his face, emotions bubbling over.

"I don't know what to say to you. I know how well-intended your words are but how can I be sure that Jenny and I won't get hurt?" she asked. "Perhaps, if we were married in name only, it might work out better. We seem to always hurt each other when we let our physical relationship dictate to us."

He was taken aback at first because he had no intentions of keeping his hands off her. She was going to be his wife in every way. However, she was right; they had to build on their trust for each other if their marriage was going to work. He had to prove to her that he could keep his jealousy at bay, that he wouldn't use her body whenever it suited him and then just walk away.

"You have my word that I'll not touch you again unless you instigate the touching. Is that fair enough?" he asked mischievously pecking the tip of her nose with his lips. "However, I must warn you that I'm a weak man and if you decide to have your way with me, I'm not immune to you."

She smirked in disbelief. "What about the ball? If Brody asked me to dance would you be alright with it?" He looked at her impatiently but understood the question.

"I made you a promise and I won't go back on my word. In spite of what you may think of me, I'm not a cad. I'll keep my word." He still held her in his arms; and without hesitation she hugged him. They had reached neutral ground at last.

"I think we should lie down next to Jenny. She needs to know that you're not going anywhere," she said questioning his willingness to stay with her. Katelyn knew that what she was asking of him was difficult but for Jenny this night was important. It was going to be a very long night. It would test them both beyond what either of them thought they were capable of handling yet, for their child, they had to try to accomplish this one task without any sexual contact.

It wasn't the first time that she had awakened to an empty bed this week and she was sure it wouldn't be the last. The only puzzling thing this morning was that she remembered going to bed last night feeling totally unfulfilled, hurting with want for Gianfranco, yet this morning she felt as if she had been made love to all night. It was as if her dreams of him were real and he had taken care of all her sensual needs. Was it a dream? Her body was telling her just the opposite.

She could hear commotion downstairs and knew that everyone was awake and walking about. The ball was today, and she was sure that Sylvia had a big day planned. It wasn't easy putting this event together and Katelyn was sure that there was still plenty to do before tonight. Mrs. Footy agreed to take care of Jenny for the evening so that problem was solved. She wasn't sure Mrs. Footy would take Jenny earlier, if Sylvia needed her help, but she would make the offer to help.

Katelyn took a shower, put on her sweats and went downstairs to offer her services. Jenny was recruited into helping sort out ribbons. Everyone was busy and didn't seem to notice her as she walked into the kitchen. She stood there for a moment and watched all the excitement. Life was good and she had very little to complain about.

"Dig in, I'm sure we can find something for you to do," Sylvia said after spotting her. They worked for about an hour or so before Kevin arrived back at the ranch. It was only then that she found out that Gian Franco had left for New York earlier in the morning.

"What do you expect?" she asked herself as she stared at her reflection in the mirror later that afternoon. Here she was wearing the most provocative

gown she had ever worn in her life and the man she wore it for had promised never to touch her again, unless she asked him to. "He left the ball in your court. You get to make the next move," she repeated aloud to her reflection. She wasn't aware that anyone had entered the room until she saw Kevin's reflection behind her in the mirror. He stood back from her, glowing openly with admiration for his sister.

"You look positively stunning in that dress. I'm almost afraid to see the reaction you're going to get from other men tonight. I'm almost tempted to lock you in this room tonight," he teased. Katelyn loved Kevin and hated the miles that kept them apart.

"I'm a big girl now, Kevin, or haven't you noticed?" She said lifting the tie that was dangling lifeless around his neck and adjusted it for him. "Now, that's better," she added.

"It's what sisters are born for, other than causing their brothers to lose sleep all the time," he teased holding her by the shoulders.

"You wouldn't have to worry if you would just stop feeling that it's your job to protect me. I can handle life all by myself." Kevin smiled and dropped his hands.

"You'll never be too old for my protection, Irish. You only have to call me and I'll be there for you. I love you and if I haven't told you lately, I'm very proud of you and the way you're raising my niece. I do have some bad news for you, though. Gian Franco just called; he's trying very hard to make it tonight but he's not sure if he can. I guess you're going to have to settle for me," he mocked lovingly.

She sat down on the settee at the end of the bed. *It should hardly matter if Gianfranco can make the ball or not. Didn't they just decide that their relationship was changing? Didn't he agree with her that a physical relationship would be a mistake?* Katelyn couldn't help but feel disappointed at what was and what should have been.

"Katelyn, I'm sure if he could help it he'd be here. I think the reaction you're having is interesting because it wasn't at all the reaction he thought you'd be having. He was convinced that you wouldn't mind it at all if he didn't show up. As a matter of fact, he was laughing when I suggested that it would upset you to have to go alone," Kevin retorted watching her and studying her reaction.

"I'm not upset at all. Everyone that knows Gianfranco is aware, that someone of his caliber will always put business ahead of pleasure," she said sarcastically. She stunned even herself with her spoiled sounding remark. It never occurred to her that she would switch places with him and become jealous of his work. She wondered if it was work-related or another woman. After all, she had never insisted that he be faithful to her. How could she be jealous? She convinced him that they would not have a physical relationship, unless, as he insisted, she initiated it. She decided she would address that flaw in their arrangement as soon as he returned.

"Katelyn, that's not fair and you know it's not true. Gianfranco would never put business ahead of you and his little girl. I know him better than anyone and I can tell you that for sure, for him, his family will always come first. He'll find a way to be here tonight if whatever he's dealing with in New York can be resolved."

"Promises are made to be broken, Kevin, weren't you aware of that?" she asked with tears threatening. She couldn't believe her saying. *Why am I feeling so emotional?* Maybe her period was coming; that would explain her odd behavior. "I'm sorry, Kevin, I don't know what's got into me. I don't mean to be so negative."

"Let's wipe all these tears away, go to the ball and have a good time. I'm sure Gianfranco won't let you down. Besides, you'll have a good time anyway. You'll know a lot of the people attending. What do you think? Are we ready to show off our new duds to our waiting fans?" Kevin took one more look at Katelyn and noticed the lone piece of hair that had come loose during her melt down. He fixed it for her and smiled. "I remember doing this for you as a kid. Your curls never stayed where they were meant to. Jenny is a lot like you." He hugged her and they headed downstairs where they were greeted with hoots and howls.

"It wouldn't be unlike him to show up in the midst of everything," Kevin said as they joined their other guests.

Katelyn gave a patented sigh as she followed Kevin into the waiting crowd of friends in the foyer. There had been no tears or regrets as she left Jenny with Mrs. Footy. It seemed her daughter enjoyed the idea of spending the night baking and making candied apples with the housekeeper. Mrs. Footy knew just what to do to keep Jenny happy and entertained.

It was time for Katelyn to decide what kind of marriage she expected from a union between herself and Gianfranco. She needed to make it clear to him just what she expected from this marriage. She would think about it tonight while she was alone with plenty of time to evaluate their future.

"Momma you look like a princess. Is Daddy going to meet you at the ball?" Jenny asked excitedly. "You could be Cinderella and he could be the prince," she added.

"Honey, I'm not sure if daddy can make the ball tonight." Katelyn bent down to try to reassure Jenny that her dad had not left them but to a seven year old, she only understood that he had left them again. "He's in New York on business and he might not be able to fly back tonight but he's going to try," Katelyn promised.

Katelyn knew that no matter how right she thought her decision to keep Jenny from Gianfranco had been, she realized now that she had been wrong. It was obvious that Jenny was having a very difficult time accepting Gianfranco had to leave town on business. Fear was written all over her face. She wanted to believe he was coming back but she was afraid to put her trust in him.

Katelyn took out a card from her bag and handed it to Jenny. It was all the telephone numbers where Gianfranco could be reached at any given time. She told Jenny that if she wanted to she could call him if she got scared and he would talk to her no matter what he was doing or how late it was. She explained to Jenny that very few people had his private numbers. She went on further to explain that he wanted to be sure that they could reach him anywhere and anytime if they needed to. Her mother's words of wisdom seemed to offer comfort to her for the time being; she took the card and put it in her little pocket.

Kevin hired cars for the evening to avoid having anyone drive after drinking. The ride to the country club was surprisingly quiet. The ballroom was packed when they arrived. All of the state's most influential people were in attendance. Katelyn spotted Brody almost immediately. He was standing in the midst of a group of men talking politics as usual. He was taller than the other men; even if he hadn't been taller, he had an aura very similar to that of Gianfranco and it was what separated him from the other men. She wondered when Nellie would make her entrance. If nothing else, she thought, she had their reunion to look forward to tonight. Brody must have felt her presence because he turned, looked in her direction and smiled as he excused himself from the pack of men.

"You look absolutely stunning," he said as he greeted Katelyn. She thanked him and together they entered the larger ballroom that was already alive with laughter and music. She took a quick glance around the room to see if Nellie had arrived but she was nowhere to be seen. She wasn't comfortable keeping what she knew from Brody but her sixth sense told her it was for the best that he remained ignorant, for now. She wanted to believe that after tonight, the man she had grown to love as a dear friend would find the happiness he deserved.

"Everything is so elegant. I don't think Sylvia forgot a thing. Do you know where you're sitting?" she asked. "Will we be sitting together by any chance?" she added as they made their way to the table that held the place cards.

Brody made his way through the crowd of people and picked up both his card and hers as well. They were sitting with Kevin and Sylvia just as he expected they would be. He did notice a card for Gianfranco Broccolini too but he knew, from speaking to Kevin, that he probably wasn't going to be able to make it. He held the cards in the air and signaled to Katelyn that they could go inside and take a seat. He escorted her to their assigned table but not before introducing her to the many people who stopped him along the way.

Katelyn knew she shouldn't, being in the mood, she accepted the glass of champagne that was offered. It no time at all, one glass turned into two and then three and then four. Brody was very polite and kept her company for most of the evening until the great surprise. Katelyn had forgotten but as soon as she saw the surprised look on his face, she knew, without following his line of vision, that Nellie had entered the room.

Brody didn't say a word as he sat silently watching the apparition of the woman that he had once loved. He believed that Eleanor had probably gotten on with her life and married some rich Parisian and yet here she was in the flesh. He didn't utter a word as she moved her hips seductively from side to side as she strolled in his direction. He didn't know what she was up to but her show was definitely for his benefit. He remembered that dress she was wearing and couldn't wait until she turned around. Whatever her reason for being here, that dress was meant for his eyes alone. He had thought that she had given up on completing it because he hadn't seen it in any of her designs and he had seen them all.

Brody didn't mean to keep tabs on her professional life but he was curious to see if what she gave up was worth what she accomplished. He needed to know that she had walked away from their marriage with no regrets. From what he had seen, she had made a great success of her life, although she dropped out of sight for the past year. He'd hired a private investigator to look into it but to no avail. Wherever she was, she didn't want to be found. She reached the table but not before Katelyn, who'd had too much to drink, stood up and greeted Eleanor, calling her Nellie.

"Nellie, I didn't think you were coming," she said feeling a little intoxicated.

"You two know each other?" he questioned and then added, "Who is Nellie?" seeming somewhat confused.

"Eleanor is Nellie, the woman who opened the new boutique that you took me to. I have to tell you she's very talented. But you would know that, wouldn't you?" she asked pointing a finger into Brody's chest.

"Katelyn, I think you have had a little too much to drink. Do you want me to take you home?" he asked.

"I'm only a little tipsy and you two have unfinished business to discuss. I'm going to leave you to it. I'll get some fresh air." She stood for a second and turned her attention to Nellie. "It was nice to see you again and good luck, I think you both deserve to be happy. It's been a long time coming," she added.

Katelyn knew, as she walked away, that all the time they had spent separated somehow disappeared. She knew, from the way Brody admired that dress and twisted her around in his arms, that he was looking for the infamous tattoo located on his wife. He must have seen a hint of it because, as he led her out on to the dance floor, he smiled, realizing that his wife had finally come home to him. *It's all well and good. Too bad happily ever after isn't in my future.*

She had almost reached the bar when a young man she didn't recognize stopped her. "Excuse me, aren't you Kevin Donavan's sister?" the cool young voice asked before introducing himself. As he stood in her line of vision, Katelyn saw that he was a tad older than he first appeared. He was young and confident, or at least he seemed to be when he spoke. She acknowledged his claim, accepted his hand and introduced herself.

"My name is Michael. I'm a colleague of Kevin's," he said letting go of her hand. He gave her a sideways glance, and looked over his shoulder and then offered her another drink. He also told her that perhaps he should help her back to her table seeing that she was slightly inebriated. The champagne was doing a great job numbing her pain but her head was becoming very fuzzy.

"I'm pleased to meet you, Michael, but I don't need saving. Thanks for the drink," she said, slurring her speech as she walked back to the table on her own accord. She sat with her back to the door and watched happily as both couples, Kevin and Sylvia and Brody and Nellie, danced. Each couple seemed engrossed in their partner. It was a pleasant sight for Katelyn. She took another sip from her champagne and noticed that Michael was headed in her direction once again.

"You're very persistent, aren't you?" she asked as he joined her, sitting in the seat that had been saved for Gianfranco. They exchanged small talk before Michael admitted to being a little curious. "Well, why don't you spit it? We both know you want to ask me something." she rebutted.

"I'm just wondering what a beautiful lady like yourself is doing all alone at one of these things?" he asked, as he drank from the glass he had brought to the table with him.

"It's very simple, really. My fiancé is out of town on business and I'm here. No mystery, I'm afraid." She smiled at him and she reached over and innocently took his hand in hers. "Michael, would you consider it forward of me if I asked you to dance?"

"I would never take such liberties but I would be honored to dance with you," he said as he touched her elbow and led her to the dance floor.

She didn't know what it was about Michael that felt wrong but she decided to ignore the little warning signs and dance with him anyway. When they reached the dance floor, she noticed that Michael didn't seem to know Kevin at all as he had intimated. She casually introduced them and was shuffled away by her escort.

"Thanks for not giving me away. I don't know your brother, my name is Michael though. Michael Bishop, I'm a reporter at the Herald and I'm here on a lead. It seems Eleanor Mulaney, the famous designer who disappeared a year ago, may be hiding in this town somewhere. Do you know anything about her?" he asked as he held her in his embrace.

"If I did, I wouldn't tell you," she whispered seductively. As he whirled her around on the dance floor Katelyn was careful not to let him see her as she searched the dance floor for any sign of Brody and Eleanor. It was pretty clear though that they had probably left to find a more private place to talk.

"Tell me something else," he said as he glanced down at her. "Your story is just as intriguing as Eleanor Mulaney's. You're engaged to be married to Gianfranco Broccolini, one of the richest men around and he's left you alone at this function. I might add, looking strikingly sexy, what gives? Everything I hear about the almighty Broccolini leaves me to wonder why he left you alone to fend for yourself while he's off doing who knows what."

Katelyn was a journalist herself and she wasn't about to fall for this trap no matter how much she'd had to drink. She used this same method herself on occasion. He asked her about the connection between Gianfranco and Kevin and didn't seem surprised to learn that they were college friends. He had done his homework, she was sure of that. He wanted a story and the only way he thought he'd get one was to trick her into revealing the life she shared with Gianfranco when she felt more vulnerable, like now.

After Michael promised to stop digging for a story, they continued to dance. He found himself relaxing and having a good time, enjoying her company. As they slowly turned to the music, a path opened toward the two of them. She couldn't figure out why until he was directly upon them.

"I see you've kept yourself otherwise occupied in my absence," the voice said from behind her. She could feel his breath; he was so close. Gianfranco was not a man to be taken lightly and right now she wasn't sure what the next couple of minutes held for her dance partner. The couples within their immediate vicinity had a lot of sympathy for the young man who would be on the receiving end of his wrath.

"I don't believe we've had the pleasure. My name is Michael Bishop," the young reporter said, holding out his hand to Gianfranco. "I've had the great pleasure of keeping your fiancé entertained awaiting your arrival. If you'll excuse me, I'll leave her to you. By the way, Mr. Broccolini, I would think twice about leaving such a gorgeous creature alone," he added before taking leave.

"I think a breath of fresh air would be appropriate. All these people are waiting for me to make a scene and as that would embarrass both of us, I suggest we go outside." He didn't give Katelyn much of a chance to defy him as he led her outside into the night air. He wasn't looking at her as they stood in the cold frigid weather of Montana. It was almost as if it would hurt him to look away.

"Let me go back inside. I'm freezing out here and I'm not having any fun. I wanted to dance with you but you had to go and spoil the fun for me," she declared once again slurring her words.

"I guess that was one small minor detail we forgot in our haste," he said, taking off his jacket and placing it around her after observing that her nipples were taut from the cold; the material of her dress so thin, it offered little protection from the cold. "That guy was a reporter and I don't know what you've said to him. Let's hope I can stop him from printing whatever he has in mind to. What were you thinking?" he asked.

His touch was gentle and yet reserved. He was holding back and Katelyn knew how hard this was for him. The physical side of their relationship was never lacking, in fact it was the only thing that kept the emotional detachment bearable for them both. He looked sexy dressed up in his tuxedo and she was finding it hard to concentrate on anything he was saying. She was soaking in his masculinity, enjoying the false sense of power the alcohol was giving her. Who said women didn't enjoy and want sex as much as man did?

173

"If I hadn't arrived when I did, Katelyn, how long would it have taken Michael, whatever his name is, to get you into his bed?" he asked heatedly.

"You bastard!" she cried out with loathing. "You'd stop at nothing to make sure you didn't look the fool in public, wouldn't you? It doesn't matter if anything is going on or not; you're angry that he moved in on your property. That's it, isn't it?" she asked as the tears welled in her eyes.

He laughed arrogantly and shook his head. "Is that what you think? You can't honestly believe that young man's thoughts weren't about what he wanted to do to you? I came between the two of you because I felt like I was being made the fool? You are practically my wife, Katelyn. I don't take too kindly to witnessing my wife in the arms of another man, especially since she seemed to be enjoying it. I'm a little tired of reminding you that your mine and mine alone," he added possessively.

"No! I belong to no one," she said as her voice was drowned out by the onslaught of his lips. She tried, with all she could muster, not to react to him but she couldn't. The effects of the champagne were magnifying her sexual attraction to him. His hands slipped below the jacket he had placed over her shoulders for warmth and he pulled her tightly into his arms. It didn't matter that there were people coming and going, he didn't care. He wanted to prove to her, once and for all, that she was his and she would give herself freely to him. His kisses were fierce and demanding in their assault. With each utter of protest, he released new passion in her.

Gianfranco realized that they had company, and as he relaxed his fierce hold on her, he held her protectively in his arms. "Excuse me, but if you two don't come up for air soon, we'll have to hose you both down," Kevin said as he joined them on the patio. "You should be ashamed of yourself, making my baby sister cry this evening. She didn't think you were going to show up tonight." Kevin stated before asking how his business went in New York. After Gianfranco gave a brief synopsis, Kevin said he'd catch up with him another time because he was freezing to death and wanted to go back inside; he suggested they do the same.

Gianfranco waited for an explanation from her but when none came he asked the question himself. "Why were you crying?" She didn't answer and her silence spoke volumes, or so he thought. "Don't even bother to think of something clever to say. I don't think I could stand to hear another lie from you. I noticed Brody and his new friend in a quiet corner when I came in. It must have upset you to see them together. I'm sorry for that. I know what it feels like to love someone so much and not have that love returned."

A cold shiver of rage and disgust came over her as she listened to him admit his love for someone else to her. It hurt like hell to love someone that much and not have it reciprocated but it was him she loved, not Brody. When will the raw pain go away, she wondered? Could she marry him knowing he wanted and loved someone else? She didn't think she could do it but she knew he'd never let her go. He would never break the promise he made to Jenny, that they would be a family.

He felt obligated to say something. He had to make this situation tolerable and he hoped she would cooperate. "Let's call a truce; I think we should go inside and dance, that way it'll appear as though whatever rift there was between us when I arrived is over. If for no other reason, we'll do it for Jenny. I want the world to believe we're happy for her sake." His voice sounded more like a plea than a command.

Katelyn's heart felt as if it were being torn to shreds. He supported her as they reentered the ballroom and even smiled adoringly at her. She felt weak as they danced but she held on to him to continue the show. If there was a way, she prayed they'd find it to make this marriage work without them despising each other in the process. If only he could forget the woman who haunted him. She wondered about this woman who didn't love him.

He lifted her chin in his hand and kissed her. He kissed her right there on the dance floor for everyone to see. It didn't start out to be a passionate embrace, not at first. "We shouldn't be doing this, not here. I'm sure if we sat down and discussed this problem we could come up with an agreement of some kind," she whispered for his ear only.

Gianfranco's eyes opened to their fullest. Without a glimmer of feeling for the people around them, his eyes darkened with disappointment. It was obvious to anyone who stood close enough that she had once again released the devil in him. "I can't go on like this Gianfranco. I'll agree to any arrangements for visitation you want. I'll accept any terms you have to offer. I'm willing to let you go on with your life. What more do you want from me?" she asked as she painfully offered him a way out out of this farce of a marriage they were getting ready to share.

"My terms…you say you'll accept my terms, Katelyn. I thought I made myself and my terms perfectly clear," he stammered into her ear as he pulled her tighter to him so that they were the only two people privy to this conversation. "Make no mistake, if we don't get married as planned, for whatever reason you can dream up, you will be the one with visitation rights, not me." His voice was low and concise as he continued to hold onto her as he threatened her with his words.

Katelyn couldn't understand his insistence that they marry when he was in love with someone else. The smart thing to do would be to confront him about the mystery woman but she didn't dare. She couldn't bear to hear him say her name. She leaned her face forward, staring obediently into his eyes. From what she could recollect, she had just hurt him. Her hands went to his face to console and comfort him with his pain. "I can't fight anymore, Katelyn. I'm tired and I just can't do it anymore," he said as he brushed a lone tear from her cheek.

"Maybe we should go. I'm sure Kevin and Sylvia would understand if we left a little early," she said as she sobered up from all the emotional turmoil. He held the hand that still rested on his face and kissed the inside of her palm.

They made their apologies to everyone and Gianfranco summoned the car that brought him to the ball. Neither of them said a word on the way home. They both needed the time to come to grips with their individual demons and to decide how they would get past what haunted them both and still be able to live together.

Gianfranco listened to the music that played softly on the car radio and couldn't help but watch, as Katelyn lost herself in thought. He could ask a thousand times and never get an answer, how could two people who once cared so much for each other, get themselves into such a quagmire? It seemed like all they ever did anymore was either fight or make love.

Chapter Twelve

Katelyn hadn't realized that they had reached the ranch until Gianfranco came around to her side of the car to help her out. After thanking Mrs. Footy for taking care of Jenny, they both looked in on the sleeping child together. Jenny was the one grace that connected the two of them. Gianfranco reached over to his sleeping child and placed a tender kiss on her forehead. Katelyn was touched by the scene in front of her. After kissing Jenny herself, they left the room together. Gianfranco touched her for the first time since they left the ball outside their child's room. He covered her hand that had already reached for the doorknob with his own, as he did, time stood still for them both.

"I made a promise to you that I wouldn't touch you again unless you came to me, I broke that promise tonight and I apologize for that. It's as though I'm consumed by you. I'm sorry that you see our marriage as an end to your future happiness. I never meant to hurt you, Katelyn. I promise I'll make it up to you somehow," he said as he let go of her hand, as if holding her any longer would lead to something else. They walked together to the bedrooms where they slept. He remained standing outside his door studying her until she went into her own adjoining room.

Katelyn thought about what he had said; the words reverberated in her head all through the night. Gianfranco was constantly in her dreams these days. She must have kept his words close to her heart because in her dreams she heard him repeat them over and over again, only each time he did he admitted his love for the other woman. He told her that he was sorry for all the pain he was causing her and that it was time for her to let him go. He said that Jenny was no longer filling the void left by his lover and, though he'd support their child, he wanted his freedom.

"What do you mean?" she cried out, still dreaming.

"I'm leaving you. I never really loved you. I want a divorce, I'm sorry. I did try for Jenny but this isn't working anymore," he said dismissively. He was being cruel and inhuman in his handling of her. She must have cried out loud because, within seconds, she awoke and found herself cradled in his arms. He was holding her, whispering soothing words over and over as he wiped the tears from her eyes.

"It's ok, I'm here. I'll always be here," he whispered softly. Their eyes met but neither of them spoke. Katelyn was afraid to free herself from his embrace. She was being selfish, she knew, but tonight she needed him. Nothing else mattered at this point except that he was holding her in his arms, sating the lingering need that grew between them.

Gianfranco joined her on her bed and, as he did, he brushed his lips over hers. Feeling his half-naked body next to hers was enough to ignite the flames that burned heavily between them. She knew he was fighting the same demons and tonight the demon would win. He kissed the hollow of her neck and as he raised his head a voice that was losing all control pleaded with her to ask him to stay.

"I promised you, I wouldn't do this. Please tell me to go and God help me, I'll find the strength," he drawled huskily as his eyes pleaded something very different.

She didn't reply as his scent made its way to her nose. She couldn't ask him to leave; it was too late. She let her fingers roam his bare chest and find the comfort she needed there. He was with her and that was all that mattered. The other problems would be there for them to deal with in the morning and they would deal with them then.

His hands searched out all the secret places of her body, the places he knew where she loved to be touched. He wanted more than anything to hear her cry out his name in sensual pain he created. The fire between them rose and, for the life of him, he couldn't understand how a woman whose body was so in sync with his own could not be in love with him. He dragged his lips back from her belly as he heard her whisper something to him; he couldn't make out what it was she said.

"Say my name, Katelyn. Call out to me when I'm inside you," he pleaded.

"Gianfranco, don't stop now; make love to me." Her voice cried out the mating song and his eyes searched deeply into her own for the answers. He would gladly give up everything he had for the chance to convince her to love him.

Her body came alive in his arms and a slave to his touch. This was the one place where she knew she had the upper hand. The one place she felt control over her life with him. She knew, come morning, this would all end but for tonight she wasn't going to let anything stop what they were sharing from moving to its completion. He was kissing every part of her body and when he was finished he focused on her most prized appendage; he tasted her sweet nectar until he was sure her body was aching so badly with desire that anything short of burying himself inside of her wouldn't do.

He moved slowly up her belly until his tongue reached the scars left over from their child, the scars that marked her perfect body. The scars caused by him. She was still as beautiful to him as the very first time he made love to her. No other woman would ever matter to him or would ever complete him as she did. She was up on a pedestal so high that no one other woman was able to reach her, in his eyes. He made vying for his love unattainable for other women. Tonight he would love her and go to a purgatory of his own making tomorrow. She had given him permission to make love to her and he was going to make damn sure she didn't forget this night.

After so many empty years of being apart from him, in spite of all his faults, she loved him still. She wasn't sure if that was enough to make this marriage-to-be last but for tonight she wasn't going to think about it. Gianfranco took her into his arms and watched as her body squirmed with shameless abandonment beneath his skilled hands.

He lifted her from the prone position on the bed so that he was kneeling in front of her as he wrapped her legs around him and entered her. He kissed her again and again as he made love to her. In this position, he could watch her as she rode him into another realm with her legs wrapped tightly around his hips. Tonight he would take her in every position he knew because, after tonight, he wanted her to believe in their future. He thought, rather selfishly, that if she did decide otherwise, he would ruin any thoughts she had of a sex life that didn't include him. She would never find anyone equal to his prowess.

After a short nap, she felt his growing erection at her back. *He couldn't want her again in such a short time, could he?* With uncontrolled disregard, their bodies moved once again savagely, one against the other, their hearts and souls crying out to one another to tame the flame that each saw echoed in the other.

"It was never Brody…" she cried out in a faint whisper, as he brought her to surrender once again.

Gianfranco held on to her tightly as his brain tried to make sense out of what he had just heard. She called out another man's name in her moment of surrender to him. He let go of her and reached for the boxer shorts carelessly thrown on the floor. If he stayed one minute longer, he was afraid of what he might say or do to her. He loved her even though he couldn't bare the humiliation of hearing another man's name on her lips as he made love to her.

"I can take just about anything from you but I can't be a replacement, for someone else in your bed. I love you, Katelyn, I always have but what you're asking is more than even I can give you. I thought, for Jenny's sake, I could but it's impossible. My pride won't allow me to be second in your life. I can't be your conciliatory accolade. I wanted to wipe his name from your memory so he'd never come between us again but I know now that's impossible. So, you win, until you can get past your feelings for him our marriage will be in name only," he stated shortly.

"I didn't…I didn't," she repeated as he made his way to the door.

He turned in the hall and stood there bare-chested, in his shorts; she was totally naked as she begged him to come back to her so she could explain.

"Whether you realize what you said or not, it makes no difference to me. You said his name in my bed!" he barked.

"But I wasn't dreaming or even thinking about Brody. I wasn't calling out his name. I was awake and fully aware as I tried to explain all the misunderstandings to you," she reiterated.

"Right now, I'm finding it very hard not to ring your beautiful neck. As mad as I am, I still find it impossible to keep my body from becoming aroused simply at the sight of you. What does that make me, Katelyn? A pathetic fool is what I am," he added completely beaten.

She glanced down at her own nudity and tried to reach over and grab a sheet to cover her nakedness.

"Don't bother; even with a sheet you would drive me insane. That's the part of myself I find so repulsive. I want you so badly that even though you want these hands that touched you, this body that buried itself inside of you to belong to someone else, I will still come back to you," he said disgusted with himself.

"You don't understand. Please Gianfranco…That's the problem, you're not listening. I do lo…" Before she could finish what she started to say, he retreated to his own room. It was hours before she gave up on sleep. She could hear him pacing in the room next to hers and knew he was dealing with the same issues. She spent hours going over and over what he had said. He was hurting that much was obvious even to her. He said he was hurting because he believed she loved Brody and that was something she didn't understand.

For better or worse, he made sure she understood that, although they would not share the same bed any longer, none of the plans he had made were going to change. Somehow, she would have to convince him that she loved him and perhaps in time he could grow to love her back. Whether he chose to believe it or not, they were good together and meant for each other. Fate couldn't be this cruel to bring them together after all these years only to split them apart again.

More to the point, she thought to herself, not only did they share a child but she was pretty sure they had conceived their second child. Each and every time they made love, neither of them was remotely interested or worried about the outcome of not using protection. The idea that they had created another child together during any of those encounters was very real. She dressed and went in search of him to talk.

"Good morning, I didn't think you were going to be up this early," he said, with arrogant pride as his eyes bore down into hers. "Jenny is outside playing. She ate breakfast and I helped her do her hair before she went out to play. I spoke to her this morning and explained to her that we'd be leaving this evening. I trust you will be ready?" he asked.

"Where are we going? Or do I not have the right to ask? I'm a little confused about where I stand in this relationship," she asked as she poured herself a glass of orange juice.

His mood, despite his lack of sleep, was seemingly under control as he smiled at her. "I expected this much from you, Katelyn. I didn't think it was possible for you not to put up a fight of some kind. I wouldn't worry your pretty head though; we'll deal with our future one day at a time. Although, I must admit though having a compliant wife for even a little while would be a dream come true. I've already taken the opportunity to warn Kevin and Sylvia that we'll be getting married this afternoon." He paused for a brief second to allow the shock to set in before continuing. "Before you say one word, I spoke to Eleanor Mulaney and she said your dress will be delivered this morning. That is actually what gave me the idea in the first place. Why wait for you to prepare for a wedding I mean?"

"Why the rush?" she asked, too shocked at the bizarre planning he had done while she slept.

"I have my reasons. Kevin and Sylvia are out handling some of the minor details. It seems everyone wants you to have the proper wedding you've always dreamed of. I also told Jenny about our plans and she's pretty excited about the idea; I'd like to keep it that way. She's happy, Katelyn, don't ruin that for her."

She couldn't believe all the planning that had gone on without her. It wasn't as if she slept for a week. It was 9:30 for goodness sake. Jenny suddenly burst into the kitchen dragging along a bucket filled with fresh cut flowers from Sylvia's greenhouse. "Momma!" she screamed jubilantly. "Did you hear? We're getting married today. Daddy took me out this morning and got me a new dress and shoes. He said we're going to honeymoon in his country. Is that right, Daddy?"

Gianfranco picked his child up into his arms and dared Katelyn to oppose him. She couldn't believe her eyes; he had won their child over in a matter of days. It was clear to her that Jenny adored him. "Honey, I was about to tell your Mom about our plans when you came in. Why don't you go and see if Mrs. Footy needs any help packing up your things?" Jenny was too excited to put up a fight. Before she walked away, she ran to both her parents and kissed them then skipped down the hall.

"I see you've already won her over. What is this about our going to Italy? How did you arrange all this? I mean the marriage license, our passports? " she asked as she saw him reach into his pocket and withdraw a long velvet black box. He opened it and handed it to her. "This is for giving me such a beautiful child. I thought, since it was our wedding day, that you would wear it for me?"

She stared down at the box and couldn't believe her eyes. It was exquisite. The necklace was a beautiful platinum chain with a starfish dangling from it. She wondered if he knew how significant the starfish was to her. She could tell when she looked up at him that he did. "I thought that if Jenny believed in wishes then so could I," he added.

Jenny must have told him what her grandfather had always told her. Wish on a starfish and you might find that wish coming true, providing of course that you let the starfish go first. With tears in her eyes, she accepted the necklace and she cried even more as he placed it around her neck. He fastened the clasp and whispered softly in her ear. "We can give life to this starfish by letting go of the past." He turned her to face him and was mesmerized by the necklace and how it looked on her neck. "It comes alive around your neck just as I hoped it would."

He held her in his arms and licked away the salty tears that fell from her emerald eyes…and then he kissed her. When his lips made contact with her mouth, he let his tongue explore and taste, ever so slightly, before gaining entry and deepening the kiss. "Gianfranco, please don't pretend that you have feelings for me. I want to be everything you want me to be for you but I can't handle the lies."

He couldn't understand her. Why did she always have to make problems for them? "If you're going to have another one of your tantrums and think that I'll change my mind, forget it. Nothing short of a nuclear war will stop this marriage from taking place today. Jake is flying in this afternoon to be here for us. I have to fly to New York tomorrow with him to wrap up the deal with Glitz but shortly thereafter the three of us will be on our way to Italy," he stated, waiting for a nod of understanding.

She glanced over at the flowers Jenny had left behind in the bucket and picked one up to smell it. She was still reeling from the shock of getting married today. She bit her bottom lip nervously as she placed the flower back in the bucket. It was obvious that he had taken care of everything and she just had to ride the wave with him. "What about my job? How can you afford to go away yourself so soon after the takeover?"

Gianfranco leaned against the kitchen countertop and, in a monotone voice said, "You're fired! Does that answer your question? You'll be my wife in a couple of hours; there's no need for you to work. You can spend all your time taking care of Jenny. As for the magazine, I appreciate your concern but as you know Jake ran *Intrigue* for some time. He worked for me then and he's agreed to do the same favor once again until we get *Glitz* up to the same standards."

Katelyn was speechless. What they said about Gianfranco was true, though she didn't believe it until this very moment. He could move mountains in the middle of the night if he needed to and no one would be the wiser. He was a big bruit and, as far as she was concerned, she was not going to make this any easier for him. She was sick and tired of his highhandedness. It was time someone taught him a lesson and, if she had to be that person, then she would.

"I've worked all of my adult life, how can I stop now?" she asked.

There she goes again. She would fight him every step of the way; it was in her nature to disobey him regardless of whether she agreed with him or not. Katelyn would always take the opposite side of the issue in spite of herself. He stood erect as he warned her again that this conversation was moot. He watched her closely with amusement as she ranted on and on. "It's very simple, Katelyn, you just will. I can afford any lifestyle I choose to live and I choose the one where you raise our children yourself. You will have my help, of course."

"Why are we going to Italy?" she asked.

"I've decided I didn't want to watch as men keep popping in and out of your life. I want this marriage on solid ground. I know that you don't have feelings for Taylor, I also know that the idiot reporter from last night meant nothing to you either. But Brody is another story all together. I admit knowing he's reconciled with his wife makes it easier for me to deal with the situation but I want to wipe him permanently from your heart. When I'm convinced that I've done that, we'll come back, not one minute before."

There was no way he could see into her heart because if he could he would know that Brody wasn't there. She had grown tired of his stubborn jealousy and even if it killed her, she would find a way to make him listen to reason. His jealousy had closed his mind but she knew she had to undo the damage if she hoped to open his heart to her again. Until now, she hadn't realized how much her relationship with Brody had come between them, through no fault of Brody's. She needed to make it clear to him that Brody was not a threat to their marriage. If they were ever going to be able to keep their friendship with Brody and Eleanor she had to convince him how she felt about him.

"This isn't necessary; I don't have feelings for Brody and I have never had feelings for him," she stated, knowing he would never believe her.

"I wish I could believe you, Katelyn. If I hadn't heard his name pass your lips myself, I might think that there was hope for us but I'm not a fool. I don't want his name mentioned in my presence. It's unfortunate that he and his wife will be attending the ceremonies this afternoon but I couldn't very well ask Kevin not to invite them. I must warn you though, other than having me right next to you when it happens, I don't want you within ten feet of him alone," he added, waiting for another fight he knew would come.

"What will happen if I disobey this order?" she taunted deliberately. "Will you send me off to another country? Oh wait, you're already doing that. This is ridiculous and you know it," she said stubbornly.

"I don't think you want to find out right here what else I might do at the risk of someone walking in but I think you know what I'll do. It's the only way I seem to be able to communicate with you. I will promise you this… my son will be growing inside you before our trip is over, if he isn't already. I want a family with you."

Voices, from the hall startled her. She jumped, unknowingly, into the arms of the man she wanted to hate. Before she could say a word of apology, he covered her mouth with his. She was sure it was for Kevin's benefit. She had heard him coming too. *What other way is there to convince my brother that this marriage is for the best?*

"I can't get over the two of you. If I had known about Jenny, believe me, I would have pushed for this wedding a long time ago. Then, maybe I wouldn't have to walk in on you mauling my sister every other minute," Kevin teased. "It's obvious to me that you two can't keep your hands off each other. How I never saw that teakwood ring all these years I'll never know. I would have figured it out right away if I had seen it."

Katelyn blinked, "Are you angry with us?" she asked with concern.

Kevin came over and hugged her tightly. Nothing would ever come between them and all that they shared. "I'm not angry, how could I be? Gianfranco is one of my closest friends. I couldn't trust anyone more for you and Jenny. I know he'll take care of both of you," he reiterated before being interrupted from behind.

"I told Kevin that we needed to get married quickly so that you and Jenny can come to Italy with me while I take care of some unfinished business there. Forgive me, Irish, but I also warned your brother that we could be expecting our second child and I wanted to be there from the beginning, this time. He agreed with our decision." Gianfranco loving placed a hand over Katelyn's abdomen and said, "This time it's my son growing in there," he said loud enough for Kevin to hear.

How, can he pretend and put on such a charade in front of her brother and all the other people they cared about? He was going to lie and vow to love her forever. If it weren't for Jenny, he would never enter into such an arrangement. His chosen lover, whoever she was, didn't feel the same for him and he thought that having a family was the next best thing. It was laughable to say the least. He was her idea of the perfect husband, sexy, virile, handsome and rich. He was the perfect mate and he was going to be her husband but would that be enough for her?

It frightened Katelyn, even as he held her in his arms, that perhaps they were making a serious mistake. It was true that physically they were a match made in heaven but could it sustain a lasting relationship? Would it be enough to keep their marriage alive, with the odds so against it?

She recalled an article she had read once that said that fifty per cent of marriages these days ended in divorce. Would she and Gianfranco become one of those statistics? He must have sensed what she was thinking because he leaned into her and kissed her again. Somehow he always knew intuitively when she needed reassurance. It must have been her body language that gave her away and when he saw the look of nausea that was beginning to overcome her, he excused them both and took her to her room to lie down.

"How could you tell Kevin that we're sleeping together? I can't believe you did this to me." Katelyn pushed him away and went to window where she stood and looked at nothing in particular, just so she didn't have to face him. She was fighting the tears of frustration that were screaming for release. What did Kevin think after this morning's announcement and all the truths she had kept from him? She had never kept Kevin in the dark about any important issues in her life, with the exception of Gianfranco.

Gianfranco's face darkened, hearing her disappointment. "I did nothing to you. The only thing I did was tell Kevin that you could be carrying my child. Kevin's knowledge of our baby helps guarantee my position." His words lashed out to hurt her and he did a great job of it. Suddenly she felt cheap and dirty; she had given herself so freely to him. She swallowed hard as she tried to pull herself together. Her toughest fight of her life was going to be keeping her sense of self, not being lost in her relationship with him.

"I didn't tell you about Jenny because you left me," she said behind trembling lips.

"You hate everything about me and now you want me to believe that you chose not tell me about our child, because I left town. I'm sorry, Katelyn, but that doesn't wash with me. If what you're saying holds any truth, why not tell me after all these years? Jenny is seven years old. Were you ever going to tell me?" he asked.

She swallowed hard, as she tried to explain. She realized she was fighting a losing battle and he still wasn't ready to actually hear what she had to say. "You don't understand," she said in frustration. She pleaded with him to at least try to listen to what she had to say. The cold

187

chilling response and the look that crossed his face said that whatever it was she needed to say didn't warrant his attention. He would never understand what she was telling him because his feelings were so raw. He couldn't forgive her for keeping their child from him and as long as that stood between them they couldn't or wouldn't be able to move forward and leave the past behind.

"Your damn right, I don't understand. What gave you the right to keep Jenny from me? You made that decision for both of us without my consent. You didn't stop for one second to consider how I would feel. You kept the truth from me and you denied Jenny a father in her life." He cursed her because she was the reason his daughter was only now getting to know her father.

"I couldn't tell you," she declared. "It would have meant that you would return to the States because of me and I didn't want that." The words hadn't come out as she intended and she watched as her words pierced him, like a knife through the heart. She did want him back in the States but not by force; she wanted him to want her.

He raised her chin to him and with every ounce of control he could summon directed these retaliatory words at her. "I'm not willing to listen to your excuses anymore. We're getting married today and I'm going to be in my child's life for the rest of my life. If you're worrying about what kind of marriage this is going to be, let me put your mind to rest. After today separate beds is looking very appealing to me." He looked at her for a long time before shooting another word of warning at her and then he left her once more to deal with her own tears.

Chapter Thirteen

"**D**o you, Katelyn, take this man, Gianfranco, to be your husband? To have and to hold from this day forward…" She heard the words and answered appropriately as she tried her hardest to stay focused on what the minister recited. With each and every word that was said, their eyes, mirroring the depth of regret they each felt, remained locked on the other. When she answered, Gianfranco gently squeezed her hand in his, leaving little doubt about what her defiance of him would mean at this point.

"Do you, Gianfranco, take Katelyn to be…?" Again she heard the same words recited for him and yet, to her, it felt as though it were happening to someone else. As Gianfranco spoke his vows to her, his face softened and his voice cracked with emotion. To everyone else in the room, he was speaking from his heart and everyone believed it, all except her.

"You may kiss the bride." She heard the announcement and was dumbfounded when, instead of a quick peck on the lips for show, Gianfranco took her in his arms and, as everyone watched, he claimed his bride. She was shocked and appalled at the same time. This was a game to him; he didn't like to lose and unfortunately for her, she was the pawn in his game.

"Stay away from Brody," he whispered in her ear as he held her in his embrace.

Her stomach jolted from nervous sexual tension as she heeded his warning. "If you don't trust me, why did you just vow to love, honor and trust?" she asked, speaking softly so he alone would hear.

"I would have preferred the old love, honor and obey rather than love, honor and trust. There wouldn't be any misunderstanding then, would there? I want to trust you but so far you have given me no reason to."

Gianfranco held her close as he led her from the small chapel, through the door and outside to all their awaiting guests and a swarm of reporters she hadn't expected. There was no doubt about the show he intended to put on since he held on to her as if his life depended on it. He lifted Jenny into his arms and, with Katelyn just as close, they posed for the reporters. The reporters repeatedly tried to talk to Katelyn but Gianfranco answered all the questions sent in her direction. He wanted to control the press and to portray the image of a happy family.

"Mrs. Broccolini...Can we get a few words? Why, the rush to the altar?"

"My wife and I have given you all you're going to get today I'm afraid. We would like a little privacy now, so we can enjoy the rest of our day with our guests." Gianfranco began to lead them to an awaiting car but didn't stop Jenny from answering a few questions shouted at her. He knew that she would blurt out, in her own innocence, that Gianfranco was her father. He didn't care what Katelyn thought about the idea, he liked it. From the look of pride on his face, she wondered if that was his intention all along.

The limousine ride to the hotel was short and brief but very comfortable. She sat back and watched as father and daughter exchanged loving conversation. Jenny was beside herself with excitement and couldn't wait to play with the other kids from the ranch, who would be attending the wedding reception. Katelyn could see that Jenny thought the moon and sun rose over her father and he thought the same about her.

Gianfranco had thought of everything. As they entered the hotel ballroom, Katelyn could see and counted a twelve-piece orchestra set up and already playing. The room was elaborately decorated, no money spared. It was done quickly and with taste and elegance; she knew that without Gianfranco's help this couldn't have happened in such a short time.

He didn't disappoint to make sure that his wedding was viewed as a major event and that everyone who attended remembered it and talked about it for a long time to come. Katelyn smiled as she caught sight of Kevin. He was standing directly across the room talking to Brody.

Gianfranco saw the change in her face as she glanced across the room and he wished that she would look at him with such devotion. Apparently, she was looking at Brody. He knew that this night was going to be difficult for her to get through but he thought that Eleanor's arrival on the scene might make the step into married life easier for her but now perhaps he had been mistaken.

The band announced their entrance as he led her out onto dance floor for their first dance. The song that Gianfranco had requested was one by Lonestar. She listened to the words and thought about how appropriate they were for them. *Amazed* seemed to have been almost written just for them. She hoped that he meant every word and could keep the promises they foretold. He held her closely as they listened to the words; he gazed into her eyes and asked her to listen to the words to the song carefully. He told her he had chosen the song for her. "Someday you'll understand the depth of what I feel for you," he murmured.

"Every time our eyes meet, this feeling inside me is almost more than I can take... I don't know how you do what you do. I'm so in love with you..." He was singing the song in her ear as though he meant every word of it. The way he held her, this felt right. It told of promises of a lifetime. She prayed that he meant the words he was declaring.

"I believe this next dance is mine," Kevin said as the orchestra ended their song and began playing a song that seemed fitting. Kevin had picked Van Morrison's, *Have I told you lately*. She was glad that Kevin picked that particular song for them. They shared a special bond and she knew she could always count on Kevin.

"I can't believe it's your wedding day. I'm really happy for you and Gianfranco. I couldn't have chosen a better husband for you myself." They moved around the floor with such ease and comfort. He held her arms high around his neck and smiled as he wiped the tears from her eyes. "I know Mom and Dad are watching us now; Dad is probably trying to tell me this is his dance," he said as he twirled her around the floor. "I want you to know that no matter what your reasons were for not telling me that Gianfranco was Jenny's father, I'd like to think I would've understood the truth."

She let out a sigh. *Do I tell him the truth?* The tears blurred her vision as she glanced across the room at her new husband who was watching them dance. Kevin followed her gaze and smiled. "Kevin, I couldn't tell you. You would have felt obligated to tell him; I didn't want him to know. I loved him but I needed to know he loved me. I didn't want him to come back to the States and marry me because he thought he felt obligated to. You know better than I do that he would have insisted we marry right away because I was pregnant."

Kevin squeezed her hands in his and said he understood. He didn't agree with her reasoning but he did understand her thought process. "You have no idea how much work he put into making this day special for you." He explained the great lengths Gianfranco had gone to making sure that this wedding was perfect in every way. Gianfranco had people flown in from all over the place to make sure everything ran like clockwork. Kevin saw Gianfranco walking toward them; he handed his sister over to her new husband, not before offering his congratulations to them both again.

Seeing her face change, Gianfranco drew her into his arms and tensed up at her reaction to him. He tried very hard to do everything he could to make this wedding everything he thought she would want and he thought he'd succeeded. The music changed. The song and the words were slow and sensual. It was a song of promise, the promise of what was to come. Or at least it would have been, if they were any other couple.

"Kevin tells me that you were the one who arranged all this…" she said with wonder and appreciation.

"Don't read anything into this, I did it for Jenny. She wanted a big Cinderella wedding and as you know there isn't anything I wouldn't do for her." His words were meant to sting and they did but it didn't make it any easier for him to witness the pain his words caused her. He didn't mean anything he had just said to her but his pride wouldn't allow him to rescind a word of it.

The reception went along smoothly for the rest of the evening. Everyone seemed to be enjoying the festivities. Katelyn became more and more relaxed as the evening went on. As if her luck had just run out, Eleanor and Brody came over to her to wish her good tidings for a wonderful future. They also wanted to thank her for whatever role she played in getting them back together.

Eleanor repeated again, "You look beautiful Katelyn. It's as though I designed this dress for you." They teased each other for a few minutes about the tattoos that Eleanor had made her aware of while at the shop. Katelyn assured Brody that she was still oblivious about where they were on their bodies.

"Oh Brody, don't be such a prude. I have a tattoo of a lock on my buttock and Brody has the key tattooed on his. He always held the key to my heart and the tattoos served as a reminder of our love for each other in a place where only we could see them. Now, if you two will excuse me, I need to go to the ladies' room," Eleanor said, kissing Brody full on the lips before leaving them alone.

Katelyn looked nervously over her shoulder for any sign of her husband. She spotted him dancing with Jenny. Seeing the two of them overwhelmed her emotionally. She hoped that he would be too preoccupied with their daughter to notice that she was standing here talking to Brody. She tried to come up with a reasonable explanation so that she could excuse herself but she was too nervous to think. He was a good friend and he would never understand why they couldn't talk without supervision. The whole situation was pathetic and yet she couldn't chance anyone questioning their motives for getting married.

"May I have this dance?" Brody asked and she didn't have the heart to turn him down. She accepted his arm with trepidation as he led her onto the dance floor. It was a fast song so she thought that even if Gianfranco saw them she would be safe enough. They danced for a short time before they were abruptly interrupted. There was a sudden change in the music that made them turn their attention toward the orchestra. They realized that Gianfranco had just requested a slow dance as he made his way toward his wife.

Gianfranco was glaring at them with such loathing; it was a miracle that other than the two of them, no one else seemed to notice.

"Is there a reason why I make him so tense?" Brody whispered in her ear.

"No, it's not you at all. He's angry at me about something that happened earlier. I should go and try to make peace before he ruins our wedding day or what's left of it," she teased regretfully. She went to Gianfranco and, as she did, she began to tremble a little at the thought of yet another argument. He shocked her as held open his arms, took her into his embrace and led her back on to the dance floor all with a smile on his face.

He had purposefully picked another slow, sensuous song because it was the only way he could keep her close. He moved with her in his arms without a thought as the crowd looked on. He was making love to her with their clothes on and didn't care who witnessed the heat they shared between them. This exotic scene was meant to prove a point and it did.

Katelyn was trembling from head to toe. She had lost the ability to think clearly and that's exactly what Gianfranco had set out to do, not to punish her but to let her and Brody know that when it came to his wife, he didn't share. He glanced down at her, letting her know with a look that any discomfort she was feeling was her own making.

Jake wandered out on to the dance floor and broke them up. Katelyn supposed from his actions that Gianfranco might have shared their secrets with him. After all, he had to talk to someone and that couldn't be her or Kevin.

"Let me dance with the bride just once before the crowd calls the fire department to get a hose to cool the two of you down. Talk about dirty dancing, did the two of you forget there are children in the room?" he asked. "I had to hold my hands over your daughter's eyes to protect her innocence," he teased. He pushed his friend out of the way and took Katelyn in his arms.

"I can't help myself, Jake. She's the most beautiful woman I have ever laid eyes on and now she belongs to me. Don't forget that buddy," Gianfranco teased his friend as he left the dance floor.

Gianfranco rejoined Kevin, Sylvia and Jenny; they appear to be engaged in weighty conversation. Katelyn couldn't tell what they were talking about but she could see that their daughter was agreeing with her father wholeheartedly. Tonight they would spend the night at the hotel alone and leave for New York in the morning for a short honeymoon before picking up Jenny and leaving for Italy, for who knew how long.

He later told Katelyn that he had booked the honeymoon suite because everyone would be expecting it. He didn't want anyone to think that their union was anything short of the loving marriage he intended to portray.

"You want to tell me what's wrong?" Jake asked as he danced with the woman who had also become his friend.

"There's nothing wrong, what makes you say that?" she asked him biting her lower lip.

Jake smiled at her as he lifted her chin lovingly. "I've been around you a lot over the years and who better than me knows that there's more to this marriage than meets the eye? I know you both pretty well; something just isn't right. Although, I must say that you're both doing a fine job of hiding it from everyone else. The tension between you both is so high that you're ready to explode. What is it, Kate?" he asked with a note of concern for them both.

"Jake, I appreciate what you're trying to do but we have to work this out ourselves." He wanted to help but he agreed to let the subject drop. She promised that if she needed him she would call regardless of his friendship with Gianfranco.

All the guests were gathering their things and, wishing them well before leaving. Kevin had a revelation just before they left. He realized, for the first time since they started planning the wedding that Katelyn and Jenny were going to be moving to Italy for a while. He was going to be the uncle and not the father-figure, the role, that he had embraced for so many years and it made him tearful. Kevin admitted that it was going to be hard for him to give up the role of protector, now that they had someone else to takeover that role but he was happy for them.

Katelyn observed as Gianfranco insisted on carrying his sleeping child out to Kevin's car so that Kevin could stay behind and help his pregnant wife. Katelyn followed close behind so that she could say good bye to Jenny once more before they left on their honeymoon. Jenny moved slightly in Gianfranco's arms as her little face glanced upward. She had felt the rain drops on her face and woke up.

"Daddy, will you and Momma be gone long?" her little voice whispered faintly. Gianfranco could see her tears well up in her eyes as she asked. He felt as though his heart were breaking his chest. Nothing would please him more than to have his little girl join them on this trip but there were things he and her mother needed to iron out before they could have her join them. After much discussion and many kisses, he and Katelyn finally convinced her that their trip to New York was going to pass quickly and that, while they were away, Kevin would keep her busy. After the car pulled away from the curb, he knew, before looking back, that Katelyn would be crying; the mother and daughter bond had been cut, though temporarily. It was probably the first time, for either of them.

They stood for a long time before the two of them went back inside the hotel lobby and joined Jake. Jake and Gianfranco talked about the magazine and what they each expected to happen over the next few weeks. Gianfranco trusted Jake to oversee the merger through its fruition. He glanced over at Katelyn who seemed bored and lonely after being left alone.

"I don't want to ignore my wife any longer, Jake. As beautiful as she is, if she's ignored for too long she might fly the coop," he said watching her with adoring eyes. "If I wasn't already in love with her, I'd fall in love with her beauty all over again." He shared a lot with Jake and as the two men witnessed Katelyn's growing impatience, Gianfranco thanked Jake again for all he had done and what he was going to do by taking over the merger of *Glitz*.

Jake hugged his friend, razzing that one day he'd make him pay up for all the favors he had done for him. Jake turned his attention to Katelyn, walked over to her and bid her farewell. He whispered in her ear that he meant what he had said earlier and then gave her a few parting words, not before looking at her with much skepticism.

"He loves you, Katelyn, trust me. I know him, give him time to get through the rest of the stuff and I'm sure it'll all work out," Jake insisted as he kissed her good-bye. With that, he started to take off but not before seeing Gianfranco take his wife in his arms and kiss her on the mouth. Jake smirked, made a face and laughed, told them to get a room and walked out of the lobby.

Gianfranco let his tongue explore the hollow of her mouth; he deepened the kiss as he felt her response. The kisses that she shared with other men had never been this intense. If it weren't for an elderly man coughing at the front desk, meant to interrupt them, who knows, what reactions Gianfranco would have aroused in her. He looked as though he was searching her soul for some understanding of what was transpiring between them. He was just as confused by her actions as he was his own. The two of them acted like horny teen-agers whenever they were together.

"No matter how hard I try to fight the urge to make love to you, I can't," he said with regret. "You're exquisite, painfully so." He had been able to keep his emotions to himself when he was with other women but with Katelyn it was impossible. Where she was concerned, he wore his emotions on his sleeve regardless of the cost. It was like he was a teenager and unable to control them.

She was well aware, as they reached their hotel room that the civility between them, had ended. The air had suddenly chilled and she couldn't begin to guess the cause. She decided, once in the room, that she would be the first to shower and change. The only problem with that was that all she had available was a sexy white negligee that Nellie had designed for her as a wedding gift. She had packed it away knowing she would never get the chance to wear it. Only now, all the safe clothes that she had packed were long gone and replaced with Nellie's newer sexier designs.

His eyes burned into hers as she emerged from the powder room. There was no attempt to hide from him because there was nowhere for her to go. He had taken off his tuxedo, as well as his shirt and tee shirt; he stood before her clad only in his pants which were opened slightly, exposing the trickling hair just below his navel. She didn't know why she was so fascinated with his body. She knew instantly what it would do to her. She also knew his thoughts without looking at him because they reflected her own; she stared into his eyes, following a path to her breasts, which were barely covered by the lace of the negligee she wore.

Thinking quickly, he handed her a glass of champagne and lifted his glass. "To us, that we may we have the luck of your Irish ancestors on our side. I have a feeling we're going to need a lot of it if we are to survive each other." He clanked his glass to hers and took a sip. As their eyes met, once again, she found her reaction to him expected but alarming. How could her body betray her to a man who felt nothing for her but sexual desire? He stood silently, watching, as if he were trying to study her and gauge what his reaction should be. The strap on her nightgown fell from her shoulder; he let out an audible sigh as he reached over to put it back in place.

He pulled his hand away from her skin, the skin that was burning from their contact. She knew her body ached for him to touch her again and she could see, from the look on his face, that he wanted her too. When she tried to turn away from him, she felt his hand gently take hold of her neck from behind and bring her back to him. His eyes were black and intense as he turned her body toward him. Nothing prepared her for the physical ache she witnessed in his eyes.

"Are you always going to treat me like this? It seems to me that the only time you're ever civil to me is when you want me in bed," she said as her breathing became labored and her body betrayed her.

He ran his fingers roughly through his hair in anguish, closing his eyes as he thought about what she had just said. "I'm sorry, you're right. I apologize to you for that. It's not what I want for us. It's just the way it is. I want you, Katelyn, and I won't apologize for wanting my wife but I do admit that I have a problem getting beyond these feelings you have for other men. I know it's my problem and I'm going to have to work that out for myself if this is going to work. I could use your help. Don't fight me so much, Katelyn. Try to meet me half way here, okay?" he pleaded as he moved toward her.

"I'm not in love with Brody or any other man, I never was. Whether you choose to believe me or not, I don't have any romantic feelings for him. This marriage doesn't stand a chance if we can't get past this. I was willing to try for Jenny but I refuse to stay married to someone filled with so much animosity and distrust. I can't see myself waking up each morning, for the next fifty years, having regrets about this decision. I made choices years ago and at the time I thought they were the right ones." She was out of energy; she couldn't fight any longer.

"Is that how you see this marriage? Do you feel regret when you look at me? I don't believe you, Katelyn. I know what you feel when you look at me and it's not regret I see there. That's the one area we do share common ground. You do agree with me on that, don't you?" he asked.

She shot him a look but quickly recovered when lightening interrupted her thought process. She had always been afraid of lightening as a child and that fear continued through adulthood. She knew that he was aware of her fear. He took the glass of champagne from her and placed it on the table. She heard the thunder in the distance and, though it scared the daylights out of her, she went to great lengths to hide her fear from him. She recalled all the nights she had put Jenny to bed and dealt with her fear on her own. On those nights when she couldn't or the anxiety got so bad, she called Jake and he had always been there for her.

Gianfranco went to the bar and poured himself another drink. This time she could see he was drinking with one thought in mind, to get drunk. He drank one followed by another. If he was going to share her bed, holding her to get her through this storm, then he would have to be drunk in order to accomplish it. There was no way he could lie next to her, have their bodies touch and not take her in his arms and make love to her.

"Do you think you should be drinking so much?" she asked nervously.

"Let's go to bed, Katelyn, I don't think I want to talk anymore. I'll hold you in my arms because I know it's the only way you'll sleep through this storm, but I warn you, don't move," he said as he led her toward the bed.

She was the first to get into bed. After he turned off the light she heard the zipper of his pants and knew that they were being carelessly discarded to the floor. She wasn't sure if he would sleep naked as he had in the past but she didn't think he'd dare tonight since they would not be consummating this marriage. She heard him breathing heavily as he held her body close to him but Katelyn knew he wouldn't push her any further.

How could he be so compassionate and understanding one minute and so ruthless the next? His fingers were soothing as he gently massaged her back as she lay over his chest, taking comfort from the storm. Katelyn wanted to reach down and find out just what he wore to bed but she dared not. She knew that touching him would mean they would once again lose themselves in a sexual rapture, they promised they wouldn't go to.

Katelyn fell asleep in his arms and, in her dreams theirs was a normal marriage. In her dream, he had just helped her get through her fear of storms by making love to her for the duration. *It's only a dream,* as she stirred from the sounds around her.

Gianfranco must have risen at the crack of dawn because she could hear the shower and it was still very early. She could smell his scent left on the pillow next to her as she hugged it, just to feel close to him again. She got out of bed and carefully laid out the clothes that she was going to wear to the airport.

When he finished with his shower, he told her it was all hers as he proceeded to make a call to his pilot. Katelyn didn't mean to listen to his conversation but she heard him tell the pilot that he wanted to leave as soon as possible. She went into the bathroom and bolted the door from the inside. She didn't know why she did it but she knew it would irritate him. It was obvious that last night had left a mark of discontent on him and he was feeling less than generous today. He would do everything he could to get them out of the country as soon as possible; he believed he would have more control in Italy.

Once the two of them arrived at the airport, Mary Alice greeted them, congratulating them on their recent nuptials. She told Gianfranco that if there was anything more she could do to make their flight more enjoyable, please let her know.

"Could you make sure my wife is comfortable?" he requested before he disappeared into the captain's cabin.

As Gianfranco made himself scarce, Katelyn took the opportunity to go to her seat and read some of the magazines she had recently purchased in the airport terminal. Mary Alice came over to her and asked if she could get her anything, informing her of the recent call that had been made to the pilot. "Mrs. Broccolini, Brody Calder called ahead, he wanted to make sure that we had enough champagne stocked for you and your husband. I assured him that Mr. Broccolini had seen to it that the galley was stocked sufficiently. He wanted me to be sure to tell you both that he had called and sent his best."

Mary Alice excused herself but not before almost bumping into the man whose orders she followed; Gianfranco had just heard every word she said about Brody's call. The eyes that raked over Katelyn's were not cold or angry, just disappointed. "Everyone on board thinks that we are on our honeymoon and that is the impression I insist we keep up. Notwithstanding, your own feelings about Brody, I'm your lover aboard this plane. Do you understand?" he asked angrily.

Holding her hand, his arm snaked around her waist, lifting her directly on top of his lap. He let the fingers of his other hand roam down her long dark hair until he reached the hollow of her neck. His hand lingered there for a short time, silence standing between them as he fought with the idea of flicking open the buttons of her top.

"I still have work I need to do but if you'd like some champagne, I will have it sent to the master suite. It may not be from your lover but it's all you're going to get. By the way, Katelyn," he said, staring into her eyes, "the pilot has warned me that we are flying into a storm, perhaps you should try the champagne. It may be good company for you," he stated harshly, accomplishing exactly what he intended. "I'm not a saint, call for me this time and I won't be so gallant," he warned.

She was furious with him, moving past him to their private quarters so she could escape. Her thoughts were rampant but she was tired of his jealousy. She sat at the desk and remembered a time when he believed in her. They were secure in their relationship back then and jealousy had no place in it. *Would he feel differently if she could convince him that her feelings for Brody were purely platonic? Or is the hostility he feels a cover for the regret he had because he married me?*

There was no way to reason with him when he set his mind on something. She decided to leave him alone and let him work through his issues himself. Sooner or later, she hoped, he would come to the right conclusion about her feelings for other men. She could feel the turbulence and it frightened her terribly so she went to closest seat and buckled herself in again until the light went on, letting her know that it was safe to walk around. After Mary Alice convinced her that it was indeed safe to unfasten her seat belt, Katelyn decided that she would try to lie down for an hour or so.

She kicked off her shoes and jumped into bed but she couldn't help noticing the silver picture frame that she had seen on her previous flight. It incensed her that he would keep the picture of the other woman he professed to love in the same room they would share while they were married. Anger was replaced by jealousy and disappointment; she didn't dare look at the face of the woman who had what she wanted.

The plane shook again and this time Katelyn panicked. She had faith that Gianfranco only employed the best but it did nothing to alleviate the fear that she had never grown accustomed to over the years. Her heart was racing and tears were nearing the surface of her eyes as she heard the door bolt open.

"Are you all right?" he asked as he stormed into the room. Gianfranco came to her, held her in his arms and rocked her, calming and soothing the fear he knew had overtaken her. "I need to talk to the pilot but I'll be back. Katelyn, nothing is wrong, I promise," he said, seeing the panic in her eyes. "We'll be in New York in no time at all." With that said; he was gone but not before promising to return momentarily.

Katelyn was shocked and embarrassed by her behavior; she would try anything to take her mind off what she was feeling. She turned her attention once again to the silver picture frame; she was taken aback by what she saw. The silver frame held an image of a much younger version of her. She remembered the day he had taken that picture; it was the day she believed Jenny was conceived.

Curiosity grew as she saw her own image staring back at her. That curiosity was replaced by apprehension as Gianfranco entered the room again and witnessed what she held in her hand. "I didn't know you kept any reminders of me?" she stated, not waiting or expecting an answer.

"It brings back memories, doesn't it? It makes me wish I could turn back the clock whenever I look at it." He shook his head in disgust as if his thoughts were delusional. "If I could turn back the clock, I would.

Maybe things wouldn't have to hurt so much now." He said gently, as he took the frame from her hand and placed it back on the nightstand.

"I remember when you took that picture," she said warmly, she smiled as recalled the memory.

"I took it down near the yacht at the pier in New York right before we set sail on the open sea. It was just the two of us on an adventure to nowhere in particular, to spend our last few weeks together. Do you think about that trip?" he asked. His hand touched the contours of the face in the frame and Katelyn wished it was the real person he was touching. She could see the sadness in his eyes as he thought about the time they spent together on that trip. "It feels like decades ago. Time has a funny way of numbing the pain and masking it until something pushes those memories forward and you're forced to deal with the hurt all over again."

Gianfranco must have thought that her puzzled look was born from the uneasiness she felt as he reminisced about the past they had shared. He had no idea how far he was from the truth. Truthfully, her preoccupation that another storm was growing was gnawing at her and the only thing she knew that would calm her was to ask him to hold her in his arms but that was the last thing she wanted to do.

"It might help if you have a little more champagne," he said as he handed her one of the two bottles that he had placed in the cabin. "I figure you take one bottle and I'll take the other. We'll skip the glasses; I don't think we'll need them. The storm didn't seem to be going away and even though they were above the clouds, she still felt the turbulence and heard loud thunder below.

She did as he suggested and sipped the champagne. She couldn't help but notice that his bottle was nearly empty. It was apparent that he handled champagne a lot better than she did. She felt tipsy from the small amount she drank while he seemed completely unscathed. It didn't seem fair, although it did give her a little Dutch courage, which she needed when it came to dealing with Gianfranco.

"I know this is a strange request but would you mind, after we reach the hotel tonight, if we slept together? One night is all I ask, I promise. After tonight you can go back to doing whatever it was you were doing, with whomever you were doing it before I stepped back into your life," she added, as an afterthought and took another sip of champagne.

He was next to her within seconds and touched her lips with his own. "I can't promise to sleep in the same bed with you and not touch you. I could never make that promise to you," he said again as he kissed her more deeply this time and hoping that wouldn't ask him not to.

"I don't want you to. Keep the promise, I mean," she added softly. It was more of a shy plea from the heart.

Everything that happened after that was a blur. Neither of them could wait until they reached the hotel. He hadn't told Katelyn yet that he owned the hotel they were staying at or that the penthouse was his private apartment. There was so much he hadn't told her yet. He had acquired a lot during his time without her and the majority of it had been obtained after their affair because he'd had little else to keep his mind off of her. He had become a nightmare of a sort to his adversaries. If he wanted your company, there was nothing that was going to stop him from taking it from it. If he was ruthless it was because Katelyn had taken the man he had been with her when she left.

Gianfranco had been a kinder, gentler man before Katelyn betrayed him. He believed in her and when everything they shared became sullied by her betrayal, he lost it. For a long time he didn't care who he hurt or what the consequences were from the takeover of the companies he wanted. Money became the bottom line for everything he involved himself in.

The pilot's voice announced that they would be arriving at JFK airport shortly and should gather their things. Katelyn turned to Gianfranco and thanked him for what he did. She knew that what she had asked of him was difficult but she was hoping to make up for it.

It was nice to be Gianfranco Broccolini, Katelyn thought. He never waited in line for anything. Their bags were magically taken to the car that waited at the curb them. She could definitely grow accustomed to this life.

They held each other hands innocently while they waited for the bell-hop to take the bags to the room. As they entered a private elevator that would take them to the penthouse, he saw that mischievous look on her face. Gianfranco took the rolling cart from the bellhop, gave him a large tip and told him he'd handle the bags himself. In the elevator, things got a little wild even for Katelyn.

He watched and enjoyed every second as she undid the belt to her coat. Before she could do another thing, Gianfranco took his own coat and threw it over the mirror that he knew housed a security camera. The last thing he needed was to have his staff witness his wife doing a private striptease. He was pleased, but shocked, as she dropped the coat to the floor and saw that, with the exception of thigh high black stockings and high heels, she was completely naked. Somewhere between the plane and the hotel, she had stripped herself of all of her clothing.

He stopped the elevator by pushing the emergency button. He had heard of this type of behavior in elevators but he had never participated in it himself. He grinned as he watched to see what his innocent wife would do next and was overtaken by raw sensual need as she ripped the shirt open from his body and worked to release the belt from his pants. He decided that, even though he was enjoying himself immensely, he would help her out. He opened his pants, pulled himself free and watched as Katelyn quivered at the sight of him.

Katelyn slithered to the floor, without waiting to be coaxed, licking and tasting him. She surprised herself as she allowed herself to move so wantonly over his naked body. He thought he was going to die; what she was doing to him was driving him crazy. He didn't want to come this way. In frustration, he lifted her into his arms and wrapped her legs around him. He delved so deeply inside her that he didn't know where she began or he ended. She was ecstatic as he thrust in and out of her with unleashed abandon.

"I'm complete when I'm with you. I can't let you ever leave me again, Katelyn," he whispered in her ear as he took her to new heights yet again. After they completed the act, they went limp in each other's arms and rested against the wall. She had never made love with anyone else; each and every time he made love to her she was sure it was the best she would ever feel. "I'm terrified that you'll never love me the way you love him," he said, as he felt her go frigid in his arms.

Katelyn picked up her coat and covered her body. *How dare he after what we shared insinuate that I could love another man?* He made her feel tawdry and cheap. He felt no embarrassment or shame as he left his pants on the floor while he talked to her. "Don't cover your body from me now. Don't make what we just shared something other than what it was."

He watched her as he waited for a reply, anything that would explain her sudden coolness toward him. Two minutes ago, she was hotter than he was and couldn't wait for him to take her. He knew her defenses toward him were gone and he was hoping to keep it that way. "There's nothing about your body that I don't remember," he said.

She didn't say a word as he lifted his pants from the floor and put them on with great force, all the while making sure he never took his eyes off her. She had her coat wrapped so tightly around her body that he thought it would take a hacksaw to get it off her. Out of the blue, she was back to being the shy virgin. "What are people going to think if someone sees us? I'm sure they already suspect that this elevator should have reached our floor by now," she said shyly.

"I've just made love to you in an elevator; do you think for a minute that I care what anyone else thinks? You're my wife, Katelyn, not some whore I hired for sex," he said tightly before adding, "Besides, this is my private elevator." He pushed the red button with force and the elevator continued to the upper floors. Katelyn wondered how much more she didn't know about her husband.

"I think we should go to our room now. I don't think I want to discuss what just happened. I may be your wife but I feel like your whore. A wife is consulted before decisions are made on her behalf, not dragged halfway around the world and told she has no choice in the matter," she said, trying to hurt him, she did. She regretted her choice of venom as soon as it left her mouth. It seemed as though the calmness they shared had been an illusion because his anger was resurfacing. Suddenly, she could imagine what the repercussions would be; she dared to push the mighty Gianfranco Broccolini over the edge and she had done it repeatedly.

"You're right, Katelyn, you have no choice. We'll do exactly as I planned we would. We'll finish up what business there is to finish and then we'll pick up our daughter and fly to Italy. We will stay in Italy as long as it takes to convince me that your loyalties are with me and this marriage. As far as any other future plans I might have, you don't have to worry as I haven't made any." He looked frustrated with her as he continued. "I'm pretty mobile; we have properties all over the world and any businesses I have are already taken care of by the people I hand choose to run them. You'll see that we have quite a vast holding."

He didn't know why he had mentioned all that other than to impress her. He knew Brody was wealthy but it was nothing comparison. Yet, deep down, he knew that money didn't really matter to Katelyn. That was what had made her so much more attractive to him. He knew she loved him unconditionally in the past and he hoped that he could secure that same love for them both in the future. He hadn't planned on leaving her alone today but he couldn't stand the thought of staying with her for another minute.

"I have a meeting with Jake in a couple of hours so I'm just going to shower and go straight to the office. I have some business to go over with him before we leave. If you need anything at all, just ask Maggie. She'll bring you whatever you need," he said, before telling her that the housekeeper was dying to meet her. "When we bring Jenny here to live, we'll bring our personal staff back with us. Right now, it's just you and me and Maggie. She's my housekeeper and my cook."

"I'd like to go to the office with you, if you don't mind? While you're at your meeting, I could go and talk to some friends of mine." She watched him glare at her suspiciously. The elevator door opened directly into the penthouse and Maggie was there to greet him. He took care to introduce her to his wife. She seemed pleasantly surprised and happy for them both. Maggie was an elderly woman and Katelyn could tell that she cared deeply for Gianfranco and had been around for a long time.

Katelyn followed him into the master suite where he dropped their bags on the floor. She reached for a piece of her own luggage that she knew would hold some bits of clothing appropriate for the office and took them out. She followed him through the large penthouse apartment and was astonished by its size. She wished she had the time to explore each and every room but she knew he was itching to get away from her and if she gave him the opportunity, he'd leave without her.

They both took quick showers and dressed. He walked out of his bathroom fully dressed. "If its Adam you're anxious to see at the office, you needn't bother. I spoke to him two days ago; I think he got the picture when I informed him that you were going to be my wife. I'm not sure if he'll still be hanging around the office. I fired him almost immediately," he said without feeling, as he put a comb through his hair.

She tried to conceal her anger and disappointment in him but she couldn't. Instead of being able to share her happiness with her coworkers, who had become her friends over the years, he was making her feel miserable. She did want to go and see Adam, not because she had regrets, she wanted to tell him she was sorry for the way she had treated him before she'd left. She still felt that she had led him to believe that they had a future together and she regretted that.

Katelyn decided that even if Gianfranco invited her to join him, at this point, she wouldn't go. He had no right to tell her what to do and who to do it with. She would stay here by herself, take a long hot bath and call Rosa. She didn't even bother to say good-bye to him as she strolled past him heading for the bathroom.

It wasn't until after she had filled the tub and gotten in that she realized he hadn't left. He walked over to her and dipped his hand in the tub, not caring that his new shirt was getting soaked until he had the bar of soap in his hand. He thoroughly enjoyed watching her squirm as he washed her back and then lathered up both hands, massaging her breasts. He purposefully dropped the soap, it expertly landed between her legs; he continued to massage as her breathing became short and rapid. He stopped just short of bringing her to orgasm.

"Maybe, when I get back, if you're a good girl, we'll continue where we left off," he said as kissed her full on the mouth before getting up and grinning as he left. He continued to laugh as she threw a wet sponge in his direction. She hated what his touch did to her. *No, I don't hate it, I hate him.* She hated his jealousy of these phantom lovers he thought she had.

After dressing and eating a light lunch, Maggie took her on a tour of the penthouse. There wasn't a hint of a woman's touch anywhere. Each room was done in a masculine motif.

"This place lacks a woman's touch and a child's hand," Maggie stated as they walked around the penthouse. "It's a little strange to see a woman here. He has never allowed a woman to enter his domain. Ordinarily, he keeps a room on one of the lower floors and goes there with floosies, pardon the expression. I knew he thought you were special when he told me to prepare the place for you. I must tell you though, I wasn't expecting that he would marry anytime soon but I'm happy to hear it. He's been alone for far too long," she added lovingly.

Katelyn was bored and after the tour of the apartment she decided to write on paper all the things she would like to change so they could make into a home fit for a family. She kept herself busy for four hours and had come up with some great ideas. All she had to do was run it past Gianfranco and see what he thought.

"Would you like something to eat Mrs. Broccolini? You've been cooped up in this office for hours, you must be starving," Maggie said trying not to get in the way.

"That would be great. Please Maggie, call me Katelyn. I hate formalities." Katelyn followed Maggie to the kitchen and helped with the preparations. It wasn't long before the two women were exchanging stories about Gianfranco and the daughter he only just found out about. Maggie couldn't wait to meet her and didn't judge Katelyn as to why she kept her birth a secret from Gianfranco. After enjoying dinner and conversation, Katelyn decided to shower and change before calling Rosa.

She stripped out of the sweats she was wearing and stepped into the most luxurious shower she had ever had the pleasure of enjoying. As Katelyn washed her body she heard the music that was piped into the shower. Gianfranco certainly knew how to live. As the music played and she washed her body she couldn't help but wish that she had packed some of her favorite toys. If her husband wasn't going to take care of her, she would take matters into her own hands. After drying her body she put on the white silk robe that Nellie had given her. She had to admit feeling the silk against her naked body made her feel sexy. She dialed Rosa's number while sitting on the edge of her bed and waited for a reply but all she received was an answering machine.

After waiting for Rosa's voice recording to end, Katelyn spoke into the phone and left her a message. "It's Katelyn; if you're there please pick up. I need a friend. It's urgent and I have a lot to tell you. Call me at 555-1789." She was aggravated as she hung up the phone; she hated answering machines. Before she put the phone back, she had an odd feeling that she wasn't alone any longer. She turned around just in time, before he had a chance to mask the annoyed look he had on his face. He was upset with her again for some unknown reason.

"I will not have you running to him; embarrassing me by explaining the reasons for our marriage." She sat up nervously, rubbing the back of her neck, tension building. "What can I offer you to keep you from seeing him? I'll do anything you ask." She heard the desperation in his voice and saw the determination in his eyes as he ran his fingers through his jet-black mane.

"I've heard your promises before and I don't trust you to keep them. Your promises are empty," she said with an added chill in her voice. He was making her uncomfortable as he stared at her barely covered body. It was hard for her to conceal her arousal from him, no matter how hard she tried to do so. He had left earlier feeling discontented. Katelyn felt like a cornered animal and as her predator moved closer, she had nowhere to go. She was sitting on the edge of the bed, his bed. He would take her again and she would welcome it.

"Why am I not telling him that the call he overheard was not to Adam at all? Maybe, if I tell him the truth he'll leave me alone. But, I don't want him to leave me alone,"

Gianfranco tugged at the lone ribbon at her waist, the only thing holding her robe in place. With two fingers he pushed the sides away and watched as it slid off her shoulders and, as if in slow motion, he bade her to stand. He reached over and kissed one bare shoulder and then the other, then he stood away from her body, first to admire his work and then to undress himself. He never let his eyes stray from her body as he held her captive in a sexual trance and made her feel the heat he knew was there between them. When he joined her in her nakedness, he kissed every exposed part of her body.

"I can make you want me. Look at you, what would you do if I left you now? I could make you want me and no one else and you know it.

I'm almost tempted to try it but I won't. You want to know why I won't, Katelyn. I admit that you are my weakness, my addiction if you will, as much as I am yours. Do you loathe yourself as much as I for that weakness?" he asked.

How can I make love to a man who only feels contempt for me? It was a question that didn't require an answer because Gianfranco stood up, stared at her naked body and walked away from her. "I've decided to give you a reprieve," he said before walking to the bathroom and turning on what she assumed would be cold jets of water for a well needed cold shower.

What am I suppose to do? She had no idea how much Maggie knew about their marriage or what he wanted her to know. She couldn't just bring her things to another room. She sat there for a long time until he came out of the bathroom clad only in a towel. She was breathless at the sight of him. "I thought you'd be gone by now," he said.

"I'm sorry to disappoint you, I wasn't sure what Maggie would think if we slept in separate beds," Katelyn whimpered as she sank deeper into the bed. For a moment there was complete silence between them and she didn't think he was going to join her. She wanted to sleep with him more than anything. She wanted more than just sleep. This would be the hardest test that she had ever had to face.

He had a look in his eyes, something between hunger and fury. Then, in a matter of one second, it turned to a more playful gleam. He laughed arrogantly as he dropped the towel that clung to his waist. "I guess this is as good a time as any for you find out how your husband sleeps."

Katelyn recalled the nights they'd shared and locked in those memories was this same vivid image standing before her. He smiled as he joined her in bed, retrieving some of the blanket that covered her body. "I think we'll share this. I may not like clothes when I sleep but when I lack the warmth of woman's body to keep me warm, I do use blankets," he added with a smirk, enjoying the discomfort he saw in her face, having his naked body this dangerously close to her own.

She was annoyed with him and the fact that he was enjoying himself at her expense was making it worse. "I guess, from what Maggie tells me, you use blankets often," smiling as she jerked the blanket back from him. She couldn't see him but she could feel the smile spreading across his condescending mouth.

"Snooping into my private life, Irish? Let me offer you a bit of advice. I enjoy making love and if you expect my fidelity, I expect you to be my wife in every sense of the word," he added, taking her hand and placing it over his erection, holding it there. "If you want, I will take a lover but I'd rather my lover was my wife," he said sulkily.

His warning was meant to scare her and it did. If she understood what he was adamantly making clear, she needed to be a compliant bride in his arms or he'd find someone else who would be. "Are your threats meant to hurt me?" She asked the question knowing full well that was his plan exactly. She tried not to show it but it was growing increasingly difficult, having this conversation while she still held his shaft in her hand. She let go roughly and tried to make him believe that it was what she had intended to do all along.

He had a look of triumph on his face, a look that said she took his bait and reacted exactly as he knew she would. She wasn't ready for him when he rolled over on top of her and pinned her beneath his naked body. "Is this how you really like it?" he asked. "I had no idea that you enjoyed rough sex. If this is what you want, I will oblige you but it saddens me that any part of this body would be marked," he added as he traced her breasts with the back of his long masculine fingers.

"Get off me," she said stubbornly pushing him aside, her actions unmerited. "I don't want you to touch me. You have a filthy mind," she added angrily. He laughed, knowing full well how aroused she was. He knew her body better than she knew it herself and he knew she wanted him. She tried turning over on her side, hoping that would be the end of it but he left a trail of kisses down her neck and shoulder as he removed the only two barriers between them. He tossed the blanket aside and lifted her nightgown over her head.

"Tell me, Irish. Tell me to make love to you and I will. I want to hear my name on your lips this time. Please, say my name," he begged as he repeated the words over again in her ear. "I loved you before I ever met you," he said, in a voice so low it wasn't meant to be heard.

Their lovemaking was always raw and complete; it didn't take long before she cried out in ecstasy. She cried out his name over and over again until she thought she would die from sheer exhaustion. Why did it have to be like this between them? Together, the sex between them was elated. It didn't take long before she was consumed by the rapture. She fell asleep in his embrace as their naked bodies clung to each other in slumber. When she finally woke, Gianfranco was nowhere to be seen. In his place was a book on erotica. Katelyn picked up the book, glanced at it and threw it across the room. *Who does he think he is? Is this another attempt to anger me?* She was a little embarrassed when, seconds later, Maggie knocked on the door, asking if she needed anything. Maggie said she'd heard a noise and when she glanced down she was without doubt embarrassed by what she found there.

Katelyn grabbed the sheet up to her neck, looked down and saw that the book was lying open on the floor. The opened page contained a truly exotic pose of two people making love. Katelyn grew more embarrassed when she realized that they had been in that same position the night before and the page was clearly marked for her benefit. *What does Maggie think of me?*

"Did Gianfranco leave for the office already, Maggie?" she asked, trying to avoid eye contact with the housekeeper.

"He left hours ago, Mrs. Broccolini. I'm sorry…Katelyn. He asked that you not be disturbed. He said you didn't sleep well last night. He left the impression that you were ill but I can see he is back to his usual teasing self," she said, shaking her head as she picked up the book and placed it on the table. "Do you have plans for today?" she asked in her Irish brogue.

How ironic that Gianfranco Broccolini employed a housekeeper who was as Irish as could be. "I haven't thought about what I would do today to tell you the truth. The first thing I have to do is call my daughter and then I was thinking about doing something to make this place feel more like a home. It needs a woman's touch."

Maggie smiled and encouraged her. "It will do this place good to have a woman and child running around. I'm sure that is just what the doctor ordered for Gianfranco, Mr. Broccolini, I mean," she said correcting herself. She was hardly able to catch herself from saying his

given name. Maggie didn't know Katelyn nor did she know how Katelyn would stand on formality, so she didn't dare take such liberties.

"Maggie, it's perfectly alright if you call us by our given names. I really want you to. For that matter, like I said yesterday, I'd prefer it.
We're going to be family around here and I don't want you to feel you're
not part of that family," she said still holding on to the sheet that hid
her body. Maggie smiled happily and told Katelyn she would leave her
to get dressed as she prepared her breakfast.

Katelyn wrapped the sheet around her body and went over to the
book lying on the desk. She picked it up and instantly she felt her
breasts respond to the memory of last night's events. He was an excellent lover and Katelyn was learning things from him that she hadn't
dreamed possible. She placed the book on the table and decided she
would have to give some thought to her revenge.

Katelyn checked out the closet filled with her clothes as well as new
and untouched outfits. They were hung neatly across from his. It was
strange seeing his things next to hers and she couldn't resist the urge to
touch the jacket that still held his scent from the night before. She closed
her eyes and held the jacket to her body as she took in his scent. Her
body longed for his touch to relieve some of the need that he had created
with his little innuendos. She took the coat from its hanger and cocooned
her naked body with it. She hugged her arms around herself as the silk
fabric inside brushed against her breasts; they tingled against the silk.

She took a cool shower and changed in order to put last night behind her. After the shower, she dressed and dialed Rosa to see if she had
gotten her message from the day before. She answered almost right
away and it felt good to hear her familiar voice. So much had happened
since the last time she'd seen Rosa and that was such a short time ago.
She knew Rosa would be shocked at all the news she had for her and
possibly hurt at not being included in the wedding plans but she knew
she'd understand. She was a good friend and she didn't want to hurt
her; somehow she'd make it up to her.

"Is that you, Katelyn?" Rosa asked into the phone. "I got your message and I was a little concerned about you but I didn't get a chance to
call you last night because it was late when I got in."

"I'm not sure how to tell you this but I should just come right out and say it. Gianfranco and I were married yesterday in Montana. I'm sorry that I didn't get in touch with you but everything happened so fast." Katelyn listened, the silence was deafening. She couldn't figure out if it was from shock or a disappointment.

"I'm happy for you but isn't this a bit soon? I'm just a little taken back by the speed of the wedding." Katelyn supposed she was right but, looking back, they had waited seven years too long.

"Rosa, if you're free today, I'd love to have you come and see the place? I could send a driver for you?" she suggested. Rosa agreed without hesitation. She couldn't wait to see Katelyn and make sure her friend hadn't made a mistake. Katelyn decided she would skip telling her about Italy for now. They talked a little about Jenny and her feelings about having her father in her life. After a short conversation, they decided to put off the rest of their conversation until later when she arrived at the penthouse.

Rosa wasn't expected to arrive for a couple of hours so Katelyn decided to use the time making the penthouse into a little less of a sterile environment and more into what a home should look like. She got busy on the phone and before she knew it she had ordered a host of things to spruce the place up; she also made appointments with interior decorators. It wasn't until Maggie came to announce Rosa's arrival that she realized how much time had passed.

"I can't believe this place," Rosa said as she looked around. "You could fit all the apartments on our floor into this one place. I'm sure there's nothing you could want that Gianfranco couldn't give you," she said, admiring the amazing penthouse. Katelyn couldn't help but keep the secret her heart wanted to scream out; she had everything except his love.

Maggie told them that lunch was being served; both women followed her as she escorted them to the dining room. Surprised, Rosa suddenly realized that this was definitely more than she had expected. She put her wineglass down but not before remarking that everything was so proper. "I'm sure this wineglass is in the proper white wine flute or is goblet? Not like at home, where we'll drink from a mason jar if we need to," she said laughing. "You deserve all of this."

"Gianfranco made arrangements for Jenny and me to go to Italy with him, in a few days. We'll be living there for an extended period of time." Katelyn could tell from the expression on her friend's face that she didn't understand the expediency of this trip. She told her that it was all so rushed, the marriage, and now moving to Italy for an unknown length of time. Rosa didn't trust Gianfranco's motives. "How could he marry you within a few days of seeing you again and then insist on taking you out of the country? Are you sure you can trust him?" Rosa asked with concern.

Katelyn knew his reasons for the trip but she couldn't share them with her friend. How could she explain that her husband of only two days didn't trust her? She wanted to share her secrets with Rosa but she couldn't. The look on Rosa's face when she told her they would be moving was enough for her to handle. They both cried as if they were losing each other forever.

"I know it's not your fault. You and Jenny have to go with your husband but you guys are my family. This is so hard," she said as she hugged Katelyn and cried again. Rosa picked up her glass of wine and toasted Katelyn and her future happiness. She wanted Katelyn to have everything she longed for and more.

They each chatted for what seemed like hours before Rosa had to leave. She told Katelyn that she would miss them both but she promised to get a passport as soon as possible so she could come and visit. It wouldn't be the same as it was before but they would both have to accept the new roles they were about to play in each other's lives. After Rosa left, Katelyn went into the kitchen and made herself a cup of tea in spite of Maggie's objection. Maggie insisted that she was there to take care of her.

"I'm going to take this tea to my room, if you need me for anything just call. I'm a little tired," she said, forcing herself to walk in the direction of the bedroom. She drank her tea stretching out on the chase lounge that overlooked the Manhattan skyline. Her emotions began to get the better of her. It was enough that he infringed on her thoughts when they were together but now he tormented her during her quiet moments. She wanted this marriage to work, she really did.

Gianfranco stepped into their room and watched stealthily as his wife wept into a tissue. He couldn't help rid her of the pain she was going through; if he did, it would mean the end of his salvation. Maggie told him that she'd had a visitor this afternoon and seemed emotionally distraught when her company left. He didn't ask who her company was but he could guess by her reaction. He went to the bar and poured himself a drink. She heard him as he moved around the room, their eyes met. He could see she was drowning with feelings of regret written in her eyes.

"I understand you had a visitor today?" he asked as he handed her his handkerchief. "Maggie didn't get to tell me who it was but, judging from your behavior at the moment I don't think I want to know."

There was only bitterness in his tone and Katelyn wasn't up to fighting with him. She was exhausted from sparring with him and told him the truth. "I'm not sure what you mean?" she asked.

He let his eyes drift to her face and then said coolly, "You mean, you don't want to tell me who was responsible for your tears," he asked touching her cheek with his thumb.

"I don't see why you should concern yourself with my feelings. You never have before," she added, knowing her words would sting. This became a game between them and she was fast becoming emotionally unable to play.

"Was it Taylor? Did you have him in our home?" he asked in defeat. Remaining silent, he took it as an admission of guilt. He understood her tears for her ex. She followed him into his study and watched as he smashed a glass on his bar. He replaced it with another, filling it with any liquor that was available to numb his pain.

Katelyn watched as he gulped down another sip and left the study abruptly. If nothing else, she knew he was jealous, thinking there was another man in her life. She didn't see him again until much later that night and when he joined her in bed reeking of alcohol. She hated knowing that he had to drink himself into a stupor in order to share the same bed with her.

During the night, his arms had somehow found her as she lay spooned with him. He was naked and fully aroused but he didn't seem to move. He was lying still and judging from his breathing, she knew he was awake. Did he want her to make the first move? He had no idea how painful this was for her to be so close and not make love to him. No matter how painful it was, she couldn't stand to lose that closeness she felt while in his arms.

He couldn't let go of her; it felt too good to hold her. He felt her tears as they dropped on his arm and that was what kept him from touching her any further. Her tears were for another man and even if it killed him, he owed her this comfort at least. She'd married him and given up her lover; somehow he would make it up to her.

Chapter Fourteen

Gianfranco had Dana make sure that their passports were all in order. Katelyn made arrangements to have Jenny escorted to the airport in Montana by Mary Alice. It was decided that Gianfranco would meet her at the airport and bring her to the penthouse to meet Maggie.

During those whirlwind two days, they barely conversed while waiting for Jenny to arrive and for Jake to take over the day-to-day operation of the magazine. She spent a lot of her time alone and Gianfranco took any opportunity he could to go to the office. But as soon as Jenny arrived, everything changed. She brought smiles to both their faces and life to a home where it had been lacking. Gianfranco loved having Jenny near him. Maggie was quite taken, seeing a miniature version of Gianfranco. She couldn't imagine what had kept them apart all these years. In Gianfranco's defense, he never let anyone blame his wife. He took full responsibility for not being in his daughter's life from the beginning.

Gianfranco spent all his free time with Jenny and after tucking her in at night, he'd go and hide in his study with a bottle that was fast becoming his friend. Each night, Katelyn grew increasingly worried about him. She decided that she would talk to him before he took his first drink tomorrow. She would do whatever he asked of her in order to make him stop because neither of them derived any pleasure from the hell they were creating.

Katelyn never had the chance to talk to Gianfranco because he came to her instead that evening. He had gone to his study as usual but apparently he had nothing left to drink. She could see that he had thought long and hard about his visit, whatever the reason. Nervously, she sat up in bed and never looked away from his eyes. "I want to talk to you about our future. I think we need to discuss what each of us expects to get out of this marriage," he added as he stepped closer to the bed. His eyes were dark and unquestionably uneasy.

He gently brushed his knuckles against her lily white skin. Never before had a woman compelled him like she did. It was as if he were under a witch's spell that couldn't be broken. His eyes burned with desire and love for her. He wanted so badly to absorb that need from her that she so easily took from him. Then, as if nothing could stop him, he kissed her. It was a simple gentle kiss and then, uncontrollably, it became demanding and hungry as always.

"I want to stay with you tonight. I don't mean to sleep with you. I need to make love to you, Katelyn. Don't turn me away," his voice begged as he gently joined her on the bed.

"Do you think it's wise with Jenny here?" she asked. She didn't want Jenny to be hurt if and when her father moved on to another lover.

"Jenny is our daughter; she knows that married people sleep together. Damn it Katelyn, I'm not going to discuss my sex life with a seven-year-old. Did you think that after we were married, I'd settle for the life you've given me so far? I'm sorry to disappoint you again but, no matter how you feel about me, I intend to make love to my wife," he said angrily, before lifting her into his arms.

He took her that night. At first Katelyn tried to fool herself into thinking that it wasn't what she wanted, but they both knew better. His touch was all that was needed to awaken the desire stirring beneath. She cried out his name over and over again until their need for each other was sated once again. These days they fell asleep exhausted and in each other's arms.

Katelyn stretched out in their bed as the sun began to rise and reached for her husband who was nowhere to be found. She heard nothing from the shower. The clothes that were haphazardly tossed on the floor the night before were gone. The only sign of life she could hear were voices in the distance. She could hear her daughter, every once in awhile, talking excitedly about her trip to Italy.

The knock on the door was brief and soft at first and she almost ignored it. After very little deliberation, whoever it was decided against leaving and opened the door. "We need to talk," he commanded softly.

Katelyn watched as he entered the room and joined her. She wrapped the satin sheet nervously around her naked body and waited for him to offer his regrets for the night before, citing an inability to control himself or the fact that he might've had too much alcohol. But truthfully, she knew that he didn't love her.

"I'm sorry about last night," he started, as expected, with regret. "I didn't want what happened last night to happen, not the way it did. I've been giving this a lot of thought and, after last night, I think I might have a solution to our problem. It may not be what we both want but for now it will have to do. I've arranged for the room off the master suite at the villa to be refurbished by the time we arrive. My staff is under the impression that Jenny sometimes gets frightened of the dark and she would feel closer to us if, when she was frightened, she slept there. But in actuality, it will be where I will sleep," he added, feeling somewhat dismayed.

Katelyn could only stare out at the sky behind him. Nothing hurt her more than his words as they sunk in. "Are you saying that you regret what happened last night?" she asked with a flicker of hope that he would answer differently.

If he told her that he hadn't regretted a minute of what transpired between them, she would think him a liar and if he told her he regretted everything, he'd be lying too. *Does he actually think that separate beds will placate the fire that burns between us?*

"I can't say that I regret anything. I'm glad for the chances we have. We need to make this work for our daughter and any other child I may have helped to create in my selfishness." His actions were forcing her to take heed to what he was saying.

Katelyn ran her hand over her abdomen for a second and realized that he had to be right. Neither of them bothered with birth control and she hadn't thought about her period or how late it was. "The car will be downstairs to take us to the airport in about three hours. All the arrangements are made and I think, for Jenny's sake, we should stick to the plan. If I could make things easier for you, I would," he said before apologizing again. He wanted to touch her and take away the pain he persistently caused her but he couldn't because he knew consoling her would only lead to heartache.

"I've got to go to the office for about an hour. I promised Jenny I'd take her, if that's all right with you?" He tried to look at things from her point of view and from where he sat she must consider him a monster. Last night he'd played upon her weaknesses to get her into bed and it might not be rape but it was definitely manipulation on his part.

"I promise I'll take care of her. She is curious to see my office," he said, beaming with pride.

"I wouldn't stop you from taking her. You didn't have to ask permission; she's your daughter too," she bit back. She'd also had enough of the combative words to each other. They had to reach a truce of some kind and soon.

He stood, studying her behavior, for a moment. If nothing else, Katelyn always kept him guessing. He had no idea, from one minute to the next, what to expect from her. He knew there was definitely something going on in that pretty head of hers but he didn't have the time or the stamina to find out what it was. Jenny came bouncing into the room and informed her mother that she wanted to go with her father to his office.

Before leaving with her dad, Jenny asked if she could take one of the pictures of her and her mom to his office. She wanted her dad to able to look at them whenever he was lonely. Jenny chose the picture of the two of them at the beach. They had been searching for a starfish that day but they hadn't found one.

"Gianfranco, Good Morning. We weren't expecting you today. Mr. Lonetree said he didn't think you would be stopping by until next month," Dana said, smiling at the little girl on his arm. "Is this your daughter?" she asked.

"Yes, this is Jenny," he said holding her hand with enormous pride. "Could you take Jenny on a tour of the office while I have a talk with

Jake?" Gianfranco asked as he bent down to speak to Jenny and explain his plans to her. "Dana is my assistant and she is going to take you around the office and then when you're finished you can come straight back to my office, okay?" he asked.

He entered Jake's office and thought to himself, *I should be handling this takeover myself, however this trip to Italy is important to this marriage and that had to come first. I don't care if I lose every dime I have,* he thought. *I have to make Katelyn mine.*

Jake was sitting at his desk with his feet up on the windowsill, his phone glued to his ear. He seemed intent on telling whoever he was talking to that if they didn't do as he asked by three o'clock this afternoon, they'd be looking for another job.

As if he could hear the slightest movement, Jake turned to see what had caused this intrusion. Gianfranco could never fathom Jake's keen sharp senses. Jake could hear or smell anything better than anyone he knew. Jake could smell you before he saw you and if he knew what cologne or perfume you wore, he knew who was coming. Perhaps they were gifts left over from his ancestors or his training as a navy seal.

"Well, look what the wind blew in. What are you doing here? I thought you'd be on your way to paradise by now," Jake asked dismissing the person on the other line.

"I'm leaving this afternoon. I just wanted to stop in and make sure everything was going along as planned. Have you had any trouble from Taylor?" he asked, knowing full well that whatever trouble came Jake's way, he could handle it.

Jake smiled and then laughed aloud as he sprung to his feet and looked straight into Gianfranco's eyes. "Come on my friend, we both know that everything is under control here. You saw to that before I set one foot in the place. That's not why you're here, so give. What's going on?"

"Dana is showing Jenny around. I brought her here because she wanted to see where her dad works. She's an angel, Jake, I don't think I could stand to lose her now," he said, with fear in his voice. He took off his coat and threw it on the chair opposite Jake. He ran his fingers through his hair as he always did when he was thinking. "Everything is so complicated. I'm not sure if what I'm asking of Katelyn is fair."

"You seem pretty upset; has something happened?" Jake asked bluntly.

"It's Katelyn, she's really unhappy. I don't know what comes over me when I'm with her but I can't keep my hands off her. I'm so in love with her, Jake, that I just want to shake her into loving me back. I'd be good for them both, I know I would. All I need is a chance to prove to her that we'd be good together. But no matter what I do, I always seem to do the wrong thing," he said pacing back and forth.

Jake acknowledged that he understood what his friend was feeling but he also knew how Katelyn felt. These two people were family to him and he couldn't believe they were having such a hard time finding their way back to each other. Jake wanted to shout out to them and tell them that each loved the other, but if there was one thing he'd learned in his lifetime, it was that fate had its own plan and whatever that was, he could not interfere.

"I think that this trip to Italy will be a good move for you both. I think all three of you need time together without outside influence. It's been years since she had given up hope that you would ever come back. She needs time to come to terms with the idea that the impossible is probable. Give her time, she'll come around," Jake said.

Gianfranco stood near the window and thought about what had taken place last night. He didn't dare tell Jake that he practically forced his wife to have sex with him. Jake would think he'd gone insane but only after he slugged him. "I'm not sure if I've ruined any chance I might have had with her."

"Don't be crazy, I've seen the way our girl looks at you when she thinks no one is looking. I would stake my life on it that she loves you. Maybe she needs to come to terms with it herself. Remember, it wasn't that long ago that she had chalked you up to history and a lesson learned. If you had arrived any later than you did, she might have married Taylor and we all know that would have been a disaster," Jake said making a face, the thought of that image turning his stomach.

Gianfranco didn't bother to admit to Jake that his return was no accident. He knew that Katelyn might have been on the verge of changing her relationship with Taylor; Kevin had told him. It was the main reason he had come back. He didn't want to forfeit his last chance. He had no idea, at the time, that he had a child by her or he would have been back long before now.

"I hope you're right. You know how to get in touch if you need me and I do appreciate this, Jake. Now, let me bring my daughter in to say hello to her uncle," he said as held open the door to the office.

"Gianfranco, don't sweat it; this is just payback for all you've done for me," Jake said before Jenny chose that moment to jump into Jake's arms. "Hey there, little one, Dana, you didn't tell me we hired a new girl," Jake teased as he hugged Jenny.

"I'm not sharing her with you, buddy," Gianfranco said as he took his daughter from his friend's arms. "We'll make one trip to my office and then we have to go home. Your Mom will be wondering where we are soon." Before Gianfranco could take Jenny into his office, Jenny had one thing she wanted to say to Jake.

"Did Daddy tell you Uncle Jake, that we're going to Italy today? Italy is another country and Daddy is going to teach me to speak Italy," she said excitedly.

"Is that right? Is he going to teach you to speak Italy or Italian? Italy is the country you're going to and Italian is the language you're going to learn little one. By the way, angel face, tell your dad that Uncle Jake needs a present," he teased brushing the curly locks from her eyes.

"I will, I promise," she whispered in his ear before kissing him good-bye and following her father on to the elevator. Gianfranco took her to his office and showed her around and let her play at his desk for a little while before reminding her that they would have to be leaving if they were going to be on time for the flight.

"Katelyn, everything has been put in the limousine. As soon as your husband and daughter arrive, we can leave. Gianfranco has arranged for lunch to be served on the plane and I bet, after the morning Jenny's had, she'll sleep most of the trip," Maggie added with a smile.

Gianfranco would be home soon so she chose her clothes with care. She was determined to win her husband back; she might as well use his one weakness to her advantage. She wore a lightweight pencil skirt. It was olive green and emphasized every curve she had. The shirt was nude in color and a little revealing at the breasts, as she wore the buttons opened pretty low and she made sure to wear the sexiest teddy, she could find, underneath. She knew when she sat down that he would see a hint of the teddy and it would drive him insane. Katelyn thought she might as well enjoy her figure now, in another couple of months she would be swollen with his child.

Gianfranco and Jenny must have arrived because she could hear her daughter's giggles as the elevator doors opened. Katelyn did notice that Gianfranco looked at her reluctantly. She could tell the dress was working its magic and when they boarded the plane, with Jenny falling asleep shortly thereafter, all bets would be off. She would show her husband no mercy as she fought to win him back. This time she would make sure he pleaded for a normal loving marriage and she would settle for nothing less.

Gianfranco kept his distance as promised. On the plane, Katelyn found it difficult to bring her plan into fruition. He was avoiding her at all costs. He managed to frequently have some business that needed his urgent care each time she got close. She had almost given up, believing that he would never make time for her the way he made time for Jenny.

Their time together at the villa was proving just as scarce. She didn't know where he went after spending his afternoons with Jenny but he didn't come near her. Two weeks turned into a month and Katelyn was about to throw in the towel when the test kit showed a solid blue line running through it. It confirmed what she had already known to be true, that they were going to have a baby. She needed to fight harder to keep her marriage together because now there would be four of them.

She felt sick to her stomach as she got out of bed that morning; she ran to the bathroom to vomit. She cleaned herself up and went to the window, watching as father and daughter played together on the beach. It was as though he sensed her because he looked up at her window and waved. She felt like screaming at him and admitting the truth but she didn't dare. Instead she decided to join them.

"Jenny and I were collecting sea shells. Would you like to join us?"

he asked as she made her way to beach. She nodded in agreement just as Maggie called from behind.

"I have Jenny's lunch ready. Why don't you two go and enjoy your walk and I'll take Jenny in for her lunch? It will do Katelyn some good to walk. She's been looking a little peaked these days," Maggie added. "Besides, Giovanni will be arriving to give her riding lessons soon."

Gianfranco looked from Jenny to Katelyn and smiled. "Maggie's right. You do look a little under the weather. Are you feeling alright?" he asked. She assured him that she was fine. "Let's go then. We should spend more time alone now and then," he added after Jenny was out of earshot.

Gianfranco had kept his distance from her long enough. If their marriage stood a chance of surviving, they needed to build a relationship that was separate from that of their daughter. The beach was quiet this time of the year and there wasn't a soul to be seen for miles. Every once in awhile, someone would pass them with a dog and say hello. The time passed by quickly and neither of them said very much in the way of conversation. "I'm not sure how to talk to you anymore. I don't want to say the wrong thing and send you off in the opposite direction," he said.

"Have ever tried to talk to me lately? We've been here a month and the only time you've said anything to me has been at dinner when you're forced to hold a conversation. I feel as though I'm a third wheel in this family." Gianfranco took her hand in his and they continued to walk on the beach.

"I never realized that I was making you feel left out. That wasn't my intention." He squeezed her hand and smiled at her. "Have you noticed how much time I spend apologizing for one thing or another when I'm with you?" he asked with a chuckle.

They both found his admission amusing and it felt good to laugh. Maybe, after all this time, they had finally taken a step forward he thought. "Tell me, what you thought when you first found out about the baby?" he asked innocently.

Briefly, she thought he was talking about their second child. After a second or two, she realized that he meant Jenny. "I was a scared teenager. You had already gone back to Italy and I was heading for California.

I don't need to tell you that I had no idea what to do at first. Instinctively, I wanted to call you but my pride wouldn't allow it. You never actually said you wanted a future with me and I didn't want to force you into marrying me. I became more confused as time passed and then, when I could no longer hide the pregnancy, I told Kevin. He was surprisingly, understanding about my decision not to tell the father. I don't know what I would have done without him and Jake," she said.

"Did you hate me?" he asked.

"No, I never hated you. There was a time when I thought I should but I couldn't. It would have been easy to hate you and blame you, but I didn't. When Jenny was born, she reminded me so much of you. That's when my opinion of you really changed. I thanked God everyday that you had come into my life. There wasn't a day that went by, after her birth, that I wasn't glad that you were her father. I had no regrets, not one," she said, picking up a shell from the beach and tossing it.

He picked up one himself and tossed it where she had tossed her shell. She could see that several emotions were warring within him. "I wish I was there for you both at the time. You do believe that, don't you?" he questioned.

"Yes, I believe you would have done the right thing if I had told you and we would be a settled married couple today. I didn't want you feeling you were forced into a marriage you didn't want," she said daring to hint that history might be repeating itself.

"Sort of like now, you mean? I wanted things to be different. I didn't want things to turn out this way," he said with a hint of disappointment in his voice. Up until now, they were moving along nicely and again they would probably take ten steps back.

Katelyn looked a little baffled at what had just happened between them in a matter of a few feet. "Are you having regrets?" she asked.

"Some, but for the most part I'm still convinced that our marriage could be a good one. It would take a lot of sharing and caring but I think we could do it. I believe that from the bottom of my heart," he said as a wave came crashing to the shoreline.

A noise escaped her lips. It was more of a sigh than a noise, he turned toward her to try and understand what it was she wanted from him. "Is that enough for you? I'm not sure that it's enough for me. I need a husband who loves me. I want a commitment for life. I want you to promise me that we will try to make our marriage last forever. Can you give me that promise? Do we even want the same thing?" she asked.

What had she meant on the beach, he wondered? If they hadn't been interrupted with an urgent business call from New York, he would have found out. The call was something Jake had already handled, but his assistant panicked when she couldn't get a hold of Jake to verify. Jake apologized to him; let him know that going forward Dana would have his personal cell phone number in order to contact him directly with any and all business.

After hanging up with Jake, he thought again about what Katelyn had said earlier. She was going on and on about a lifetime commitment and settling for nothing less. *She would never find another man more committed to her than I am,* he thought. He would talk to her about it later. As he walked down the hall, the phone was ringing. When it rang a second and third time, he picked it up and was surprised that it was a medical office verifying Katelyn's appointment.

What appointment? Is Katelyn sick? If she is, why is it a secret? "Is this my wife's appointment for her cold?" he asked with nervous curiosity.

The young voice on the other end laughed. He could tell she hesitated before answering him. It was obvious she was checking Katelyn's file to make sure that she had permission to talk to him. After verifying that he was her husband and he was on the sheet in front of her, she answered his question. "Well, she should mention her cold to Dr. Bank because I'm sure he would want to know. Be sure she doesn't take any over the counter medications in her condition, without talking to the doctor first. Even cold medicine could be harmful to the baby," the nurse added. All he heard were the words 'baby' and 'her condition'. *He couldn't believe that Katelyn was keeping this from him, again. Could she be hiding this information from me because she isn't sure who had fathered her child? No, fate wouldn't be that cruel.* The thought was so foreign that he couldn't think about it.

His suspicion escalated with each passing hour and it wasn't until she stepped out of the shower that she noticed him. He glanced down at her flat abdomen. He wanted it to be his child. He couldn't handle any other outcome. He watched as she grabbed for her robe and tied the belt. "I wasn't aware that you had come in," she said, emanating sexual appeal in waves.

"I came to discuss something with you." He moved closer and watched as she listlessly moved across the room. He was almost afraid to bring up the subject with her in her condition. He was also reluctant to have this conversation fearing the outcome. If he found out the child was not his, but someone else's, he knew even he couldn't mend a broken heart, his own.

"If it's important, maybe I should put on some clothes," she teased lovingly. Her matter-of-fact attitude bothered him.

"I don't give a damn about the way you're dressed. I want to know why you didn't tell me about your visit to the doctor. More to the point, is this baby really mine?" he asked.

She was vaguely conscious of the fact that she had raised her hand to strike him, until she heard the echo of the slap and saw the imprint of her hand on his face. He pulled her body into him and kissed her full on the mouth. He was once again claiming what was his. His hands dropped to untie the robe and he let it fall to the floor. He kissed her and then ran his fingers lightly over her erect nipples. His touch again, setting her body on fire. They both needed this more than anything right now.

She yanked him free of his shirt and opened his pants without hesitation. They were both tearing at his clothes now, out of sheer desperation. He was lifting her breasts in his hands, tasting and suckling them until neither he nor she could take anymore. They never made it to the bed, instead he was desperate as he lifted her off the floor and lowered her body onto his waiting body, limiting the amount of foreplay. They were kissing each other and crying out their undying love for one another. "I love you, Katelyn. I wish I didn't, but I do," he said.

Did she hear him correctly? *Did he say he loved me?* Or did she so desperately want to hear the words that she heard. "What did you say?" she asked as he held her above him with their eyes locked on each other. It was time for the truth and if it hurt she needed to hear it.

"I love you. I always have. When I left to go back to Italy seven years ago, it wasn't because I wanted to. I left because I thought you needed time to grow up. It wasn't fair of me to take your youth from you. You were barely a woman; in one sense you were a woman because I made you one. I had always planned to come back. I didn't want to be in the same country, while you dated other men. I could never stand it, especially if I had to watch," he added, telling her what would have happened obviously. He couldn't control his jealousy.

"Do you mean to tell me that you returned to Italy, because of me? You had every intention of coming back? Why?" she asked. *All this time he had been in love with me and somehow I had never believed it possible.* Was he saying all this for their unborn child?

"Katelyn, I love you. I love you more than anything in my life. I just proved how hopelessly in love I am. My first reaction to the nurse telling me you are pregnant was, please let it be mine. Now, I don't care if this child is ours or not; we'll raise it as our own. I will love this child because it's a part of you; I can't lose you again," he said, placing his hand on her belly.

She touched his shoulder and she could feel the muscles as they tightened. There were no words to describe the feelings of relief and happiness she felt at this moment. "Gianfranco, we are such fools; there were so many things we should have talked about before now. This baby is yours. This child was conceived out of love. I love you too. I've always loved you. You're our baby's father, without question, because you're the only man I've ever made love to. There's never been anyone else," she stated with great conviction.

It didn't take a rocket scientist to see that the expression of love and shock on his face was genuine, tears of joy running down his face. "You waited all these years for me? What about Brody and Adam?" he asked shocked.

He lifted her from his body and wrapped her gently in his arms. Nothing could spoil this moment for them. He stood, with her in his arms, and thought. *She is really mine.*

"I never loved Adam. He was just a friend," she said as she leaned back against his naked body.

"I can't believe I almost lost you because of my stupidity," he said. Suddenly, he remembered the ring. He reached over to his jacket and pulled out the chain that held the wooden ring on it. "I got this from Jenny. I should have told you the significance of it years ago. When I gave you this ring, I made a silent promise to love you forever. Jake and Kevin have the same rings. When the Indian woman gave them to us, she told us each to choose the woman we gave the ring to very carefully because we would be bound to her forever." Gianfranco held her tightly and she could feel her body responding to him again. "I have to tell you, I thought I was cursed forever. I love you," he said again and again because he loved the sound of it.

They both spent the next few hours rekindling lost love. Finally, it was time to tell Katelyn why he had brought her to Italy in the first place. "I want you to understand everything, before we go on. When I decided to bring you here, it was with selfish motives in mind. I was convinced that if I got you here I could make you fall in love with me. I believed that, with the right amount of time and lovemaking, I could wipe Brody and Adam from your mind."

"Brody is in love with Eleanor. They were married once and I never had feelings for him, other than friendship. I wanted to tell you about Jenny so many times. Every time I had a hard time with her or things got tough financially, I would reach for the phone and then hang up. I didn't want to have to force her on you," her voice said, it cracked as she confessed what was in her heart.

Gianfranco pressed his hand to her abdomen and asked her jokingly, "When is our son due?"

"I'm sure this child was conceived the very first time we made love after seeing each other again. The night you came barreling back into my life," she teased as she kissed him. He kissed her back and wondered if he could ever get enough of her. "Does this mean you're going to sleep with me tonight, my husband?"

"I don't know about sleeping but after today we'll never be in separate beds again. That is a promise, one I fully intend to keep."

Chapter Fifteen

"Jenny, I think it's time to take Momma home to America. The baby is coming and Momma wants to be near her doctor. Wouldn't you like your brother or sister to be born where you were born?" he asked his little girl, hoping she would agree.

"I guess but I do like it here. Maybe we can come back here when the baby gets older? Do you think we're going to have a girl baby or a boy baby?" she asked as she kissed her father on the cheek. "I think it's going to be a boy baby. Our baby can play with Uncle Kevin's baby. They could be best friends Daddy; like you and Uncle Kevin," she added giggling.

"I'm not sure what God has planned for us, Jenny, but I want you to know that whatever we have, you're still my baby girl and I love you," he said as she hugged his neck even harder.

Maggie and Katelyn stood nearby watching the exchange as father and daughter discussed the pros and cons of moving back home again. Katelyn wondered if Gianfranco would reconsider the move if his daughter insisted they stay here. *She has her father wrapped around her little finger.* Katelyn was showing now and the trip would be less traumatic for the baby if they left sooner rather than later. Everyone was thrilled to hear they were coming home; Jake was the only one who knew what the trip home meant.

Jake was at the airport waiting when they arrived. He was more than happy to have Gianfranco resume control of the magazine. It was time for him to move on. He had stayed at the magazine longer than he'd intended. Maybe it was his Indian blood but he hated being cooped up in an office, staying in one place for too long. He was rich but only because he was a great investor. Being independently wealthy gave him the opportunity to move around and do whatever he fancied.

"Jake, thank you again for all you've done for us. If there's anything we can do for you…," Gianfranco didn't get to finish his sentence because the tall, dark man that stood before him finished his thoughts for him.

"I'm glad everything worked out for you both. Maybe in a couple of months when I start the camp up again, I'll call in that favor. I was thinking of expanding to include more kids and I thought that if you did an article on the camp maybe I could reach out to more reservations. That will be payment enough," he said.

"Then there's nothing more to say, consider it done. When you're ready, give me a call and I'll assign my second best because the first is going to be busy," he teased her, pulling Katelyn into his arms. "Did we tell you baby number two is on the way?"

Jake grinned from ear to ear as he gazed at Katelyn's growing belly. "Only about one hundred times, my friend," he said.

"I'm going to be a big sister, Uncle Jake. I hope my brother isn't bad though. Momma said I could hold the baby too. Maybe you can too?" Jenny asked with the wonder of a child.

The months that followed went by so fast that Katelyn barely had time to breathe. The penthouse was more like a home now and since Gianfranco had given his daughter free reign there were toys everywhere. He was pleased with the home Katelyn had made for them. He was beginning to think she enjoyed being home with Jenny and he wondered if she would insist on going back to work after the baby came. He wouldn't stop her but he was hoping she would stay home with their kids.

Katelyn hadn't mentioned it to Gianfranco yet but she decided that she was perfectly happy at home. She knew he wouldn't mind at all; they had more money than they could spend in a lifetime. She picked up the picture of Amanda Catherine Donavan, her newborn niece and smiled. She had just received the picture in today's mail and was tickled pink to see how much she resembled her grandmother. Kevin and Sylvia were so happy to have a child. She was their gift from heaven.

It was at that moment that the baby chose to kick abruptly and Katelyn was reminded that her time was growing nearer. If the doctors were correct, she would have another baby in three weeks' time. The noise of the helicopter overhead brought Katelyn's attention to the window. She watched with interest as the helicopter circled and then flew away. It was a strange fascination she had; she hoped that one day she would like to learn to fly a helicopter but didn't think she would ever have the opportunity.

"You look as though you're a million miles away," Gianfranco said as he wrapped his wife in his arms. For him every day that passed was better than the previous. There was nothing he could want more than what he already had. He adored his wife and daughter and was excited about their other child on the way. He was looking forward to being there this time, from the beginning. He placed his hand over her stomach where his child lay cocooned. Katelyn was more beautiful and alluring now than before but he knew she would be even more beautiful after the baby was born.

He found it difficult to bring up the subject of her career but they needed to talk about it. He didn't want her to return to work and he hoped she wouldn't want to either. She surprised him with a strange look in her eyes as he watched her stare at the sky above them. His private helicopter was circling above after dropping him off and she looked at it in awe. "You're not thinking what I think you're thinking, are you?" he asked.

He might give in to her every wish but this would never happen. Katelyn had a way of wanting things that most women never dreamed of. That was why he loved her. She was so different than the women who passed through his life.

"I know it's crazy, I've always wanted to learn to fly. Do you think that after the baby comes, I could take lessons?" she asked, glancing up at the helicopter.

She did it again. Every time it seemed as though they were having a normal quiet life, Katelyn sprung something insane on him. He had thought their first fight since the baby blowout would be about returning to work too soon. He certainly never expected this. He was selfish and greedy and was afraid she would get hurt. "Flying lessons, are you crazy? When did this idea spring into your head?" he asked.

"I've always wanted to fly; I just couldn't afford it. I promised myself that if I were ever in a position to afford it, I would learn." She felt an odd sense of anxiety as his expression changed. "You see, I thought that since I wouldn't be returning to work, I would need a hobby. It would be something that I could do for myself. We can certainly afford it," she added with a childlike smile.

"You don't want to return to work?" he asked. This was more than he could have hoped for. There would be no arguments and it was her idea. But flying lessons could be dangerous. "For the first time, I curse my money. Flying a helicopter could be dangerous for you," he stated briefly.

"I thought you would support the idea," she added stubbornly.

"Katelyn…" He stopped her mid-sentence and kissed her to keep her from speaking another word. "Of course, I want to support anything you want to do, but flying lessons… I'm not saying no and I'm not saying yes either. I need to see how dangerous it is first. If it's relatively safe, I'll agree but if it isn't, Katelyn, I can't go along with it. I didn't wait all these years to lose you now," he said leaning toward her so that she could feel what she did to him. "Is that a hint?"

"Only if you want me…" Gianfranco knew they were alone for another hour or so and he knew just how he wanted to spend that hour. Lovemaking was getting tricky but nothing he couldn't handle. His wife still had it. He found her irresistible even now.

Gianfranco decided to surprise Katelyn so he asked Jake to help him to set up the flying lessons. Jake was more than happy to help Gianfranco arrange for the lessons. He had a friend who gave lessons from a small airport upstate; he would be happy to provide the services. Gianfranco couldn't think of a better gift to give her after the birth of their child.

He would wait until after the birth to tell her because if she was told any sooner, pregnant or not, she'd be driving him crazy.

"The baby is due soon, isn't it?" his secretary asked him.

"Yes and it can't come soon enough," he said pulling a file from the cabinet. The closer Katelyn's delivery date came, the more useless he was becoming on the job. He had to try not to let it bother him but he knew she was growing more tired and more uncomfortable with each passing day. This morning when he left, she was trying, without success, to cope with back pain that wouldn't go away. When he suggested he stay home with her, she sent him away.

Maggie's voice on the phone quickly sent him into a panic. "Katelyn was having so much back pain that the doctor had her go straight to the hospital. She asked that Gianfranco meet her there. Don't worry about Jenny. I will take care of her and Rosa has gone to the hospital with Katelyn. Good Luck son." Maggie added lovingly.

As calm and collected as he usually was, this was one of those situations where he was glad he had a chauffeur. He didn't think he'd be able to find the hospital by himself. On the way there, he convinced himself that he was the cause of the back pain she was suffering. After all, wasn't his idea that lovemaking might help bring on delivery.

He arrived at the hospital and was ushered into a birthing room where Katelyn was already practicing her breathing techniques. He entered the room, dressed in the hospitals finest and at first she didn't realize who it was until those ebony eyes met with her own. "I'm glad you could make it. I didn't think I could hold out much longer. Are you ready?" she asked after he kissed her softly on the lips.

One hour after his father's arrival to the hospital, Kevin Quinn Broccolini was born. Jenny picked the names herself. She wanted her brother to be named after her two favorite uncles. Kevin and Jake, whose real name was Quinn. No one knew that Quinn was his real name; that came as a shock to everyone when Jenny announced it to them. It was a secret he shared with Jenny. Kevin was thrilled and honored that they named the baby after him. Gianfranco was happy to bestow the honor on the two men who took care of his wife and child when he couldn't be there for them.

Katelyn held Kevin in her arms and smiled down at the face of her son. He was dark like his father, with his jet black hair but his eyes were a deep blue like those of his grandfather, her dad. She was so happy and certainly her parents were happy too, knowing that her and her new family had found such joy.

Gianfranco pulled an envelope from his pocket and handed it to her as he took their newest child from her arms. As she opened it, she couldn't believe her eyes, directions to the location of her first lessons. She was beside herself. He couldn't have given her anything more special than this because she knew how hard this was for him.

Gianfranco was happy with his family and, if he could just get past the baby's christening, he knew he would make it through anything. He wanted his wife so badly that it hurt. He knew that the doctor would allow them to resume sex around the time of Kevin's christening so he began counting the days.

"Katelyn, I'm so glad we could come. I wouldn't miss this for the world. Brody wasn't sure if Gianfranco would want him here but Gianfranco had already apologized up and down for misunderstanding your relationship with Brody. They are downstairs now talking like old friends," Eleanor said, pointing to the two men talking on the grounds below. They had chosen to christen the baby in Southampton since the estate could house all their friends for a long weekend.

Katelyn took the baby from her breast and placed him in his crib. Their son was beautiful and such a happy baby. She covered him with a blanket and turned her attention to her friend. "I wanted all our closest friends to be here to share this day with us and that meant the two of you as well. We might have started off rocky, when it comes to the men in our lives, but we're good now. I know Brody took the brunt of all the trouble from Gianfranco but I'm sure my husband is eating crow as we speak." Katelyn hugged Eleanor and led her to the window where they could watch the people gathering below.

Their Southampton Estate was quite large besides having so much beach frontage available to them it had an enormous yard for Jenny to play in. They made time to come as often as possible. "I'm happy for you and Brody. I've never seen him so content. I'm sorry we couldn't make your wedding but it was impossible for me to travel." Katelyn was so happy that Brody and Eleanor had found each again. The more she thought about it, the more she realized that the four of them had a lot in common.

Eleanor was glowing and everything about her today was a little bit different. She looked elegant in the suit she wore and Katelyn was sure to tell her. "You look great. Something is different about you, I don't know what? Is this one of your designs?" she asked pointing to her dress. It was one of her own designs and Eleanor was proud but she was glowing for different reasons.

"I'm trying out my new maternity line. What do you think?" Eleanor asked proudly.

"You're pregnant?" Katelyn asked, before congratulating her. "How wonderful, I can't tell you how much a baby will add to your life," she said staring down at her sleeping son.

Her eyes grew wider as her sixth sense clicked in as he walked into the room. Nothing would ever change, the way he made her tremble with want when he was around. Gianfranco came over to her and held her close.

"I offer my congratulations as well, Eleanor. There's nothing more rewarding than becoming a parent. Believe me, I know," he said as he kissed his wife on the side of the neck. Eleanor gave them both a friendly kiss and left them alone. Gianfranco followed her, locking the door behind her as she left.

He turned to his wife again and kissed her until he thought he would die. "I'm trying, I really am. I don't think I can wait much longer. The doctor did say that it was safe, didn't he?" he said groaning. He sighed and made a face of disgust. "I'm sorry, I shouldn't be punishing you."

"Everyone is waiting for us downstairs. Do you think you could carry Kevin for me?" She handed her sleeping baby to his father and followed him as they started down the stairs. Jenny ran up and joined them while Jake came up and took his nephew and godson from Gianfranco.

Katelyn had a mischievous look on her face as her husband turned to her to take her hand. "I've asked Maggie to care for Kevin and Jenny tonight. I told her that we were in dire need of alone time. She was happy to oblige. She's been dying to get him to herself since the day he was born. I thought we'd excuse ourselves from the party at a reasonable hour." He stopped his descent down the staircase.

"Please, tell me you mean what I think you mean? You did say 'we' when you mentioned sneaking off to our room, didn't you?" He was sure, from the smile on her face, that his life was about to get almost perfect.

Kevin and Sylvia, with Amanda in her arms, stood at the bottom of the staircase. The baby was sucking on a toy rattle and Kevin was busy showing her off to anyone who would stop to talk to him.

Katelyn was so happy for all their friends and family. It seemed as if this had been the best year for them all, with the exception of one tall, dark Indian who stood out in the crowd. Jake had great power to love and she wondered if he would ever find a woman who would take that teakwood ring from him. She noticed that Jake had always worn the ring around his neck. He was a bit of a wild man but, with the right woman, she was sure he would gladly settle down. Someday, he would find her, if he hadn't already with no one the wiser.

Gianfranco walked over to Jake and tried his best to show his appreciation for everything he'd done. "Jake, I want to thank you for listening to me and sharing your thoughts. If it weren't for you, I'm not so sure I wouldn't have destroyed everything between Katelyn and myself. I don't need to tell you what that would have done to me," Gianfranco said as he handed his friend a drink. "I've been thinking about that article you wanted; I have an idea."

"You're the expert; I trust you'll do the right thing," Jake said as he gulped his beer.

"Don't worry, I won't let you down. It's been a top priority since getting my own life in order," he said as he peaked at his wife across the lawn. He couldn't stop wondering about the promise tonight held in store for them. He wanted the same kind of happiness for Jake and he knew just the person for the job.

They all had their little secrets and Jake was no different. He'd never told another soul, other than Gianfranco, about Joey Davis. She was

Joey Davis, alias Jocelyn Davis. She was the daughter of the man who took in the young Indian boy when his grandmother died. Joey was also the reason why Jake left home to go to college and later became a Navy Seal.

He hadn't told Jake that he had found Joey or that he hired her. Apparently, Joey had become a war correspondent and was quite good at her job. Gianfranco wondered if Joey had been subconsciously searching for Jake all this time. Up until he made the call to her to offer her a job, Joey had thought Jake was still a member of a Navy Seal Elite Squad. She was happy and relieved to hear that he was back in the States and doing very well. She didn't give away too much information but Gianfranco suspected there was more to this story than she wanted anyone to know. It was funny, even to him, how fast she accepted his job offer when she knew Jake was no longer overseas. As far as Jake was concerned, Gianfranco decided to keep him in the dark about hiring Joey. It was better, at least he thought, he would let nature takes its course.

"Send me a journalist who will take the job seriously. You know how important this camp is to me. Whoever you send has to know, going in, that only our native tongue will be spoken and that includes in front of him or her. I won't make any exceptions to the rule, not even for you," he added without haste.

"I know, if nothing else, I learned that the hard way." He remembered those long summers they spent at the camp helping Jake out. Jake neglected to let him and Kevin know what they were in for. They each learned to survive at a place where no one spoke their language so in order to get by they had to learn to adapt. Nights at camp were lonely and all they had to get them through were pictures and letters from Katelyn, sent to Kevin. They shared everything and those close friendships they formed taught them very valuable life lessons.

Yes, Joey will be the perfect reporter to send to the camp and Jake won't know what hit him. It would be even more interesting to see if he would keep her in the dark, just as Jake had done to them so many years before. She will think she's going right into the middle of an Indian reservation from the 1800's. If there is one person Gianfranco believed would be fair to the story, it would be Joey. Soon they'll find out if the sparks still existed between them and if there was a valid reason to keep them apart any longer. Gianfranco wondered if that ring around Jake's neck would be there for much longer.

Acknowledgments

Thank you to Kevin, the love of my life and my own personal hero. Thank you for your unending support and encouragement.

To Ed & Eileen Moore, the inspiration behind writing romances.

To Pete & Eleanor Brady, we miss terribly and know you would have been proud.

To my family and friends, thank you for all the support and encouragement.

To my Mom, for loving each manuscript I gave her to read more than the one before.

To Barbara, my sister and friend, thank you for being my loudest cheerleader, my soundboard and my super promoter.

To Kathy, Rosa, Barbara, Katie, Erin and Jen thank you for the support and love.

To my editor, Dennis DeRose, who pushes me to do better and is always looking for a new way to help me realize my dream. Thank you.
Finally, to my children, Jennifer, Katelyn and Kevin Jr.; I love you all and appreciate your faith in me. Thank you.